Two pair of eyes, two guns, both pointed at me.

I froze, determined to drop at the first twitch of their fingers, determined to outmaneuver not one but two bullets.

Behind m̶̶... ... ...
and determ̶ ...

The guns̶ ...
if through w̶ ...
of the stairw̶ ...

I'd never seen her look so fierce, so full of strength and power. I realized in that split second how much I loved her, how much I needed her now that I'd lost everything else.

Then the bullets hit . . .

Praise for *Amazon Ink* by Lori Devoti

Also by Lori Devoti

Amazon Ink

Amazon Queen

LORI DEVOTI

Pocket Books
New York   London   Toronto   Sydney

Pocket Books
A Division of Simon & Schuster, Inc.
1230 Avenue of the Americas
New York, NY 10020

This book is a work of fiction. Names, characters, places, and incidents either are products of the author's imagination or are used fictitiously. Any resemblance to actual events or locales or persons, living or dead, is entirely coincidental.

First Juno Books/Pocket Books paperback edition May 2010

JUNO BOOKS and colophon are trademarks of Wildside Press LLC used under license by Simon & Schuster, Inc., the publisher of this work.

POCKET and colophon are registered trademarks of Simon & Schuster, Inc.

For information about special discounts for bulk purchases, please contact Simon & Schuster Special Sales at 1-866-506-1949 or business@simonandschuster.com.

The Simon & Schuster Speakers Bureau can bring authors to your live event. For more information or to book an event contact the Simon & Schuster Speakers Bureau at 1-866-248-3049 or visit our website at www.simonspeakers.com.

Design by Lisa Litwack. Illustration by Steve Stone.

Manufactured in the United States of America

10 9 8 7 6 5 4 3 2 1

ISBN 978-1-4391-6772-4
ISBN 978-1-4391-6775-5 (ebook)

For my children. I would walk through fire for you.

Acknowledgments

Thanks for making this book a reality go to my agent, Holly Root, editors Paula Guran and Jennifer Heddle, and many others at Pocket Books whose names I do not know.

Special thanks to Pat Rice and Sasha White for their input on an early version of the first few chapters of this book. I'm afraid little of the original survived rewrites—thank you for that! Also to Ann Voss Peterson for reminding me of things I really shouldn't need reminding of.

I'd also like to thank Rob Francis for answering my fire questions and the Castle Coalition for answering questions on eminent domain, even though eminent domain did not make it into the final book.

Preface

Descendants of the god Ares and nymph Otrera, the Amazons were blessed with strength, longevity, and mystical powers. As their divine bloodline was weakened by mating with humans, they learned to focus and maintain their powers through the use of body decoration, mainly tattoos.

Despite their descent from Ares, the Amazons worshipped Artemis, the goddess of the hunt, forests, and hills, and the womanly concerns of virginity, fertility, and childbirth. As the world outside of their community moved to worship gods over goddesses, their desire to stay separate—and exclusively female—grew.

Dividing eventually into twelve tribes each identified with a protector animal, the Amazons lived in the area around what we now call the Black Sea for centuries.

Then the ancient Greeks encountered a few of their settlements. Their stories of a tribe of woman warriors began to draw the interest of the outside world. To survive, the Amazons became increasingly nomadic. Although they dispersed in all directions, most moved to the steppes of Russia.

The animals that had identified their settlements became family totems, a reminder of their past greatness. These totems were tattooed on each member of the tribe, tying them together magically when the Amazons weren't together physically. The tattoos became known as *telioses*.

Amazons fall into four basic talent groups: warriors, priestesses, artisans, and hearth-keepers. Amazons may have aspects of power from all of the groups, but there is usually one that is obviously dominant. Their personal power tattoo (the *givnomai*) is chosen to enhance those powers, helping to lock them into their role for the tribe. It is rare for an Amazon to have significant powers from more than one group.

Warriors possess superhuman strength and flexibility. Priestesses can harness elemental powers—fire, wind, water, earth—without use of objects. Priestesses also call upon the goddess Artemis for guidance for the tribe. Artisans create objects that store power: tattoos, fetishes, and jewelry. The power these objects have is based on what they represent: a bear fetish would provide strength, a coyote stealth, a fox cunning. Some artisans can put the power into the object; others can only create the object and must have assistance from a priestess to embed the power. Home, food, and child care are provided by the hearth-keepers. Their powers are protective and medicinal.

Although not immortal, Amazons do live for hundreds of years and retain a youthful appearance for several centuries.

Even in the New World, the Amazons kept their nomadic ways. The twelve tribes continued to keep a low profile by traveling around the country, much like modern-day gypsies, settling for short periods of time in one of six "safe camps."

Camps are located on enough land to provide a buffer between them and the human world. Each has a hearth-keeper, priestess, and queen (from the warrior talent group) assigned to them by the high council. These queens maintain order within the camp and work to protect it from human detection through both magical and mundane ways. They stay longer than the other Amazons, but still shift to a new camp every few years. Individual Amazons move freely between these camps, never settling for too long in one place.

Amazons mingle with the human population on a limited basis. Just like their ancestors, they take human lovers but do not marry. Since most Amazons believe themselves superior to humans, most have no issues with stealing from humans or conning them out of money. Their seminomadic lifestyle aids them in evading confrontations that might come from such an existence. A few do offer legitimate—or semi-legitimate—services at area fairs and bazaars such as selling craft items, such as fetishes and jewelry, telling fortunes, or offering self-defense classes. They do not, however, take jobs that require them to work day-to-day in one place or get to know any humans in depth. If anyone begins to get too close, they move on.

The Amazons have never trusted men, nor brought them into their camps. They even feared their own male offspring might rise up and try to control them, as Greek males had tried in the past. Because of this fear, their male children were put to death. Over time they stopped the killing and instead maimed the infants by breaking an arm or leg, then leaving the boys where humans could find and raise them.

Some of these offspring survived; many didn't.

Around the turn of the nineteenth century, Bubbe Saka, a priestess, was instrumental in stopping all of this. Male children thereafter were left unmaimed at human churches and hospitals.

Although the Amazons were unaware of it, even before the maiming stopped, these sons had begun gathering together. Also unknown to the Amazons, their sons possessed similar powers to their own.

Through an encounter (told in *Amazon Ink*) with Melinappe (Mel) Saka—Bubbe Saka's granddaughter and an Amazon who had left the tribe—the Amazons discovered both the sons' existence and their powers.

For the first time in their history, they are forced to face the fact there is a group who can match them power for power.

What the Amazons don't know is if that group will choose to try and destroy them.

Chapter 1

Full noon sun in the middle of a busy downtown street, and I was about to steal a baby.

An older white two-door, with a bumper that obviously wasn't original to the car, angled its way into a parking spot. I whistled, signaling the two warriors I'd brought with me that our target was close.

Thea Caras, our new high priestess, opened the door to our Jeep and set one foot on the pavement. I motioned for Tess, a hearth-keeper and our driver, to be ready. Then I followed suit, trying to look casual, although Thea with her full-sleeve tattoos was not your usual downtown Beloit shopper. For that matter neither was I, nor were the two warriors hidden in shaded doorways nearby. Still, I grabbed a hoodie from the seat beside me and threw it at Thea. She frowned but pulled it on.

It was the middle of July and hot, but better she be sweaty than flashing her unusual art.

The men took their time getting out of the vehicle. I glanced over my shoulder, checking to make sure the fifth member of our team, Lao, a three-hundred-and-fifty-year-old hearth-keeper, was in position to take the child once we had retrieved her from the sons who had stolen her.

Finally the men exited the car. The tallest reached into the backseat and pulled out the carrier. I could see the baby inside, fast asleep with a blue-and-white checked blanket tucked around her. The shorter of the two, maybe six foot three to the other man's lanky six six, scanned the street. I ducked down in a pretense of checking my tire. Thea cut around behind the back of the Jeep to approach them from the street.

Back on my feet, I signaled Areto. She was short for an Amazon, with no visible tattoos. Dressed in mom shorts and a scoop-necked T-shirt, she blended nicely with the humans. Fumbling in a purse we'd picked up at Goodwill before setting this stage, she walked between the sons and stopped.

Disguised as a man, complete with a trucker hat, Bern moved too. She headed toward an old VW Bug that Lao had hotwired earlier and parked at the corner.

With Bern and Areto in place, Lao was next. Pushing a rolling shopping cart, she moved into the tall son's path, then stumbled and fell. The cart tipped over. Onions and peppers rolled across the concrete. Lao lay sprawled across the sidewalk, the picture of elderly distress.

Areto rushed to Lao's "aid." Falling to her knees, she stared at the Amazon son. "She needs help."

I joined Areto and placed a hand on Lao's shoulder. "She's hurt," I cried. "Her arm is bent. Can one of you help me?" I moved as if struggling to flip the older Amazon onto her side.

Neither male moved.

Eight feet behind the man with the infant, Thea lifted a blowpipe. Something shot from its end. The man slapped at his neck, then took an unsteady step to the side. Confusion clouding his eyes, he set the carrier down.

Also confused, I blinked. I had assumed Thea would use magic to divert the men; I hadn't expected the priestess to use a weapon and what appeared to be some kind of drug. However, in the middle of our mission, I didn't have time to analyze the priestess's unusual choice.

The shorter man had missed the exchange. When I looked back at him, his attention was still on me.

"Mateo, Amazons!" he yelled, leaping toward us.

I stood, meeting him head-on, and jammed the heel of my hand into his nose. He cursed; blood streamed down his face.

The first son, the tall one, was barely standing; only his arms, locked at the elbows and wedged against the cars beside him, kept him from falling. His face drawn, he lunged toward the carrier, but it was too late. Tess had already pulled up behind his car and Thea, the baby carrier firmly in hand, had already leapt inside.

With a shriek of the Jeep's tires, they raced away.

The son whose nose I had just busted cursed. He took a step toward me, but the taller son yelled there was no time. The first son headed toward me, hesitated, emitted an angry growl, and flashed his teeth. The taller one staggered to their car, then slapped his palm against the door.

With a last snarl, the shorter man jumped behind the wheel and they sped off after the Jeep.

They got to the corner before Bern placed her foot on the Bug's front bumper and pushed it into traffic in front of them.

At the shriek of tires and metal, she turned and strolled toward us.

Lao was already on her feet. She made a *tch*ing sound. "Must have forgotten to put the damn thing in park. It's hell being old, Zery."

"Lucky we have another ride," I replied.

"Yep." She grinned. "It most certainly is." She climbed into the truck we'd parked only a few spaces away; Areto slid into the center, and Bern hopped into the bed. I stood by the truck and watched the action.

Police had arrived almost immediately. Both sons stood tense and silent; neither, I was sure, willing to say they had been outsmarted by Amazons. Not only would that have been humiliating, but as far as humans knew, we were nothing but myth. Plus the sons had no proof the baby we'd taken from them was theirs—telling the authorities would have had no benefit anyway.

We had won, and they knew it.

The shorter son turned. His eyes found me. For a second I thought I'd been mistaken, that he would say something to the cops.

But as he stared, I realized he wasn't thinking of pointing me out to the humans. No, he was thinking of what he would do to me when he caught me.

With a smile, I swung my body into the truck and pulled the door closed with a click.

He could think all he liked. It wouldn't change that these men—men who claimed to be sons of Amazons, sons who had inherited our powers and long life spans—would never be a match for the Amazons—ever.

Our safe camp was only an hour's drive from Beloit.

When we pulled in the drive, most of the camp's current occupants were outside waiting for us. Everyone except Thea and the baby.

I jumped down and strode toward Tess. The young hearth-keeper was sitting on the old farmhouse's front porch next to the baby's seat. She was holding some kind of stuffed animal—a cow, a flat cow. I raised a brow but didn't comment.

"Where's Thea?" I asked. The priestess had joined our camp only a week earlier, two days before the call came that two sons had stolen a high-council member's child and was headed in our direction.

Tess dropped the stuffed toy back into the empty carrier. "She went to the clearing with the baby."

I frowned. Thea had taken the call telling us about the

child. As queen of this camp, I'd have preferred to have been part of the conversation myself, but I had been out and the high council had chosen to tell Thea—it wasn't my place to quibble.

Now, though, I wasn't sure what we were supposed to do with the child. I assumed we would reunite her with her mother, but I didn't know when, where, or how.

I didn't like not knowing, and I didn't like Thea disappearing with her.

"I think she was doing some kind of blessing," Tess offered. "She had a bowl and some oil."

A bowl and oil . . . sounded to me more like Thea was planning to make salad.

I grunted and turned to go into the woods. At the last minute I went to the truck and grabbed a staff, one of my shorter ones for easier maneuvering in the trees.

I didn't normally walk around armed, but these were not normal times. The sons had grown bold, stealing the child. Who knew what they might try next?

It was a bit cooler in the woods than it had been in the open sun, but it was still hot and humid. My shirt stuck to my skin and bugs zipped around me. I waved them off with one hand and mentally cursed Thea for dragging the child to the clearing in the middle of the day.

The blessing could have been done at the farmhouse, or Thea could have waited until dark. Artemis was a moon goddess; any blessing from her would be strongest then.

Muttering another curse, I tugged on the elastic band at the bottom of my jog bra and let it snap against my skin. The three seconds of cool air that provided was no relief. My palms were sweaty too, making it harder to grip my staff. I took a second to wipe them on my shorts and blow a lock of blond hair out of my eyes.

A few feet away something crunched through the underbrush. Heat forgotten, I regripped the staff, but there was no further sound and no other signs anything might be amiss.

An animal, then, maybe a stray dog. We saw plenty of them, raccoons and possums too. *Could be anything.*

Still, the interruption made me remember my task.

I gripped my staff with renewed earnestness and kept walking.

I stepped over a fallen log, paused and listened again. There was no movement in the woods, though, and little sound. The animal I'd heard earlier must have left the area. I swung my back leg over the log and kept moving. I was close to the obelisk now.

Just before entering the clearing, I stopped. I wanted to see what Thea was doing, what had been so important that she had fled with the baby as soon as arriving back at camp.

The obelisk that marked the center of our place of worship was black and glossy in the sun. Thea stood next to it; as Tess had said, she held a bowl. She had lost the hoodie and her tattoos were now clearly visible: Medusa dominated one arm, an owl the other.

I had commented on the Medusa when we first met.

It wasn't idle conversation. Her choice of the snake-haired female was unusual. Amazons tended to animals and other symbols of nature, like the moon on the back of my neck or the owl on her other arm. Even our *telioses,* tattoos on our lower backs that depicted our family clans, and our *givnomais,* personal power tattoos on our right breasts, were all animals.

In fact, while we couldn't shift into animals like the sons supposedly could, we did get strength from the animals we chose, at least the ones we chose for our *givnomais.*

But Thea had seemed to have a different theory on tattoos than I did. She claimed body art didn't have to relay power, that Medusa reminded her what could happen if you acted with passion instead of logic.

I hadn't bothered to reply. All of my tattoos had a purpose. And I didn't consider personal reminders a purpose. Besides, logic was fine, if you had time for it. In battle you frequently didn't. Gut instinct had saved my hide more than once.

The sun shone through the trees onto Thea's short dark curls. Her eyes closed, she murmured something over the bowl, then dipped her fingers into whatever was contained inside it.

Her fingers glistening, she looked down. I realized then the baby was on the ground, wrapped in her blanket and snoozing.

I hesitated, unsure whether to make my presence known or not. It was obvious Thea was in the middle of some ceremony, and despite my annoyance that she had whisked the child off without consulting me first, I didn't feel right about interrupting her.

Something rustled in the woods. The priestess froze, only her eyes moving as she scanned the trees. Knowing she would spot me soon, I stepped forward.

"Zery." She glanced at the child, then set the bowl onto the ground and wiped her hands on her shorts. She took a step back, her foot hitting something white.

I tilted my head. I couldn't make out what the object was, but the way Thea was standing gave me the distinct impression she had no desire to show it to me. Which of course meant I had to see it.

I strode forward. "You left before we could talk."

She flipped both of her hands palm up. "The child needed to be accepted by the goddess."

"Accepted?" I'd never heard the term.

"Presented as a gift. Children are the most precious gifts, you know."

It sounded like the kind of worn sentiment you'd find on a two-for-a-dollar greeting card.

"I've never heard of a child being 'accepted' before."

She shrugged and glanced at the baby. "Perhaps your former high priestess preferred doing the ceremony in solitude. Many of us do."

A barb for interrupting her. With a frown, I took another step into her space, then kneeled, placed my staff on the ground, and scooped up the infant. She opened her eyes, curious and blue, and stared up at me. I had the strange urge to pat her on the chest or run my finger down her face. I grimaced. I'd never held a baby before; as a warrior, I'd never had the need or desire.

Seeing my discomfort, Thea held out her arms. "I can take her." I moved to shift the burden of the child's weight to the priestess's arms, but as I did, my eyes locked onto the white object lying behind her: a knife, made of bone.

I pulled back. "What's that?"

She stiffened, then followed my gaze . "Oh, the knife." She bent to retrieve it. "Have you never seen one of these either?"

A knife made of bone and carved in the shape of a small spear lay across her two hands.

She smiled. "It's a ceremonial knife. Carved over a thousand years ago. About as dangerous as a wooden spoon, as a weapon anyway, but full of magic. I use it to stir the oil."

I could see now the tip glistened. She picked up the bowl and held it out. An inch of oil covered its bottom.

So, I *had* interrupted something. Still, she shouldn't have wandered off with the baby we had just gone through so much effort to reclaim, not without telling me where she was going and why.

"Are you done?" I asked.

She tapped one finger against the rim of the bowl. "For now. The magic is gone; I'll have to recall it another day."

A prick to make me feel guilty, but it didn't draw

blood. "Or perhaps after she is returned to her mother, she can be 'accepted' then," I parried back, but I wasn't done. I had another question for our new priestess. "What did you use on the son—the dart? It wasn't part of our plan."

Thea's jaw tightened. "Do you have a problem with the outcome? We did get the child." With her thumb she twirled a ring around her finger. It was gold with a black enamel spider clinging to its band.

Despite myself I shuddered. Last fall the Amazons had been attacked by a son. I'd been staked out in a yard, a spider's web of magic stretched over me, keeping my warriors from me, holding me down *helpless*. I had never feared anything, still didn't, but spiders . . . I couldn't help but associate them with that nightmare, lying there vulnerable and exposed . . . I pulled my gaze from the ring as I realized Thea was watching me.

"Perhaps," she replied. "Here." She held out the knife. "You're a queen. Someone should have shared this part of our history with you before."

I glanced at the weapon, reluctant to take it but still eager to pass off the child. Finally I slipped the baby into Thea's arms and took hold of the knife.

The handle was smooth and warm and seemed to pulse with life inside my grip.

"Do you feel it?" she whispered.

Running my thumb down the blade, I nodded. She was right; it was dull. I felt nothing . . .

A shriek, loud and harsh, startled me from my

thoughts. I stepped back, my attention dashing around the clearing. Another shriek, this one closer and overhead.

A bird, bigger than any I'd ever seen or dreamed existed, soared toward us. Its wings, probably eleven feet tip to tip, blocked the sun. Its head was featherless and red, its beak hooked.

I froze, my brain not moving fast enough to process what was happening, to form a defense or an attack.

Thea cursed and my instincts snapped into place. I threw the knife, but the blade wasn't crafted for tossing. It fell with a thud to the ground.

I bent to pick up my staff and swung it overhead, like a child batting at a piñata.

The circling bird barely seemed to notice. His focus wasn't on me; it was on Thea and the child she held.

The child . . .

"A son," I yelled. The bird was a shape-shifted son, probably one of the two whom we'd tricked in Beloit. How they had found us this quickly I didn't know, but I had no doubt the monstrous bird wasn't natural . . . at least not for northern Illinois.

Something blasted from the dirt beside me. My staff, caught in the explosions, flew from my hand.

I coughed and rubbed dirt from my suddenly streaming eyes. Rocks flew from the ground and shot into the air like missiles. Thea stood in the center of the minefield, her arms held out and her lips moving. She was trying to down the bird with rocks previously buried beneath the soil.

But she had set down the child.

"Thea!" I yelled, trying to warn her to get to the baby, to take her and run. I could fight the son, but if we lost the child . . .

The priestess didn't hear me. She seemed lost in her fight. Her hands formed claws and dug down in the air, like she was digging in the dirt; then with a quick twist she flung her hands back up overhead and a new batch of rocks flew into the sky.

Realizing it was up to me to grab the child, I fell forward into a somersault and rolled, landing in a crouch next to the infant. Relief washed over me. I reached for her, ready to grab her and run, but she had been moved, bumped aside by a growling, snarling animal.

The thing stood next to the now screaming child, almost over her. Its body was stocky like a bear but smaller, maybe forty pounds. His teeth, attached to snapping jaws, were sharp and jagged, obviously built to tear flesh from bone. A wolverine.

I knew he was the shorter son as soon as I saw him, but his expression left no doubt. He stared me down with a hatred so intense, it felt personal. Animals don't emit emotions like that, but humans do . . . and sons do.

I'd wronged him, and he meant to make me pay.

A mix of a growl and snort escaped his jaws.

The knife was close, had fallen less than a foot from

where I kneeled. I leaned out, willing my hand to close over the bone handle.

It pulsed against my skin. I loosened my grip, then, remembering why I needed it, tightened my hold again. The internal reminder took only a second, but when I looked up, ready to pounce, the animal was gone.

A man stood in his place. Naked, he looked more muscular than he had clothed.

A tattoo of a wolverine covered the top half of his shoulder, but I didn't spend long studying his art. My focus latched onto his hands instead, on the squirming, screeching child he held over his head.

Chapter 2

The knife in my hand, I leapt and landed on the son's back. He smelled of male and woods, musk and humus. Earthy and enticing. Except I wasn't enticed; I was enraged.

He didn't bend or move to protect himself. He stood straight and tall. I thought I had him, thought I'd won. Then the bird, whatever it was, swooped low, grabbed the bundled baby in its talons, and soared away.

Thea cursed again, louder and rougher than before. I felt her scrutiny, hard and accusing, but I didn't glance at her.

One elbow locked around the son's neck, I pulled back my free hand, the one holding the knife, and thrust down toward his chest.

I landed without warning on the rock-strewn ground.

The impact surprised and jarred me. My jaws snapped together and my fingers flew open. The knife fell to the ground and I tumbled onto my back. Unarmed, I didn't pause; I shoved myself up and, seeing it now only inches away, grabbed my staff.

I pivoted slowly, looking for the son. He was close and back in his animal form. We were alone now; Thea had left, in pursuit of the bird, I assumed. I had no idea how she meant to catch it, or if she could, but here and now I had my own battle to fight. I focused on the son.

I moved forward, my staff low and positioned to strike against his now smaller body. The snorting growl I'd heard earlier grew louder, and his eyes glittered with dark emotion.

I swung. With a sickening thud, the end of my staff collided with his head. He slid backward, his claws scrambling at the ground and his growl growing so loud it was almost a roar.

In seconds he was back on his feet. He circled to my left, his teeth snapping. He was watching me, calculating my next move.

He bared his teeth, declaring a challenge.

Deep in the battle, I released a yell, sidestepped, and jabbed at his head—this time with enough force to kill.

My staff collided with dirt and rock. The impact reverberated up my arms and into my body. I jumped back as if electrocuted and surveyed the ground, searching, wondering what the hell had happened, how I'd missed.

A hand shot forward and grabbed my staff, or tried to.

I sidestepped, twisting the staff up and over my head, then lashed sideways, aiming for where a lifetime of practice told me a throat would be located.

The son, a man now, again completely naked, dropped to a crouch. My staff flew harmlessly over his head.

I recovered again, pulling the staff back and bracing my legs for my next thrust.

"Give it up. We won't let you have the baby." He stood slowly, his eyes telling me not to swing, that despite his calm words he was ready for my next move.

"Won't let us have what is already ours? Perhaps you'd like to think again."

His eyes glittered, not the same eyes I'd seen staring at me from the animal's face, but the expression . . . the hate . . . it was a perfect match.

"Yours?" he asked and snorted. "You can't own a child, can't do with it as you please, Zery. Not as long as the sons are here to stop you."

Despite my best intentions, I jerked. He knew my name.

I tightened my jaw, then pulled my lips into a smile. "I don't remember being introduced."

"Don't you? Zery Kostovska." He tilted his head and studied my face. I kept it void of all emotion. "I feel like we've met. I know so much about you . . . how even in a house full of Amazons, you keep yourself apart. How you come here to the woods when no one else does. How you pride yourself on being the perfect Amazon queen." He laughed at the last.

"Who are you?" I asked.

"Me?" He grinned. His teeth were even and white. "I'm your fairy godfather. The sons assigned me to watch over you and your little camp of Amazons. Do you feel special?" He shook his head, a mocking imitation of motherly letdown. "I was so disappointed when I saw you in Beloit, realized you were part of their plan." He looked at me again, his scrutiny intense. "You really should try not to disappoint me."

He moved then.

I swung my staff.

And the son did the impossible. He caught it with his bare hand.

I'd had my blows parried before, but not by many and not easily. But the man staring at me had caught my staff without moving more than his arm. Even the cocky slant of his brow hadn't altered.

Then he did something no one had dared to do before. He jerked my staff toward his body, jerking me there too. His arm slipped behind my waist and he held me tight against his naked form. My breasts already compressed by my workout bra were crushed more. The only things separating us were my thin tee and shorts and the staff we both still held.

I didn't struggle; my eyes met his. The weak struggled; the strong simply escaped . . . when they were ready.

"One question. Why? Why are you doing this? Oh, I forgot . . . that's how the Amazons stay strong, isn't it? Preying on the most defenseless?"

Anger flooded my body, but I forced calm into my voice. "The Amazons stay strong because we are strong."

He laughed. "Of course. And only the strong deserve to survive."

"Basic law of nature—the strong survive. You have issues with that?" I asked.

"Yes." He jerked me closer. "If it's at the cost of someone else's survival."

He was talking nonsense. "You threaten me, I'll fight back. You steal from me, I'll steal back. If you expected something else, you don't know the Amazons."

His lips quirked, but without humor. "Oh, I know the Amazons. Way better than I'd like. Take my mother, for example . . . I know her, know she cast me aside, not because she couldn't raise me, but because she thought I was beneath her. At least that was all she did. She didn't kill me or maim me. I suppose I should be grateful for that. Other sons weren't so lucky. Some of us curse our mothers, but me?" He shrugged a shoulder. "You can't hate a rattler for being a snake, can you? Just like you can't hate an Amazon for being a bitch."

The venom in his voice was harsh, but our reality was harsh. An example of why the sons didn't belong with us. My mother didn't raise me, but while I couldn't claim to love her, or miss her now that we made no pretense of familial care, I didn't bemoan my fate. Being raised by surrogates, one after the other, had made me strong, taught me early on what emotional commitments did to you, how they weakened you.

But I had no interest in explaining any of this to this son and, based on the rage simmering behind his dark eyes, he had no interest in hearing anything I had to say.

He leaned closer; his breath—it smelled of spearmint—stirred my hair. "What about you, Zery? You ever curse your mother?"

Then he pulled back and his hand moved, from my waist to the back of my neck . . . to one of my tattoos . . . if he touched the others I'd desert my submissive act.

"You wear Artemis's crescent, but do you follow her, Zery? Really?" His fingers brushed over my skin.

The tattoo was a gift, one I'd received when I'd accepted my role as queen. It tied me to Artemis, awakened some of her strengths inside me. All queens had them, high priestesses too, although theirs was on the inside of one wrist.

His fingers touched both the ink and the magic buried there; a tingle swept through my body.

Another surprise.

I hid my reaction.

His fingers moved again. Somehow, without being able to see the tattoo, he was tracing its border.

A shiver erupted from my core. I gritted my teeth.

He cocked his head. "You really don't let people get close, do you? Have you ever? Maybe that's what's wrong with the Amazons . . . what they need to change." He leaned in. This time his lips brushed my ear. I stood still. I could take him down at any moment. Knowing that was enough, gave me the patience to stand there and listen . . . to learn. I hoped to get him to talk more, to give me a clue how many of the sons watched us and where they lived. And then, after I stole the baby back, I would kill him. He and his fellow son had stolen one of our own—he couldn't live, not after that.

"Has anyone ever gotten close to you, Zery? Have you ever loved anyone or anything? Or can't you, because no one has loved you? Because your own mother doesn't give a damn about you?"

It wasn't his words that angered me, but his tone, the mockery in them—I'd had enough, waited enough. I lifted my knee to deliver the most basic, but fulfilling of attacks.

Behind me an owl called. The sound seemed to startle him; he froze.

I smiled . . . a mistake on his part.

His hold on me disappeared. My weight shifted, but my knee was already moving, guaranteed to hit its mark . . . but once again I struck nothing but air, because the man was gone and the animal I'd first encountered was back.

He looked at me, his eyes free of emotion now. Then he did what I'd imagined he would when I'd first seen him; he opened his jaws and chomped into my calf.

Then, just as quickly, he let go and was gone.

Blood streamed down my leg. I took a step forward or tried to, but my knee buckled. I cursed and used my staff to force myself to stay standing.

With each step, I forced my brain not to register pain, let the adrenaline flow unimpeded through me. It kept me going, but the son hadn't taken the path as he escaped. He had dived into the thickest brambles, using his animal form and instincts to get him quickly through areas that, even unwounded, I'd have had a tough time negotiating, at least without a sword to clear my way.

Also, I had lost blood. The pain might have been muted, but my leg was rubbery and my knee wasn't answering the demands of my brain as it should have. I placed my palm against a birch and mumbled my frustration. I would heal, much quicker than a human, but it would take a day or so, not seconds. Amazons were descended from a god; we weren't gods.

"Zery!" Thea yelled from the clearing.

I pushed myself away from the tree and scowled after the son. He was long gone now, and hard as it was to face, in my injured state I had no hope of catching him.

I swallowed that truth, then returned the way I'd come. Though short, it was a hard trip. The adrenaline that had pushed me forward before, now ebbed. And with its waning, my leg began to throb. But I was used to pain, was trained to handle it. I blew air out of rounded lips and limped on.

Thea stood next to the obelisk, her hands empty and a scowl on her face. As my eyes met hers, as my foot hit the flattened grass and dirt, the pain, manageable seconds before, ripped through me. With no explanation or warning, I lived the attack again, in slow motion. *The ani-*

mal's teeth punctured my flesh a millimeter at a time, his jaws crushed against my bone. He pulled; my leg screamed; my mind screamed.

I staggered, and a shudder shook my body.

Then the pain was gone, not completely, but down to a gut-twisting ache.

I stared at the high priestess, wondering if she'd seen what had happened, had some explanation. But if she did, she didn't offer to share.

She tromped to the obelisk and smashed her fist against the stone. "You lost him." Her head lowered, she muttered something.

"*We* lost him," I corrected. I assumed she meant the wolverine son and not the bird, but she had obviously been no more successful in stopping either than I had been.

Her gaze dropped to my leg, then back at my face. There were words behind her expression, angry words. I waited for her to throw them, or something else at me. Then we could face the wrath that boiled inside both of us, the frustration of our lost battle. I flexed my fingers, then curled them back around my staff . . . ready.

Her eyes stayed flat and her lips tight for a flicker of a second. Then she shook her head. "The pressure of losing her after we had just saved her, and before I could present her to the goddess . . . I didn't mean to. . . . How could you have expected an attack from above?" She glanced again at my leg, letting her gaze linger there for a bit.

I adjusted my stance. "True, we couldn't expect it, but

it shouldn't have happened. The child should have been safe inside the house, surrounded by the tribe." She had endangered the baby by bringing her here. Apparently she needed to be reminded of that.

"I was so close . . ." she murmured. "To presenting her to the goddess," she finished as if in explanation. Her jaw tense, she picked up the bowl and walked to the edge of the trees with it. Her back to me, she mumbled a few words, then spilled the contents of the bowl onto the ground.

She seemed to miss that *she* was the reason the child had been stolen, that *she* had brought her here. So what if the baby had been "presented" before the sons grabbed her? She still would have been taken. I bit down on the inside of my cheek. "Did you see where the bird went?"

She shook her head; anger, loss, and disappointment warred in her eyes. "I had my . . . I followed him as long as I could, but he was too big, too fast. It was impossible to keep up."

"What direction did he go?" I made no pretense of politeness. It was obvious we both thought the other had failed.

She pointed to the north. "Toward the town."

Our camp was twenty miles from the nearest small town. "He could have been headed to Deep River, or the highway, or Canada." I smashed the end of my staff into the ground. There was no telling.

Thea twisted her lips to the side and a shadow passed over her face. "What about the other one? What was it?"

she asked. "It looked like a wolverine. Do you have wolverines here?"

I shook my head. "Not that I know of, but that doesn't matter. The sons can shift into whatever animal their *givnomai* is."

"So it's true." Despite the fact she'd just seen a bird the size of a small plane swoop down on us, she looked skeptical.

"You saw for yourself how true it is," I replied, realizing she hadn't believed the stories, not before today. "You saw the son I battled, saw him shift."

She shook her head. "I saw the wolverine, then I saw the man. That doesn't mean they were the same. But the bird . . . obviously what it did wasn't normal. *It* wasn't normal." She looked at my leg again. This time she knelt down. When her hands touched me they were cool and covered in whatever oil she'd been stirring, then spilled on the ground. As she rubbed the oil over my wound, the smell intensified, but I didn't work with oil either for magic or cooking. I couldn't identify the scent.

"Trust me. He shifted," I said.

"I'd heard the stories, but . . ." She held up a hand. "Give me your shirt."

I pulled it over my head. She folded it around her hand and wiped oil and blood from my skin.

I continued, "What did you think the bird was, if not a son?"

She refolded the cloth and wiped some more. "A bird. An agent of someone, his moves orchestrated."

"Orchestrated? By who?"

"The sons obviously, eh."

"But you believe it now? Believe they can shift?" I hadn't seen a son shift before today either. I had to admit it was hard to believe they could. Amazons couldn't shift. Why could their sons?

She tilted her head side to side in grudging agreement. "I believe I underestimated them. I believe next encounter I'll be ready."

On that we both agreed.

She returned to my wound, tying the cloth around my leg. When she stood, her expression was tame, almost soft. "The damage isn't bad, puncture wounds only. I expected much worse."

"Because it was a wolverine?"

Her eyes unreadable, she replied, "Because it stopped you from doing your job." Then she strolled from the clearing.

With a growl, I followed.

Amazons had owned the safe camp since the area was settled. We—not me, being in my nineties, I wasn't born yet—built the farmhouse not long after.

When Thea and I arrived at the house, the yard was empty. Thinking everything was under control, not knowing we had lost the child yet, the Amazons had gone about their normal tasks. It was approaching time for dinner. The hearth-keepers would be in the kitchen. The warriors were exercising the horses in one of the lower fields, and the one artisan staying with us was off doing whatever artisans did . . . drawing or carving or something.

"Do you have a plan for retrieving the baby?" Thea asked.

Her voice startled me. I wasn't used to being questioned, not even by the high priestess. But Thea wasn't Alcippe, our old priestess; she was younger, probably used to being bolder and sharing more responsibility in how a camp was run.

That, of course, didn't mean I had to answer. Especially since the answer was no. I had no idea how to find the sons now. And even if I did, I was fairly certain getting the baby back this time was going to be a lot harder.

And I wasn't sure how much time we had. But after talking to the son in the woods, I had an idea *why* they wanted the child . . . revenge, pure and simple.

Payback for every son an Amazon had killed or maimed in the past.

Chapter 3

I stayed up most of the night, pacing outside. I had gathered the tribe as soon as they had returned to camp from their various tasks. It had been awkward telling them we had lost the child, that the two sons had stolen her back, but they deserved to know.

There had been a few dark looks darted from face to face, but that was it. No one questioned us. It wasn't their place. They knew if their assistance was needed, Thea or I would tell them. Until then they were to just go about their regular lives.

After the circle broke up, I'd stayed outside . . . thinking, wishing I could go back in time and stop what had happened.

I tilted my face up to the sky.

The moon was full. Artemis was strongest at the crescent, on the sixth day of the new moon. That was when I could count on being filled with her fierce energy, but any night the moon was in the sky, I felt her. And tonight I needed her.

The baby was back in the hands of the sons. I didn't know how long they'd had her before we rescued her the first time or exactly what they had planned for her, but knowing they had her, could put in place whatever scheme they had at any moment, ate at me.

I wanted to rally the tribe and race out to defeat them. Problem was, I had no idea where the sons might have gone. The council had given Thea the address in Beloit. I had put in a call to my contact, Kale, when we got home, asking for more assistance, but calls to council members went to voice mail, and mine had yet to be returned.

I stared up at the moon for a moment longer, praying Artemis would look down on me and gift me with some skill to find the sons and save the child.

But I knew it didn't work like that, knew Artemis had already gifted me with all the skills I could expect to have. New ones didn't just drop down from the trees.

So if I wanted to find this baby, I would have to find the talent to do so inside myself.

I just hoped for the child's sake that wouldn't take too long.

After only a few hours of sleep I awoke later than normal, but still early. I checked my wounds before leaving bed.

I'd discovered a second injury on arriving home last night—a bloody slit in my thumb. It throbbed a bit this morning, but was obviously nothing to be disturbed by. I spared a glance at it before moving on to the bigger concern—the bite on my leg.

As I pulled off Thea's makeshift bandage, I saw she had been right. There were four distinct puncture wounds, two seriously deeper than the others, but none dangerous to me or my leg.

And none nasty enough to explain the pain I had felt when I stepped into the clearing. The incident was already fading from memory, though . . . perhaps it hadn't been as bad as I recalled. I was tense at the time. That amount of anger and frustration could easily have amplified my reaction. I was calm now, though, and ready to find the sons.

I left the wound open to the air. It would heal quickly. I could already put weight on my leg with no pain, and I didn't need a bandage as a reminder of what had happened.

I left my room and stepped into the hall. There were sounds coming from the kitchen—the hearth-keepers fixing breakfast and preparing goods for the farmer's market in Madison, Wisconsin, in three days. It was a weekly event during the summer for us. Technically everything sold at the farmer's market was supposed to be a Wisconsin product, but we weren't big on technicalities, and a small piece of land the tribe owned in northern Wisconsin provided a convenient address for the paperwork. Marketgoers knew us as Amazon Farms, and they loved us. Who wouldn't?

I personally didn't frequent the market; Lao handled it and handled it well. I seldom went to Madison at all.

But Thea had said the bird last night was heading north. Madison was north, as were the only two sons I knew how to find. I'd met both of them in the fall, or seen them at least. We hadn't exactly sat around the fire and exchanged war stories.

One worked for my friend Mel in her tattoo shop as an artist. The other, his mentor, was an older man confined to a wheelchair. His handicap was the result of the old Amazon ways, when we still killed or maimed our sons to keep them from becoming threats.

If the council didn't call this morning with a new direction, searching out whatever sons I could seemed a sensible step. So a trip to Madison would clearly be in order.

First, though, I needed to track down my new high priestess. I walked through the living room. Except for the two threadbare couches and a few dirty coffee mugs and plates, the room was empty. The front door, however, stood open.

Thea stood in the yard with her hands raised above her head. Her hair was wet and her dark curls glistened in the early-morning sun, but it was the expression on her upturned face that stopped me. Her eyes were closed, as you would expect with the sun streaming down on her, but she still looked rapt, like she was soaking in the rays, recharging, growing stronger before my eyes.

For some reason, I found the idea disturbing. I stepped onto the porch.

Most of the other occupants of the house had formed a half circle around the new priestess. When I walked out the door, they turned faces filled with curiosity and a bit of wariness toward me.

I suddenly felt out of place—as if I'd stumbled into something uninvited, but that was impossible. This was *my* camp. I was queen here and had been for over a decade. Despite the fact that many of the Amazons present were newcomers to this house, I was the one steady factor. Their expressions were unfathomable.

Unless someone had told them something to make them doubt me, to question my reliability. I scanned their faces, looking for any sign of censure.

Thea dropped her arms and turned. "The queen joins us."

The words were innocent enough, but there was something about Thea's tone that caused my body to stiffen.

I opened my mouth to utter a rebuke, then saw her expression. While not friendly, it wasn't mocking either. I snapped my jaws shut. She was new; we were still getting to know each other. I could easily have been reading her wrong. Most important, though—now was not the time to be taking our aggression out on each other. It would only get in the way of doing our jobs.

Still, I couldn't bring myself to smile. Not that I smiled much anyway. Life was too serious.

I walked down the two steps that separated the wide front porch from the yard, then moved toward our new high priestess with my shoulders back and my footsteps tapping on the concrete walk.

The Amazons who had surrounded the priestess took a step back. I stopped a staff's length away.

She tilted her head. "We are enjoying the sun. It helps me feel centered, ready to take on any challenge." The fingers of her right hand brushed over her left arm, over Medusa.

I registered the gesture, realizing it was a habit of hers. What I didn't know was why she did it, what emotion she was feeling at the time.

"I'll be going to Madison today." I paused, wondering if I should ask her to come along. After only a second of consideration, I added, "It would be best if you stayed here."

It was normal procedure. It wasn't often the high priestess and the queen were both absent from a safe camp. And I preferred to handle the trip to Wisconsin's capital city on my own. Mainly because I didn't want her with me when I visited Mel's.

Mel was an outsider now. My relationship with her was not necessarily looked on kindly by others in the tribe. Plus I needed Mel to help me get access to the sons. Bringing a high priestess she didn't know along would not be a help.

My plan announced, I turned to the other Amazons. The circle had broken into parts. The hearth-keepers were wandering back inside or toward the garden. Our one artisan was still at Thea's side. As I turned away, she began talking to the priestess. The warriors had clustered together under a nearby maple. They were obviously waiting for something . . . direction from me, I assumed.

They were all fairly new arrivals. I knew them from Amazon gatherings, but most had only been staying at the camp since spring. I had, however, been running them through their paces for weeks. Not only did we have a martial arts exhibition at the Illinois State Fair in a month, I needed a lieutenant. I had lost my last lieutenant to our run-in with a son last fall—our first encounter with them. I hoped one of these warriors could fill the position.

I called to Areto. She was only five ten, small for an Amazon, but she was quick and limber. I'd had the group scale the side of the barn earlier in the week with nothing but a rope and Areto had arrived at the top minutes before the rest. She also reminded me of Mel; it might have just been a superficial resemblance, her dark hair and short height, but I didn't think so. I thought I could trust her, as much as I could trust anyone.

"You're in charge of the exercises today. Let me know if anyone slacks." She didn't question why and she didn't glance at the high priestess I knew was still standing only a few feet behind me; she just raised her hand in signal to the rest of the group and led them toward the barn.

Thea was still behind me, still waiting. I walked toward the house. I needed car keys if I was going to drive to Madison.

"Are you going to inform the high council of what happened?" she asked.

I turned. My voice steady and sure, I answered, "I have a call in, but we can't sit around and wait. We need to get the baby back."

She inclined her head in agreement, then motioned for Sare, our lone artisan, who still stood beside her to move along. The girl picked up a leather bag from the ground and wandered off to sit in the sun and do her work—carving totems, I guessed. They sold well at fairs.

"You can't go alone," Thea said, her voice low.

I exhaled through my nose. I was not used to being ordered, at least not by anyone below the high council. My arms hanging loosely at my sides, I addressed her. "I don't expect to find the baby in Madison, just information."

"And you can't get that with a phone call?"

I couldn't. I needed to see Mel face-to-face if I wanted any hope of convincing her to help the Amazons. She didn't trust us. She might even believe the child would be better off with the sons.

"No," I replied, then walked away.

My foot had barely hit the step when she called again. "It was my failure too. I'll get the knife and meet you here."

I paused. My first instinct was to turn on her, to tell her exactly who was queen and what my orders were, but when I processed her actual words, they stopped me. She had admitted fault. She suffered guilt for it. I could appreciate that, could see how she would want to be part of righting what had happened in the woods. I still didn't want her in Madison, but I couldn't deny her the right to fix what she had been part of screwing up. Not without hearing her out.

I continued on into the house, torn on what to do.

Thea was crouched on the ground next to Sare when I came out. I could see that the artisan was drawing rather than carving as I'd guessed earlier.

As I approached, Thea took a piece of paper from her and rolled it like a scroll.

Ignoring them both, I got into the safe camp's car, a ten-year-old Jeep Cherokee. The Amazons who came and went had their own vehicles; this one was communal property, meaning for today it was mine.

Despite my complete lack of acknowledgement, Thea climbed into the passenger seat. I took my hand off the key. I'd told her she needed to stay at the camp. While inside the house, I'd realized no matter her guilt or desire to right her part in our mistake, she needed to comply.

She tapped the rolled-up paper she'd gotten from the artisan against her leg. "What is your plan?"

"I am going to Madison. You are staying here."

My direct response didn't seem to bother her.

"You haven't explained why you think going to Madison is the answer. Seems more likely we would find out something around here." Her thumbnail flipped the edge of the rolled paper.

I hadn't explained because I didn't need to explain. I still didn't, but remembering her admittance and not wanting to put more pressure on our strained relationship, I replied, "We know the sons have the baby. We just need to find out where. There are two sons in Madison. Seems logical they might know something about the pair who has the child."

"And you think they will tell us?" She twisted her lips to the side.

I tapped my fingers against the top of the steering wheel. "Probably not, but if I ask right, maybe someone else will. Worst case, I can watch the Madison sons. Madison isn't that far from Beloit—the sons who stole the baby probably know the others. With their Beloit cover blown, they may be in contact for help."

She nodded. "Makes sense, but it seems like there might be a more direct approach." She unrolled the scroll.

And there was my fairy godfather staring up at me.

I cursed myself silently. She'd described the son to the artisan and the girl had sketched a portrait. It was a good idea, a much more direct plan than spending two hours in a car and hoping I'd be able to get information out of the sons in Madison.

"He might live near here or at least have gone into town to get supplies, eh?" she asked.

"He does," I replied without expression, and then I started the car.

The depth of my potential failure was making it hard to speak. He was my fairy godfather, of course he lived near here. Probably within walking distance of the safe camp. Hell, he might live in our woods in his wolverine form, be the creature the hearth-keepers were constantly trying to keep away from our chickens, for all I knew.

She smoothed the drawing, ran the pads of two fingers over his face. "You've seen him before?"

I put the vehicle into reverse, then headed down our drive. "No, but I know he lives close by." I couldn't kick her out of the car now. Besides, it didn't appear I'd be going to Madison, at least not right now.

She angled her head, obviously waiting for more of an explanation, but that was all I was giving.

Finally she looked away and started digging in a corded bag she'd brought with her—the kind that could be used as a backpack too. It was yellow, a bright sunny yellow.

She pulled out a cell phone and started punching buttons. "If he has the baby, he will need supplies."

I watched her out of the corner of my eye. Amazons had a long-standing resistance against technology. We had a landline in each of our safe houses, and I knew a few Amazons who had those pay-as-you-go phones, but that was about it. "What are you doing?"

"Searching the Internet. Trying to see where he might go for baby supplies."

"It's a town of three thousand. There aren't that many choices." Her thinking to have the artisan re-create the son's image had shaken me, but I was past that. "We don't need the Internet."

She placed the phone on her lap. "Have you ever used it?"

I hadn't. I wasn't even sure what it did. I stared at the narrow highway in front of me. We were out of the wooded area where we lived and traveling through the more typical terrain of fields and more fields.

"It won't help us find the son."

I flipped on my turn signal and turned the Jeep into the hub of life here in Deep River—Walmart's parking lot. When I slammed the Jeep's dented door closed, Thea's cell phone had disappeared. I rewarded her with a jerk of my head toward the store.

We only had the one picture, so we headed first to the photo department and had a few more made. Then we split up. I let Thea take the baby section. I headed to the cashiers.

After an hour of complete failure, I was feeling much better about my initial plan to visit the sons I *knew* I could find.

I went to the in-store cafe where I'd arranged to meet Thea. She had her phone out again and was talking to someone. When I walked up, she punched END and stood. "I found him. He's living in a cabin about ten miles by road from the safe camp, maybe two cross-country."

Success, or at least a step closer.

Thea held up her phone and smiled.

My fairy godfather was about to get a visit he wouldn't forget.

The son's place wasn't hard to find. It was, as I had guessed, close to the safe camp if you traveled through our woods anyway. By road it was a good distance, but it was off the main highway.

I turned onto a spindly dirt road. There were two ancient steel mailboxes stacked on top of each other right at the highway, meaning there was at least one other house on the road. If the other house was occupied by humans, this might complicate things. Humans got jumpy when weapons and magic were tossed around. I preferred to keep our encounter with the sons under the human radar.

As we were pulling in, a compact hybrid was pulling out. I moved to the side to let it pass.

It didn't look like what I imagined my tattooed godfather would drive, but I stared down the driver anyway. A woman peered over the steering wheel as she approached. I relaxed against my seat. Unless the wolverine could also shift into seventy-year-old schoolteachers, I was pretty sure it wasn't him.

I waited to move until she was completely past, then looked to Thea for further instructions.

"It's at the end of the road," she replied.

"How long is the drive?" I asked. After seeing the son had a neighbor, I wondered if we wouldn't be better off returning to the camp and approaching the cabin on foot through our woods.

As soon as I asked, we passed another vehicle, a truck . . . the kind with dual tires on the back end. It was parked nose out. Trees crowded around it, but I could make out an oversized fifth wheel behind it and a log house beyond that.

"Not there," Thea commented. "It's a bit further."

A man in his fifties was standing beside the truck, seemed to be tinkering with some device on his dashboard. As we rolled past, I noticed a woman too, loading boxes into the trailer.

I made a point of not looking at them as we went by and I don't think they paid much attention to me. They seemed too occupied with whatever they were doing. Right past their place there was a huge pothole; as I maneuvered around it, the truck started up and the pair pulled out, the trailer hitched up behind them.

With our potential witnesses gone, I relaxed a bit. We drove probably another quarter of a mile, then pulled off into the grass.

Thea got out first. I took my time. The son had picked a good spot. Even knowing he had a neighbor a quarter of a mile away, the place felt isolated. Of course, that didn't mean we were alone—the son or sons could be there. I hoped they were.

With that in mind, I pulled a knife from under the backseat and signaled for Thea to creep toward the house.

The forest closed in on the short gravel drive as we approached, narrowing to nothing but two bare ruts in the grass with trees pressed in so close the branches overhead mingled into one thick canopy. The cabin, tucked in between some massive maples, was small. I guessed nothing more than one main room . . . maybe a small bedroom and bath. There was a carport thing instead of a garage; it, like the cabin, was made of unstripped logs. It looked like the son had built the place himself.

The wolverine had a little Grizzly Adams in him. A bit of old farmer too . . . the place was littered with old pieces of machinery. The kind you normally see rusting in fields as you drive down county highways.

"What now?" Thea stayed partially hidden in the trees.

The property seemed quiet. I was fairly confident our arrival would come as a surprise . . . if anyone was home. There was no vehicle parked under the carport.

Of course the bird son could have taken the car and my fairy godfather could be inside, or he could be sitting in the underbrush in his wolverine form watching us. Or another son in a different animal form could be watching us. I glanced around the clearing; a rabbit paused not far from the carport to nibble at some grass.

I froze . . . over a rabbit. My reaction was unsettling. But it was more unsettling to realize I could be staring right at my enemy and not be able to tell. If I ignored the rabbit, walked toward the cabin, he could shift and I could find an arm wrapped around my throat.

I looked at Thea. "Do you sense magic?" Sometimes priestesses could tell if magic was being worked. Of course, if the rabbit was a son, he might not be using magic right now. Maybe they used it only to shift, not to hold the shape. Not being an expert on Amazon sons or magic, I really didn't know.

Thea closed her eyes and held out her hands.

Finally she opened her eyes. "Nothing."

Which told me the same—nothing. Still, it wasn't her fault I knew so little of our enemy. I hid my annoyance.

I pointed, letting her know I would circle to the back of the cabin; she was to stay where she was, to alert me if anyone approached and to stop anyone besides me from leaving.

Hoping I wasn't just playing bird dog, that the son would be home and choose to face me, not rush for an escape route, I slipped through the trees lining the clearing.

When I was even with the cabin's porch, the rabbit heard me and ran. I watched him escape into the trees and prayed I wasn't making a mistake by assuming he was simply what he appeared to be.

With the horrible rabbit threat gone, I crept toward the cabin. There were two windows each about four feet off the ground. They were easy enough to peer into, but the inside of the cabin was dark. All I could make out past the grime was the rough shadow of some furniture, a couch, and an oversized chair. I moved to the second window. This one looked into the bedroom. The actual room was dark, but a light had been left on in a small attached bathroom making the contents of the space much more visible.

There were two rifles and maybe six rifle-shaped boxes lying on the bed.

Guns. Amazons don't do guns.

We have never had a reason. We haven't had a real enemy since before firearms were invented, and certainly haven't since before they'd become the reliable killing machines they are today.

But now we had an enemy, and he was armed not only with the ability to shift, but also with rifles, maybe more weapons I couldn't see through this window.

It pissed me off. Not because we couldn't destroy the sons, we still could, but because the males were an even less worthy adversary than I had thought.

Were they so sure of their weaknesses they were afraid to face us using traditional weapons? I shook my head in disgust.

"What is it?" Thea had crept up behind me.

I stiffened. I had told her to wait.

She cupped her hands and stared through the glass. "Guns."

I nodded.

"We should take them."

I didn't move; I couldn't. "Take them?"

"They are superior weapons to what we have now." She glanced at the knife I held.

"So we should take them and use them," I repeated.

She opened her mouth to reply, but I was already past her, already headed for the back door. I didn't bother to check the lock. I lifted my foot and kicked in the door.

There was a click. Instinct told me to move a step to the side, but heat smacked me in the face and a force flung me backward. After that all I was aware of was noise . . . an explosion and the sensation of my body flying through the air.

The cabin had blown up.

Chapter 4

I was thrown twenty feet, into the woods. My back hit a tree seconds before my butt hit the ground. I cursed and tried to stand. Pain grabbed me, like someone had slipped my spine into a vice and was twisting down the handle, trying to twist me too. I gritted my teeth and tried to convince my mind it didn't feel the pain, didn't feel anything at all.

Doubled over, I staggered forward.

The cabin was an inferno; smoke billowed from the hole that had been the roof. The leaves on the closest trees, curled from the heat.

"Thea?" I called. Amazons were hard to kill, harder than humans anyway, but a fire like this? Nothing could survive it. Still bent at the waist, I jerked off my shirt and wrapped it around my face, then I lurched toward the fire. She hadn't been in the cabin, hadn't even been as close as I had been. Surely she had survived.

Heat slammed into me. Fire roared forward like a live beast unleashed and set on destroying its captors. There was a crash. One of the cabin walls had fallen in; ash and bits of red-hot coals sprinkled the ground and my bare skin.

I brushed them off and circled to the right. Entering the building without knowing the priestess was inside would be suicide—entering it at all would be suicide, but if I could hear her, knew she was there, I'd do it. It wouldn't even be a choice.

I paced slowly over the area near the back door where I'd last seen her, listening and searching for some sign.

After five minutes I had to stop, had to bend lower to find air not clogged with soot. There was none. Even outside the actual fire, I felt as if I had been dropped down inside a potbelly stove.

I'd decided walking back and forth like a trapped bear was getting me nowhere when two old farmers in a pickup with a water tank in the back arrived. Based on the hoarse yells of the ragtag pair, I gathered they'd had a hard time making it down the drive. I also knew if one of them had called in the fire, I had fifteen, twenty minutes tops to get out before the real fire department arrived.

They started spraying the trees closest to the cabin. I'm sure the structure itself appeared to be a lost cause.

I marched forward, doing the best job I could to hide

my still-throbbing back and held out my hand for the hose. The man stared at me as if I'd stepped out of the fire with the complete intention of pulling him back in with me. Frustrated, I grabbed the hose and soaked myself down, shorts, hair, and the shirt tied over my face.

Then I dropped the still-flowing hose onto the ground and headed back to the fire.

The other man found his voice. "You can't go in there."

I ignored him, made it all of three steps before it began to rain, soft, almost a mist. It felt insulting, like a god was laughing at me, teasing me. I turned to stare at the cabin. It was already consumed by the fire.

I had to face that even an Amazon couldn't have survived that.

And the fire truck couldn't be far away.

I wasn't too worried about the farmers being able to identify me with my face covered by my shirt and my body by soot or that they would have paid much attention to the Jeep, but the firefighters were a different matter. I would have to move the Jeep before they came down the narrow road and spotted it. I was a witness, chances were they'd at least want to hear my version of events.

Without looking at the self-appointed heroes again, I pointed my body toward the main road. Somewhere in the short trip back to the Jeep, my back pain changed from a steady throb to intermittent shrieks—shorter and more spaced out, but breathtakingly severe.

At least this new pain made me forget my leg completely. It didn't, however, make me forget Thea or stop thinking about what I would do after hiding the Jeep.

Not that I needed to worry about hiding the Jeep.

When I returned to where I had left it, it was gone.

I'd disappeared into the woods just as the fire truck rumbled down the road. The pothole had slowed the massive vehicle some. I figured by the time they got to the son's house, it would be nothing but ash.

Which suited me fine. I didn't know what the story on the guns was, but I wanted the sons for myself. I didn't want them being locked up in some human prison before I could get to them.

It took me an hour to get back to camp on foot. If I'd been whole, I could have made it in a quarter of the time. I guessed it took the son in his wolverine form even less than that.

I approached from behind the barn; the horses were out, but there was no sign of any Amazons. I was glad for the quiet, glad I didn't have to face any of them just yet. The past twenty-four hours had taken a toll on me. I needed to at least look strong when I gathered them together and announced Thea was missing. I hadn't worked out yet what had happened to the Jeep. My guess was the sons had seen us arrive and stolen it.

A mare approached and nuzzled my neck. I wrapped my fingers in her mane and used her for support.

My face against hers, I inhaled. The sun-heated scent of her skin was calming. Closing my eyes, I pulled on her strength, pulled on the strength of my *givnomai* too. Then I straightened my back, swallowed my physical pain, and strode out of the paddock.

The gravel crunched as my feet came to a halt.

Sitting in a line next to the five or so other Amazon vehicles was the Jeep.

It hadn't driven here on its own. And I didn't think the sons had delivered it to us.

Our new high priestess had deserted me, left me wounded and alone at the cabin.

My temper soared. All thoughts of avoiding a confrontation with her fled.

I tromped toward the house, not sure what I was going to say or do once I reached it, once I reached Thea.

But the building was empty. The grounds were empty.

I walked back through the house, this time armed with my staff. I checked each room carefully, looking for some sign there had been a battle, but everything looked to be in place.

Back in the yard, I considered my options. The Amazons had to be near. All the vehicles were present, and all the horses were too.

A houseful of Amazons didn't just disappear, not without a struggle, one that would be impossible to hide. Which meant they were nearby, just not within sight.

I entered the woods.

It was early evening now. The sun wasn't as strong as it had been during my last trip to the clearing, but the air felt thicker, humid and cloying.

Ignoring the sweat that instantly beaded on my upper lip, I positioned my staff as I had the last time, perpendicular, so I could walk the path more easily. The late afternoon rain had softened the ground; it gave under my feet, cushioned each step, and made the pain in my back less obvious. I murmured a thanks to Artemis for blessing me with the small gift.

As I approached the obelisk, I heard voices. Hidden behind a tree, I paused and listened. I recognized Thea's voice first, then humming or chanting. With a frown, I peered out. The occupants of the camp were seated in a full circle, not the traditional partial circle or crescent we normally used when worshipping.

Thea stood near the obelisk; in her hands was another bowl. She crushed some kind of leaf over it, letting the crushed pieces fall in, then passed it around. As each Amazon took the vessel, she mimed with her hand for them to dip their fingers into the mixture and dot the oil onto their foreheads. First in line were Tess and another hearthkeeper, both young and used to being told what to do.

Lao sat five Amazons to the right of the two hearthkeepers. As the second girl smeared oil on her forehead, Lao stood and folded her arms under her well-endowed chest.

Her back stiff, she addressed Thea, "I've worshipped under a number of priestesses and I've never seen a one waste good olive oil by daubing it between their eyes." She lowered her chin.

Thea straightened. "Have you ever lost a queen?"

Areto stood then. "If Zery is lost, we should be

looking for her. Artemis blesses those who take action."
At Areto's words the other warriors rose too. The
hearth-keeper who held the bowl set it onto the ground.
Her eyes shifted back and forth between Thea and the
Amazons who had stood.

Thea sighed. "Once we have . . . the goddess's blessing,
we will search for Zery."

"How exactly did you *lose* her?" Lao again. I was beginning to think the older Amazon had a lot more warrior in
her than I had suspected.

Instead of answering, Thea stared at her. Lao blinked,
then frowned, and Thea turned back to the hearth-
keeper who had set down the bowl. She motioned for her
to continue, but I'd seen enough.

I was in charge of this tribe.

"I was wondering the same thing." I stepped into the
clearing.

The group turned as one. Lao crossed the circle to
where Tess sat with the bowl. She jerked it from the girl's
hands and moved toward the path with strong steady
extensions of her denim-clad legs. When she reached the
path and the younger women weren't behind her, she
yelled, "Those pies won't make themselves."

The hearth-keepers scrambled to follow. Within seconds the three had disappeared down the path. I jerked
my head in the direction they had gone. Without a word,
the remaining Amazons, all except Thea, crossed the
clearing and hiked out of view.

She held out her hands, palms up. "You're alive."

I stalked toward her. "And you left."

She blinked. "Of course. What else was I to do? The cabin exploded; I was knocked backward, stunned cold for . . . I'm not sure how long." She turned and lifted up her short hair. There was an ugly red gash in her scalp, and I realized now her shirt was stained with blood. "When I came to I realized how bad things were . . . the house was ablaze. I didn't see you . . . thought you'd been lost." She closed her eyes briefly as if reliving the moment. When she opened them, she murmured under her breath, a prayer, I assumed. "I knew you wouldn't want the car discovered. If it was, the tribe could be tied to the son. So I drove it back here and gathered the camp to decide our next move. I was afraid we would be calling the council, asking for a new queen."

"Not yet," I replied.

"No, not yet . . ." She tilted her head and studied me. "You are strong."

The words felt odd, less compliment and more assessment. I ignored them, because, despite the fact that she was right, I wouldn't want the Amazons tied to the explosion or the son, she shouldn't have left me behind—shouldn't leave any of us behind, ever.

"We protect our own," I said.

"Of course . . ." Her lips thinned. "You aren't saying I should have forgotten protecting the tribe, are you?"

"Of . . . no." My fingers twitched on my staff.

"Good, because I was sure I was doing what you would want, what the council would want. I'm just glad I don't have to call them . . . not about getting a new queen anyway." She cupped her hand over her neck, as if massaging away a pain. She seemed to have forgotten I was standing in front of her.

Suddenly my back spasmed. Determined not to show I was injured, I flipped the staff around in my hands, made it appear I was twirling the weapon rather than twitching in pain.

She glanced at me. The spasm continued, but I ground the end of the staff into the earth and squared my shoulders. My face calm, I replied, "No, no need to call the council. I'm fine."

Her expression darkened. For a second I thought she might argue the point, but she didn't. "How *did* you survive?" she asked. "The cabin . . . it was there one minute and a raging hell the next, eh?"

"The explosion threw me clear. I hit a tree, but I'm fine." It was more than I wanted to say. I was still struggling to get a grasp on what my reaction should be. Pain, anger, and something strangely close to reason warred for control of my attention—some little voice telling me Thea had done the right thing, returned to camp, gathered the tribe . . . What more could I have asked of her?

My jaw tensed. To find me? To let me know she had survived?

Another spasm grabbed my back. I gritted my teeth and held my breath until it passed.

"Did you see the son?" she asked. Her gray eyes were level now, her focus solid.

The spasm over, I was able to shake my head. "Humans showed up. That's all."

"Are you sure?"

I hesitated. *Was I?* But finally I nodded. Neither of the farmers had struck me as anything more than one-hundred percent human. Not that that guaranteed they were. The sons had apparently been fooling the Amazons for the past century. We had learned, unbeknown to my friend Mel's mother, Cleo, that Mel's father had been a son. I respected Cleo . . . I didn't think she would have been easily fooled. But that had been before Amazons knew the sons had powers similar to their own.

We were more aware now. And I was positive neither of the men fighting that blaze had been sons. Now, the rabbit? Much as I didn't like to admit it, I still wasn't sure about him.

Thea twisted her lips. "I wonder how he knew we were coming?"

"Knew?" Caught up in my anger at Thea, I hadn't thought about why the son's cabin had exploded. "You think he booby-trapped the place with us in mind?"

"You think it was coincidence?"

No. She was right. Houses didn't just explode, at least not very often. "He knew we were coming," I repeated.

"How?" she asked.

I shrugged and another spasm clawed through my body. I paused, then kept going, hoping she hadn't noticed. "He knew we would come looking for him. What else would we do?"

"So he tried to kill us." She said the words softly, then raised her eyes as if expecting a reaction.

I didn't have one. It was a sneaky way to fight a war, but then, we were talking about someone who had a stockpile of guns.

The guns. I'd forgotten about them. My brows pulled together. Why would he blow up his own collection of firearms—many still in their boxes?

"What?" she asked.

I shook my head. "Nothing. We should get back to camp." I turned and another tremor gripped my back. I muttered a curse. I wasn't used to feeling this much pain. I'd been injured before, many times, but the effects had never slowed me, not like this.

I closed my eyes, wondering if Artemis was sending me some message.

Thea's hand ran down my back. I stiffened.

"You're hurt?" Her eyebrow twitched. "I can help."

Caring for the wounded was one of the high priestess's jobs, but for some reason I didn't want Thea's touch or help.

I stepped away and walked as straight and solidly as I could manage toward camp. With the help of nothing but stubborn resistance, I even kept my staff from dipping toward the ground.

My fairy godfather had tried to kill us. Someone should take back his wings, rip them off an inch at a time.

Hopefully, that someone would be me.

Chapter 5

The sons had won again, at least for a while. After my collision with the tree and my run-in with Thea in the woods, I'd gone back to the farmhouse to discover Kale, my council contact, still had not called. I had called Mel instead, only to find she'd taken her daughter to Michigan and wasn't expected back until late Friday night. After that I'd asked for Peter, the son who worked for her. He was gone too, was with her apparently.

I'd hung up the phone confused and concerned. Mel leaving the tribe had killed our friendship for a decade. We had just started to patch it back together. I was afraid the issue of the sons would soon blast it apart again.

But the call helped solidify my plan. I would head to Madison Saturday morning. The farmer's market gave me a convenient excuse for being in the city—much better than just showing up on Mel's door and demanding to talk to the sons.

I'd gone to bed and slept a solid four hours. Now I was standing in the bathroom admiring my increasingly haggard appearance.

I turned my face away from the mirror, grabbed a wet towel, and scrubbed it over my skin. As I twisted my torso, my back shrieked.

The damned injury had been nagging me again . . . since Thea woke me up at four, asking if I was ready to resume our search for the baby.

I'd ignored her and eventually she'd gone away, but the other pain had remained. I'd stayed in my room a couple of hours stretching and thinking, but neither had done anything to lessen the pain.

I ran hot water on the towel and pressed it against my back. After a few seconds I threw it into the bathtub. It landed with an angry slap.

My injuries and recent failures were piling up and weighing me down, but I had a day to kill before heading to Madison.

Normally I would have exercised, but my back was in no shape. I left the house and passed by the barn with its room full of weights. It was early, but everyone was up. The hearth-keepers were working in the garden and warriors were clinking weights together in the barn. The camp would be busy for the next few hours, then things would settle down for lunch. During the heat of the day we would run errands and work on less physical projects.

In the evening we'd be outside again, working the horses and practicing for the exhibition at the fair.

I stepped into the woods.

"Zery!" Thea appeared on the path. She was carrying her bowl. I could smell the same oil I'd smelled before, olive oil. At least that's what Lao had said it was last night.

"I was looking for you earlier. You didn't answer your door."

I tilted my head and took another step down the path.

"I found the son's name, the one who owns the cabin," she said.

I paused.

"Jack Parker. He's lived there five years. Has probably been watching this camp."

She was right. He had told me as much.

"I'm searching for more information, for other places he might go now that his house is destroyed, but so far nothing. He seems to have no history."

"Like an Amazon," I replied. Amazons did everything they could to stay under the human radar. We sometimes shared identities, had more fake IDs than a bar full of teenagers. I guessed the sons did the same.

"You don't know where he might go, do you?" she asked. The bowl she held dripped oil onto her shoe. I stared at the round stain for a second, considering my answer.

My voice steady, I replied, "None. I'd never seen him before yesterday."

"How about your friend? The one in Madison? She has connections, doesn't she?"

"She's out of town."

A shadow passed over Thea's face. "But she'll be back. Soon?"

"No. I called last night. She's gone for a while. The sons are gone too." I'd decided last night I wasn't taking Thea with me to Madison. I had no qualms about lying to her. I just hoped lying was enough to keep her at the safe camp.

She didn't like my answer, but she didn't question it.

With Thea gone, I returned to my walk. I had plenty to think about. I was going to Madison, and I wasn't sure what I was going to do when I got there. It all depended on Mel and exactly how connected to the sons she had become. If she had thrown in with them, stood with them *against* the Amazons . . .

My stomach clenched, but as my body warmed from my walk, the ache in my back subsided. Thankful for that, I rolled my head left then right and forced any possibility that Mel had gone to the other side from my mind. I would find out tomorrow, no need to dwell on it today.

The path I was on led to the obelisk. There was another trail that wound through the fifty acres we owned. All except the two acres the house sat on were wooded. Amazons and animals alike used these paths. In fact, parts of it predated our ownership of the land. There was more than one "thong" tree, trees manipulated by Native American tribes to point to places of interest, off this path. All pointed toward our obelisk.

We had raised the stone, but we didn't make the woods sacred—that energy had been there forever. And we weren't even the first to recognize it.

I got on the longer trail behind the barn. It wove around the back of our property, eventually branching into three paths, one continuing until ending at a barbed-wire fence erected by a neighbor, one going out wider around the outskirts of the neighbor's holdings, and one that led to the obelisk. I took the outer path. It was cool this morning and the air smelled of leaves, flowers, and earth.

Birds were out too, lots of them screeching at each other and me to keep away from their nests. As I approached an oak that had been struck by lightning a few springs back, something stirred high above my head. I glanced up to see an owl fluttering overhead, like a very large brown-speckled butterfly. He seemed to watch me, his eyes flaming.

He hovered a second longer, then took off, flying up and out of the trees.

I ran my fingers up through my hair and stared after him, not sure what I expected to happen next.

Nothing did. I lowered my hands and shook my head.

The sons were making me jumpy. Every animal, no matter how small or safe, I now saw as a potential threat.

I didn't like it. I had two weapons on me today. I reached to the small of my back where I had stored a pair of nunchakus. They were a weapon I wasn't as skilled with as others—my staff, for instance—but I had been practicing and they were easier to carry with my strained back. I also had a belt on that concealed a blade disguised as a buckle.

So, the first wasn't my strongest choice and the second wasn't my fastest. Deciding on the nunchakus, I pulled them free from my pants and held both ends in my right hand. If a son surprised me, I could quickly drop one end and attack.

With my fingers wrapped around the weapon, it was hard to relax my body or my brain. I kept moving, every inch of me on alert.

It was just as well. Maybe nine yards further along I heard voices, murmurs. I had left all the Amazons back at camp.

My arm tensed as I moved closer.

There was a flash of blue and yellow, and bodies jumped out at me from nowhere. I spun, raising my arm automatically over my head and my fingers letting go of one end of the nunchakus. My back complained; I twisted my face in response.

"Oh dear. We surprised her."

"Did you see him? Did you?"

An elderly woman with a pair of binoculars pressed to her eyes searched the sky above my head. "They are so rare. Emily, do you have the camera?

"Karen, how about the recording? Did you get him?"

I staggered backward, my gaze dashing over the group. There were six of them, all dressed in T-shirts, khaki shorts, and a variety of head gear. The one with the binoculars shoved her hand flat against my chest and pushed me back a step.

"Damn. He's gone." She lowered the binoculars and glared at me. "Without the picture, we can't prove anything." Her hair was steel gray and she was carrying an extra forty pounds around the middle, and it didn't seem to occur to her or bother her that I not only towered over her, I was holding an actual weapon.

The free end of the nunchakus rapped against my knuckles, and a muscle tightened in my jaw. "Who are you?" I asked, my arm still raised.

She glanced at my upraised arm and poked me in the chest. "Don't be threatening me. We have every right to be here. Who are you?"

As she poked me, I realized she looked familiar . . . the woman I'd passed yesterday pulling out of the drive shared by the son and the camping trailer's owner.

Her four companions closed ranks. They weren't all as old as she was, or as heavy, but not a one was over five foot seven in height. And even though the expressions they laid on me were deadly, I knew *they* couldn't be.

I lowered my arm. "You are lost."

One in pink, wearing a pith helmet, shook her head. "Can't be. The GPS says we are right where we planned to be." She held out a small black box.

The numbers on the screen meant nothing to me.

She pointed at them. "Here, see? Longitude and latitude exactly. Right here." She stamped her white-tennis-shoe-clad foot.

I reestablished my grip on the nunchakus. "Where you are is on private property. You need to leave."

"Karen, you idiot. She's right. That should be a three, not a five." Binocular Lady punched Ms. Pink T-shirt in the arm. "We want to be over there." She pointed to their right, toward the obelisk. They started to move.

I stepped in front of them. "No. You need to leave."

Binocular Lady stepped up again. "Listen, the International Friends of the Birds gave us the coordinates for this location. And they were right. We spotted one." She nodded her head as if that declaration said everything.

I pressed my lips together. "One what?"

They exchanged knowing glances. "We'll be gone soon." Binocular Lady tried to shove past me again.

I growled. I wasn't used to dealing with humans, at least not humans who were as completely unintimidated by me as these women. I wasn't quite sure what to do. If they had been other Amazons or sons, it would have been easy; I would have used the nunchakus that my hands itched to set free.

But six unarmed women dressed in shorts and pastel shirts with kittens and puppies on them? How exactly should I go about defending our property from them?

I copied her move; I placed my hand on her shoulder. I was tempted to put it on her forehead, but I resisted.

"You need to leave." I put as much force into the words as I could muster, and annoyed as I was, that was quite a bit.

She rolled her eyes to the side, staring at my hand, then looked back at my face. "Maybe we did get off track, but there's no harm in us just checking the location. We'll be gone as soon as we do, right, ladies? The owl . . . he can't have gone far." Her eyebrows disappearing beneath gray bangs, she glanced at her crew. They nodded. As one unit, they closed in again until they formed a tight half circle in front of me. Then they turned their stares on me.

I looked back, from one to the other. None of them said a thing; they just stood there staring.

I leaned to one side, half expecting them to lean too.

Instead, Binocular Lady placed her hand on my arm and said, her voice deep, "We'll only be a minute."

I tapped my nunchakus against my thigh. "No." Then completely out of patience, I grabbed her by the upper arm and quickstepped her toward the shortest route off our property.

"What? You should have—" She snapped her lips together.

I didn't ask her what I should have. I didn't care. My fingers still wrapped around her fleshy bicep, I looked over my shoulder at Karen. "Which way to your car?"

Eyes round, Karen pointed to the right. Within ten minutes we were at our property line. I jerked up the barbed-wire fence separating our acreage from the farmer next door's field and motioned for them to belly crawl out of there. One by one they complied until only Binocular Lady was left.

I leaned down and hissed in her ear. "Owl or no owl, this is private property. Keep off of it." Then I shoved her to the ground and waited as her friends on the other side helped tug her under. Before her feet cleared the wire, I dropped my hold on the fencing. The taut wire sung in response.

Without another word, I turned and stalked back to the path. We had never had much of a problem with trespassers . . . now two sons and a group of bird-watchers in less than two days.

I preferred the sons.

After leaving our visitors behind, I gave up my stroll.

I was almost to the house when something hit me from behind. I struck the ground hands first. The nunchakus dug into my palm, and my back screamed. I grunted and sprang back to my feet.

When I turned, the wolverine son, in his human form and fully dressed in a gray T-shirt and camouflage pants, was waiting.

"You destroyed my house," he muttered.

"You mean that eyesore of a hovel? Was that yours? Who knew?" I kept the nunchakus hidden for now, held up behind my forearm.

He stepped to the left; I did the same.

He didn't appear to be armed, but his pants were baggy with numerous pockets. There was no telling what he had hidden inside them.

"Where's the baby?" I asked.

He shook his head. "I really underestimated you, or

maybe overestimated. I can't believe you are part of this. I really didn't think you were such a sheep."

"A sheep?"

"Is that your *givnomai*, Zery? You have Mary's little lamb tattooed on your breast? Is that why you follow instructions so blindly?"

My temper flared. I raised my arm and let go of one side of the nunchakus. Spinning the weapon, I leapt toward him.

He jumped to the side, but not fast enough. The wooden club struck him in the side of the head. He grunted.

"Be careful. It wouldn't do for a sheep to take down a wolverine." I spun the rod and moved forward again, but my back had suffered from my last swing. The muscles there contracted, hard. I stumbled.

He bent at the waist and rushed toward me like a football player planning a tackle. Ignoring the pain shooting through my back, I slashed downward. The rod struck him again, but he didn't stop. His shoulder hit me in the stomach. My feet left the ground and for a second we were airborne. We hit the ground with a thud.

He was on top, but only for a second. I grabbed his hair, jerked back his head, and pressed my thumb into his eye. The ache in my back encouraged me to push harder.

He cursed and flipped so we were both on our sides. The hand I'd been using to push against his eye became trapped under his head, my thumb no longer reaching his socket.

He twisted his face and bit me. Pain shot through my hand where his teeth had sunk into skin and muscle.

Then before I could react, he shoved the side of my face into the earth. I inhaled dirt and dead grass, was forced to open my mouth to breathe.

I still held the nunchaku. I lifted my arm and swung down, aiming for his face and neck, but my efforts were weak. He reached for my attacking arm and grabbed me by the wrist.

My curse was swallowed by the earth.

I tried to twist my wrist free, but at the current angle and in my current condition, I couldn't. So I resorted to the trick that had worked before; I lifted my knee and aimed for his groin.

He rolled again. My knee hit his thigh, but my face was free. I could breathe, which meant I could fight. I balled my fingers into a fist and smashed him in the nose.

He grinned. His face was stained with blood, mine and his, and he grinned.

I struck him again.

"Maybe a butterfly? Is that your *givnomai*? Your touch is so gentle . . ."

Again he rolled, slinging one thigh over my legs as he did, trying to hold me in place. I groped the ground as we rolled and my fingers found a rock. I concentrated on his taunts and slammed it into his skull.

This time his grip loosened.

I shoved him to the side and staggered to my feet.

My nunchakus were gone, but I still held the rock, and as he sprung up after me, I held it where he could see it.

"Nice," he murmured. Blood flowed from his scalp an

inch or so behind his temple. He touched two fingers to it. "But your aim was off. You want to kill me, you will have to try harder than that. I won't lie still, helpless like a baby." He stared at me, taunting me with his words.

"You won't get away with it. The Amazons will hunt you down."

"Really? Seems to me if that were true, I wouldn't be standing here now."

We were both moving now, slowly sidestepping around an invisible circle. My breath was ragged and a mix of sweat and dust coated my body. I wanted to cough or spit, to get some of the dirt that had found its way inside my mouth out. But I wouldn't give him the satisfaction. I followed his example and smiled too. "I'll rectify that soon enough."

He grunted. "Threats. You forget you aren't the first Amazon to try and kill me . . . there was my mother. Left me in a trash pile, in the snow. I survived. I'll continue to survive, and I'll do everything I can to stop the Amazons from destroying any more sons."

"As if the sons were the innocent ones. I lost my lieutenant to a son last fall and two others—teen girls. We weren't targeting him. We didn't even know he existed."

"*One.* One son. Are you saying the Amazons have no bad within them? That the tribe is so perfect one of your kind couldn't do what that one son did? Go out on her own?"

I snorted at his ignorance. "Amazons have structure. We follow the high council. It is what has kept us strong."

He stopped and placed his hand on his forehead. Then he laughed.

Anger flickered inside me. I tightened my fingers on the rock.

He shook his head and then held up a hand. "Enough."

But I wasn't done and I certainly wasn't going to let him dictate when I would be.

I fingered the stone. It was rough and jagged, as if it had broken off from a bigger mass rather than having been formed on its own, it edges worn off by erosion and time. I found the sharpest point. Then I lunged.

He grabbed me by the wrist and stared down at me, his dark eyes snapping. "I'm not giving you the baby. You need to accept that, and if I think you are close to finding that baby, or harming another infant, I will forget my job is only to watch and report."

I swung my free fist.

He grabbed it too.

We stared at each other as if trapped in some kind of unwelcome dance. Then he jerked me toward him, twisted my arms behind my back, and lowered his face to mine.

My mouth opened to yell curses, but his lips were already over mine. Wisely he kept his tongue out of reach of my teeth. I snapped my jaws together and arched my body, trying to escape.

My inability to do so was infuriating.

I twisted my face to the side, the curses he'd stopped began flowing from my mouth, and I bucked my body against his. Somehow he moved my wrists to just one of his hands and reached into one of those pockets I'd worried about when he first arrived. Realizing he was going for something he intended to use against me, I slammed my foot down on the top of his. He grimaced but didn't drop his hold. Instead he twisted toward me again, something silver shining in his hand.

A gun or a knife . . . I put everything I had into the struggle, forgot my pain, forgot everything but attaining freedom. I rammed my knee into his thigh over and over, turned toward him so my mouth was level with his shoulder, and bit down as hard and viciously as I could.

I was rewarded with the warm taste of blood through his T-shirt, but as quickly as the moment of success came, it was gone. There was a snap and cold metal closed around my wrists.

He shoved me to the ground.

I panted for breath, my mind whirling, wondering how with only my feet free, I could kill him.

It was little reward, but he was winded too. His chest heaved. He rubbed the back of his hand over his mouth as if scrubbing the area where our lips had touched.

Then he turned and headed off in a lope. Six feet away he stopped and called back. "Don't be a sheep, Zery. Be headstrong and stupid if you must, but don't be a sheep."

I let out a yell and scrambled to my feet, but he was already gone.

Chapter 6

It was another long walk back to the farmhouse. I had
tried to remove the cuffs on my own, but the son had
snapped them tight and all I got for my efforts were
scrapes to add to my already torn palm where he had bit-
ten me. So I was forced to walk back to camp cuffed.

And the yard was full. Areto was running the warriors
through their exercises, Lao had the hearth-keepers on
the front porch tying bundles of herbs together, and
Thea was sitting under the oak next to Sare. Today she
was carving fetishes. As I approached, Thea held a falcon
up to the sun. When she saw me, she dropped it onto the
girl's lap.

I walked past her. "Lao, meet me in the kitchen."

The hearth-keeper took care of minor home repairs.
She was my best bet for picking the lock.

"What happened?" Thea, of course. Alcippe, for all our disagreements, understood when I didn't want to talk.

My new high priestess, however, seemed clueless in this arena, or more likely she just didn't give a damn.

Lao had stood and was brushing bits of herb off her hands. When Thea asked her question, the hearth-keeper scowled. Mumbling, she stepped over a stack of lavender and tromped toward me.

"There should be a paper clip in the junk drawer. Should do the trick."

Without answering Thea's question or even glancing at her, I followed the hearth-keeper.

"Zery," Thea called. "You had a call earlier. I told her you were out. Her name was Mel. Isn't that your friend? The one who is out of town for a long time . . . ?"

My shoulders lowered. I stared at the safe-house door, scuffed and badly in need of a fresh coat of paint.

I didn't know why Mel had called. She wasn't supposed to be back in Madison until tonight. Maybe she had called from Michigan. No matter, I didn't have to explain anything to Thea.

I kept walking. I was still going to Madison tomorrow and I still wasn't taking Thea with me.

She would just have to deal with it.

I followed Lao. Behind me Thea cleared her throat.

My strides strong, I stepped over the threshold.

My back spasmed.

I hesitated, feeling almost as if I had been poked.

I looked back. Thea still stood where I had last seen her, her arms hanging loose at her sides and a challenge on her face.

I kept walking.

Lao picked the lock on the handcuffs, then gave me a rag to run over my face while she got some medicine for my hand. I tried to wave her off, but she jerked my palm toward her and used her chest to cradle my hand as she dabbed medicine on the wound.

"Don't know what bit you and I'm not asking to know, but there's no reason to walk around torn up."

After that I didn't fight her. I just sat quietly as she put a piece of gauze over the wound and wrapped a bandage crosswise over my palm—not that different from how a pugilist wraps her hands before a fight.

She opened and closed my fingers, in and out of a fist. "Fine, won't even slow you down." She thumped on the table with her open palm, stood, and gathered up her supplies. She looked at the cuffs for a second before holding them out to me. "You probably have more use for these than I do."

Chuckling, she shook her head and dropped them in my lap. Despite her humor, the gesture reminded me of Thea dropping the fetish in the artisan's lap. I stared at them for a second. When I looked up, Lao was watching me; her eyes were serious.

"Best get out there."

I waited, thinking she would say more, but apparently

she was done. First aid kit in hand, she walked from the room.

Best get out there. Four simple words. She could have said them any day, but for some reason I didn't think she'd said them casually today.

I pushed back my chair and headed out into the yard.

Thea was sitting beside Areto. I'd say she was whispering in her ear, but that was more a feeling than fact. As I stepped off the porch, both stared at me as if expecting something—an explanation, I guessed.

It was a fair expectation. I didn't arrive at camp in handcuffs too often. Unfortunately for them I wasn't feeling driven to be particularly fair at the moment.

"There were women in the woods earlier," I said, addressing Areto. "I expect them to come back. Set up some patrols starting now and keep them going until I say to stop."

"Through the night?" Thea asked.

"Go," I said to Areto. She nodded and trotted off.

"What kind of women were they?" Thea took a moment; she seemed to be inspecting me. I still looked rough; I hadn't bothered washing anything except my face with Lao's rag. I hadn't even bothered looking in a mirror. So I didn't know exactly how rough I looked, and I didn't care.

"Bird-watchers." Down by the barn Areto had gathered the warriors. I turned to join them.

As I walked away, Thea followed.

"Are you going to tell me what happened?" The question didn't come across as pushy, more bored curiosity.

However, I wasn't much in the mood for sharing.

The warriors stood in a row. Two were probably my age; two were older. Bern cracked her knuckles as I approached. She was pushing two hundred, in both pounds and years. Her skin was cocoa colored but her eyes were bright green, like new grass. The contrast alone made her stand out. Add her size, how she carried herself, and the fact that she'd chosen to dye her hair bright red, and just looking at her would cause most humans to cross the street. It was why I had assigned her the job of backup when we had gone to steal the baby from the sons.

"Put Bern on the dusk shift." I figured the birders were looking for the same owl I'd seen right before I stumbled upon them. Most people thought of owls as being nocturnal and many were, but I'd seen mine not long after dawn, which probably meant he was one of the few who preferred the grayer skies of dawn and dusk.

I was guessing the birders would know that too, and I hoped seeing Bern come at them even completely unarmed would send them scurrying back home for good.

Areto didn't question me, but Thea did.

"Bird-watchers got you in handcuffs?" Her eyes showed interest and disbelief.

I slid my jaw to the side. The role of queen had some privileges, like not having to explain anything you did at camp. I answered to the high council and Artemis. That was it.

I took a step toward the barn.

I needed to fill Areto in a bit on what had happened, to make sure she knew the real threat wasn't the birders I'd mentioned, but the son.

I wasn't making the announcement publicly, because there was no reason for most of the camp's occupants to know. It was the warriors' jobs to protect the rest of the tribe.

Areto followed, as did Thea.

Looking at Areto, I said, "I want you to patrol for the birders, but there's another threat too, a son. One of the sons with the baby. He's been watching us. I don't know for how long."

Areto answered with only a silent incline of her head; she knew I would tell her all she needed to know and wouldn't pry further.

Thea, however, was a different matter. "That explains the handcuffs, eh?" She darted her gaze at Areto. The warrior looked straight ahead, waiting for whatever else I had to say.

Her reaction reassured me that I was making the right choice regarding the position of lieutenant.

Still, I had decided I needed to tell Thea what had happened. "On my walk, the son returned."

Her brow quirked. "Alone?"

"Yes."

She pursed her lips and looked to the side.

I tightened my jaw. One son had got me into the cuffs. It was a truth I couldn't deny.

"I'm leaving in the morning for Madison, with the hearth-keepers," I announced.

"And me?" she asked.

"Knowing the son is around, we can't afford to both be away from camp."

A muscle in her neck twitched.

"My council contact hasn't called back. The sons in Madison are our best hope."

"The sons who are out of town? Who won't be back for some time?" She watched me from the corner of her eyes.

"They may not be. I don't know, but Mel is coming back early. We spoke last night." We hadn't and it wouldn't be that hard for Thea to find out I was lying, but I felt no need to be completely honest with her. Basic need to know facts . . . I was going to Madison to get information on the sons or the baby. She was staying here to help Areto protect the camp.

I turned my attention back to the warrior. "You will be in charge until I get back."

Areto's eyes flicked to the side toward Thea, but if the high priestess was annoyed by my decision, she didn't show it.

"Your friend left the tribe. What makes you think she will help us?"

I smiled. "I don't . . . or at least she won't do anything *because* it helps us, but if I can convince her a child is at risk . . ." I shook my head. "Goddess bless the son who gets in her way."

* * *

I was asleep, or as asleep as I get, when two soft taps of someone's knuckles on my door awakened me. I was on my feet, my staff in my hand, before a third could sound.

Dressed only in an oversized T-shirt, I padded to the door and waited. Two more raps, silence, and then another. Code to let me know a warrior was waiting on the other side.

Keeping the staff ready, I opened the door.

Areto, her mouth grim, greeted me. "Bern. She found a body. One of the birders, we think."

I jerked on a pair of shorts and followed her.

It was maybe one in the morning. The full moon was past, but the night was still bright enough to make out the two people in the yard. Bern stood with her arms hanging stiffly at her side. Thea stood beside her looking authoritative and in control.

When I stepped onto the sidewalk, she strode toward me. "One of your bird-watchers?" She motioned to where a human-sized hump lay under the oak that dominated our yard.

I glanced at Bern, but even with the moon's light her expression was unreadable. As if sensing my thoughts, Thea flipped on a flashlight. "Bern says she found her next to the obelisk."

I cut my gaze to the silent warrior. "Dead?"

She inclined her head slightly.

I returned her nod and looked back at the body. "Were there others? Any sign more had been there?"

A shake this time.

Processing this, I walked to the body. I recognized her instantly—the woman who had challenged me, the leader of the group. She was dressed as I'd seen her earlier, same cheery yellow T-shirt with suns and daisies, same khaki shorts.

"Heart attack?" I asked, this time of Thea.

"No. It looks like she was strangled with these." In her hand was a pair of nunchakus. The pair I'd lost in the woods while fighting with the son.

"Are they . . . ?" She twisted them over. A crescent moon was carved on the end of one stick. I didn't need to answer; that told her they were mine.

"Of course, Bern . . . Areto tells me she's an expert with these." Thea paused as if waiting for me to say something . . . to jump on the story, to lay blame on Bern?

I looked at the warrior who still stood silently watching. "Did you kill her?"

"No." Her first word, and I believed her.

I looked back at Thea. "She didn't do it."

"But if she didn't, then who . . ." She glanced at the crescent, then pressed her lips shut.

"The son?" I offered, although I didn't believe that either. The son had no gripe with the birders. Why would he kill one? Unless it was to make trouble for us.

I bent down to study the body. The skin on her neck was waxy, almost transparent in places, but her face was a dark angry red. I picked up her hand; her fingers were limp. I motioned for Thea to direct the flashlight beam closer. As she did, I pressed my fingers against the flesh of the bird-watcher's underarm. The white imprint where my fingers had touched shone white. I checked her eyes next. They were open and flat looking. I touched her skin there too, checking for stiffness. There was none; rigor mortis hadn't set in. She hadn't been dead long.

I glanced at Bern. "How was she when you found her?" It was a test; I did believe her, but it didn't hurt to run a check or two.

She motioned at the body with her hand. "Like that, mainly. I think she may have been dragged a bit."

She must have seen the question on my face.

"Look at her heels. When I picked her up, dirt fell onto me."

I checked the woman's shoes, Bern was right. Clumps of moist earth were caked on the heels of her practical white walking shoes.

"Someone bigger than her, then," I murmured. Which narrowed down the possibilities by about zero.

I checked her neck then. From what Areto had told me—and the state of the birder's face—I knew she had been strangled, but I wanted to see for myself. There was a line of bruises that ran from the front of her neck to the sides, where it angled up slightly. It was thinner in the front too, just like you'd expect from the nunchakus— the chain cutting into the front of her throat and the rods pressing against the sides.

"What should we do?" Thea asked.

I'd been asking myself the same question. A woman was dead. I knew she had friends, and chances were she had family too. Someone would notice at some point that she had gone missing. When they did, I couldn't have them coming here.

The question, however, was: should we destroy the body or leave it somewhere with hopes of directing the investigation away from us? I sure as hell wasn't calling the human police to my camp.

I flipped off the flashlight and stood. With Thea in my sight, I asked. "Can you clean her up? Make it look like she died somewhere else?" I didn't understand magic, couldn't work it myself, but I knew with wards almost anything was possible.

The priestess stared down at the body. "The evidence will still be there, but I can make it so no human will notice it. Deflect their attention away from anything that would lead back to us."

I nodded; it was what I wanted to hear.

"It won't change what other people know, though. If anyone knew she was coming here, and they saw you yesterday, they can still report to the police."

Bern stepped forward. "Not if they already have the killer."

Thea nodded. "That would be for the best, and simple enough to set up."

Shocked that Thea would agree with what Bern was suggesting, I twisted my head to look from one to the other. "No. Bern didn't kill her; I won't pretend she did."

"Not"—Thea glanced at Areto—"even to save the tribe?"

My grip on the flashlight grew slippery. My grip on reality too, but I shook my head. "We've survived worse." I snorted. "It isn't like humans haven't noticed us before, been suspicious of us before. It isn't even like I haven't been arrested before."

"All the more reason Bern should stand in for you. We can move the body, make it look like Bern robbed her." She glanced around our tiny circle. "Did she have a car? Do we know where it is parked? Bern could take it, get caught with the body in the trunk. They'll think it was robbery, clean and simple. Then you and the tribe are off the hook." She held out one hand to Bern. "Give me your totem. Besides your tattoos, it's the only thing tying you to us. And the humans won't understand their power, or . . ." She reached into her pocket and pulled out her phone. "Sare might have time to change your *givnomai*. The *telíos* will pass. Lots of human females have tattoos there."

I grabbed her phone. She blinked at me, but didn't object.

"Lots of humans have tattoos on their breasts too. No one is messing with Bern's tattoos." The very thought of stripping an Amazon of her tattoos, taking away her personal power or her tie to her clan . . . it sent a chill through me like a frost-covered spear. "And Bern isn't throwing herself on the sword—not for this. It isn't her place; it isn't her responsibility."

Something flickered in Thea's eyes. She lifted her head. "Then whose is it?"

Mine. Of course it was mine.

But because of my past arrest and what Mel had told the detective who had arrested me, turning myself over wasn't so simple. The police in Wisconsin already knew a closed group of women, all women, lived somewhere in northern Illinois, and also knew my friend Mel had left us. They hadn't wanted to let me go the last time, but with the true criminal, the murderous son, handed to them all but gift wrapped, they'd had no choice.

If I got arrested again, they wouldn't miss the opportunity to look a lot more deeply into exactly what kind of group I ran.

I looked at Areto. "Wake the others and find the woman's car. Take Lao with you in case you can't find the keys."

My attention back on Thea, I continued, "Do whatever you can to cover up where she's been. Make it look like a robbery or, better yet, an accident."

I smiled. "An accident." *Binoculars.* I reached down and shuffled inside the birder's jacket; sure enough her binoculars were hidden inside. "Make it look like these got caught on something and she fell."

"So where should we do this?" Areto asked.

I paused, then smiled. "I have an address for you. A cabin just burned down. There's some old machinery lying around. See if Lao can figure out a way to make it look like the cord got caught on something, and leave the body there."

With that, Areto ran off to wake Lao and the warriors, leaving me with Thea and Bern. The warrior made a move to leave too, but I stopped her.

"I'm heading to Madison in twenty minutes and you're coming with me. Tell Areto and do whatever else you need to do. I don't know how long we'll be gone."

A slight shift of Bern's eyebrows told me she heard me before she too jogged into the house.

"You're leaving?" Thea asked.

I ignored the incredulity of her tone. "The high council hasn't called with information?"

"No."

"Then we still have a baby to find." I dropped her phone on the grass, my heel grazing it as I went to make sure the warriors understood what they were to do.

Chapter 7

It wasn't even four in the morning when we arrived in Madison. The trip had been quiet. Bern wasn't much of a talker, but then, neither was I.

I took the John Nolan exit off the Beltline, going toward the capitol. I knew stopping at Mel's this early would do me no good. In fact, it would just increase the suspicion I was sure would be waiting for me. I knew Mel and she knew me. She would know I hadn't come to Madison for a simple reunion.

The farmer's market was a horribly thin cover, but hopefully enough of one my friend wouldn't be on alert immediately. I just needed her mind open long enough for me to explain that I was here to save a child, not just seek revenge on the sons.

This route took us over Lake Monona. The water was still, blue, and if you looked in the right direction, endless. Just like I'd always believed the Amazons would be.

"Thank you."

Bern's sudden burst of conversation startled me. I glanced at her.

"For not asking me to give up my *givnomai*." She touched her breast where her personal power tattoo was located. I didn't know what Bern's *givnomai* was; if nothing else the first run-in with the sons had taught us keeping that secret was important. But based on her personality and the strengths she bore, I would guess she chose a bull or perhaps a bear, something strong or solitary.

"I couldn't do that," I replied.

She looked at me, her green eyes piercing. "You could. You didn't."

She was right; I could have. Thea would . . . did argue I should have taken it to protect the tribe. But what was the tribe? Not a faceless group, but individuals. Wasn't my duty as much to each of them as to the whole?

"Lao will be a while." I wasn't sure how long. It depended on what she had to do to make the birder's death look like an accident. The other hearth-keepers were following us with most of their market goods. Lao would drive up alone when she could. "We'll take her place and help direct the setup."

The warrior turned to stare at the lake.

I knew she was wondering why I had brought her. But I hadn't wanted to leave her behind, hadn't wanted to tempt Thea to push her to take the fall for the birder's murder.

"Then later, when things are going well, we will go see a friend of mine."

She glanced at me then, but went back to her silence. Maybe she had nothing to say, or maybe she was thinking of something Thea had said right before we left how Mel had left the tribe and not to trust her.

I didn't bother probing the warrior to see. It didn't matter. Mel was the only lead I had.

The market was set up in a giant circle around the capitol building. It took us a while to find our spot, squished in between a local dairy and a nursery selling what looked like grass they had pulled from some field.

By the time we found it, the hearth-keepers had arrived too. I put Bern to work lugging tables while I taped hand-lettered signs to boxes of tomatoes and herbs. When I was done, Bern and I helped pull the tarp into place over our booth. The weather looked fine, but you never knew, and having shade from the sun was good too. As I tied the tarp's cord around one of the poles we'd brought for that purpose, I saw two hearth-keepers who weren't from our camp whispering to Tess.

She glanced up, but when she saw me watching, she dropped her gaze. I looked at Bern. She shrugged. "They're impressed you're helping. Most queens wouldn't."

I frowned. I didn't work with the hearth-keepers

much, but it wasn't because I thought I was too good for their work. It was just, well, *their* work, and if I were to be honest with myself, I wasn't good at it.

But then maybe that was because I did shy away from it.

With that in mind, I took a little more care with the rest of my duties and when the market opened at six, we were completely set up and ready for business. I was bagging a bunch of radishes for an elderly lady when Lao arrived.

As I handed the woman her change, I noticed a light of approval in the older hearth-keeper's eyes. When a mother with two toddlers in tow asked for a dozen tomatoes, I helped her too. This time when I glanced at Lao there was a smile on her lips.

"Business is good," she said.

I nodded, feeling awkward. I shoved a bag I hadn't realized I'd held back into the cardboard box where the hearth-keepers stored them.

"So things went smoothly?" I asked.

Her face turned somber. "Yes. Although . . ."

"What?"

She shook her head. "Nothing."

I could feel there was something she wasn't saying, something she wanted to say but perhaps felt she couldn't . . . or shouldn't.

Suddenly I wanted the older Amazon to talk to me like she would anyone else. I was tired of being queen twenty-four/seven, of having everything I did and said analyzed because of my position.

"You can tell me, you know," I said as casually as I could. I didn't want her to think my comment was an order. I wanted to know what she was thinking, but I also wanted her *to want* to tell me. In the middle of rolling radishes over in their box, so they showed at their best, I paused.

I hadn't felt like this in a long time . . . didn't let myself feel like this.

Lao, unaware of my moment of sudden insight, placed her hands on her hips and stared toward the domed capitol building that dominated the square. "I'm not sure about that high priestess. She's got ideas . . ." She dropped her attention to some basil and muttered under her breath.

"What?" I prompted.

When she looked up, her eyes were clear and direct. "I heard what she wanted to do to Bern. How you wouldn't let her."

I shifted my eyes then and pretended to study a group of college kids dressed in cutoff sweatpants and skin-tight tanks. "It isn't Bern's responsibility to protect the tribe; it's mine."

Lao nodded. "Thea mentioned that too . . ." Then she wandered to the other side of the booth to help two soccer moms who were oooing over a small collection of hand-carved fetishes Sare had sent along.

My fingers tightened on the radishes, snapping their green tops off into the bin.

Thea had talked about me to Lao, or at least in front of Lao and, I guessed, questioned my choice.

My time with the hearth-keepers and my desire to put my role to the side for a while was quickly forgotten.

I was beginning to doubt my decision to leave Thea behind and beginning to wonder what I would find when I returned to camp.

At nine, Bern and I left. Mel's shop didn't open until eleven, but I wanted time to talk to her alone—before the son showed up for work, assuming he was working today and he and Mel hadn't taken their relationship to a level I didn't want to think about.

Based on the fact she'd gone with him to Michigan, I was fairly certain that was a lost hope.

Peter was attractive; there was no denying that. When I'd first met him, I'd actually encouraged Mel to hook up with him, but that was before I knew he was a son. Now I hoped she'd wised up.

But I doubted it. Mel was too stubborn for that, and as I said, I already had evidence to the contrary.

Bern rode shotgun again, a silent shotgun.

When we pulled into Mel's lot, I gestured for her to grab the basket filled with produce I'd taken from the booth—a kind of peace offering.

With Bern walking behind me, I paced toward the building.

I was nervous. It was a strange thing to realize and

admit even to myself. I hadn't seen Mel in a while, and our time together then had been volatile, but for a long, long time Mel—and her family, but mainly Mel—had been one of the most important people in my life. Even more important than my own mother. A lot more important than my mother.

We'd made some ground in repairing our relationship last fall, but I knew if she had bonded with the sons, what I was going to ask of her would split her loyalties. And there was every possibility she would choose the sons over the Amazons.

I wasn't looking forward to it.

Mel's shop and home was in a hundred-year-old school set on about an acre on the Near West Side of Madison. She'd bought the place from the city ten years earlier. There were two buildings on the property—the old school itself, where Mel and her family—her mother, grandmother, and Harmony, her teen daughter—lived and worked, and the old gym/cafeteria. That's where I along with a couple dozen other Amazons had stayed last fall.

We entered the main school from the side, through the basement. The shop's door was in the front, but it would be locked. The basement was where Mel's grandmother, an ex–high priestess, ran her fortune-telling and other new age arts business. It was also where Mel's mother, a warrior, kept her gym.

I was hoping to see either of them first, as a warm-up of sorts before facing Mel.

I opened the door and walked into a room filled with

the last thing I'd expected to see—babies. There were at least a dozen of them, tucked inside round-bottomed plastic seats. The kind of combination seat/carrier the baby I'd lost had been in.

I froze; it was like walking into a nightmare.

Behind me Bern muttered, "Babies."

My body relaxed, released the air I'd been holding in my lungs. She saw them too. For a second I'd really thought . . . well, Bubbe, Mel's grandmother, was a powerful priestess. I wasn't completely sure she couldn't have known I was coming and plotted the perfect greeting. Be planning to make me sort through the lot of them to try to discern the baby I sought as some kind of worthiness trial.

As if on cue, the old priestess walked into the room. She had a baby propped up on one shoulder and was rubbing some kind of root over her sleeve. When she saw me, she stopped.

"You are here, *dorogaya,* Zery . . ."

One of the babies on the floor began to fuss. With a shake of her head Bubbe walked over and shoved the root into his mouth. Loud sucking noises followed and the infant quieted immediately.

She moved to another seat, this one empty, and placed the child she held inside. Standing, she said, "My days of watching babies, they should be over, but Dana, she has convinced my daughter to run a program for new mothers in the old gym. And me, I'm left with these . . ." She gestured to the seats and sighed. Her gaze on me, she asked, "How about you, *solnyshko?* Have you a wish for a baby?"

I wasn't sure how to answer. I wanted a baby, a particular baby, but not for myself. I hoped Mel's grandmother wasn't looking into my future . . . near or otherwise.

"You know me, Bubbe. My only wish is to keep the tribe strong. I do that by being a dedicated queen."

She puckered her lips. "If only that were such a clear path." Her blue eyes were sad, reminding me what she had done to protect the tribe. She'd stolen Mel's son and made her think he had been born stillborn. All to keep his birth and Mel's desire to keep him from driving a wedge between her granddaughter and the tribe.

It hadn't worked. Mel had left anyway and Bubbe had borne the secret for years. She'd revealed the truth to Mel last fall, but I didn't know what had happened after that or if Mel had forgiven her.

I studied the older Amazon, trying to read her body language, but she was, as always, inscrutable. I'd given up and was turning to introduce Bern when another female rushed into the room. This one was young, flushed in the face and stinking of old milk: Dana, a hearth-keeper who had come to live with Mel when she learned she was pregnant with a son. I hadn't seen her since then.

"Zery!" She rushed toward me, her face glowing.

Before I could dodge her enthusiastic greeting, Bern had stepped forward and shoved the basket full of produce between us.

"Oh." Dana stopped short. She glanced at Bern, her eyes filled with curiosity but zero intimidation. Dana was one of those rare beings who found good in everyone so saw little to fear from anyone.

It was strangely reassuring to see that hadn't changed.

"Have you seen him?" She stopped next to one of the carriers and scooped a bundle from inside. The baby was red and ugly, with eyes that were screwed shut against the light. "I named him Pisto," she murmured.

Named after my lieutenant who had been killed by the son . . . my lieutenant who was also Dana's sister.

Thinking of Pisto, I reached out a hand.

"Don't touch him." Mel's voice rang out from across the basement.

I curled my fingers into my palm. My friend hadn't changed much, not that in nine months I expected her to. She was dressed much like I'd seen her last, with a few minor tweaks—wearing shorts instead of jeans and a sleeveless instead of long-sleeved tee. On her head was her favorite Badgers cap and in her hand was a staff.

That was different—not only that she held a staff but that she held it with such ease. I'd always known she had the talent in her, but she'd denied it for so long . . .

"Looks like Harmony isn't the only one who's been working with your mother," I remarked.

She paced forward, the staff in front of her. "Why are you here, Zery?"

"We are friends, remember?" I motioned at Bern to set the basket on the ground. She complied, then stood with her hands shoved into her pockets and her body looking deceptively relaxed.

Mel, however, wasn't fooled. She shot a glance at the warrior, then laughed. "Which am I supposed to be swayed by? The gifts or the intimidation?"

"Neither. I just want to talk to Peter. Is that wrong?"

She tossed the staff from one hand to the other, then leaned it against the wall. "No, not at all. Let me ask you a question. What do you love, Zery? Really truly love?"

I opened my mouth, but nothing came out. I hadn't expected the question, wasn't sure I had an answer. Then I realized I did. "The Amazons." The tribe was my life.

"Really? The Amazons? Or the tribe? Do you want to help and protect each individual or some myth that exists only in your mind?"

I held up a hand to stop her. "We've had this argument before. You don't like the tribe, don't want to rejoin, fine. I accept that. I'm not here to bring you back."

She took a step toward me. Her hands were at her sides, empty. For any other artisan it would be an innocent stance, but Mel wasn't any other artisan. Her father had been a son, and as I'd learned during our last time together, she had not only artisan but warrior and priestess talents too.

She was, I realized, a prime example of why mixing with the sons was dangerous. There was no predicting how strong a baby from a son and an Amazon would be. Which reminded me of someone else. Mel's daughter had a son for a father too.

"How's Harmony?" I asked

Mel tensed, every inch of her except her fingers; they wiggled.

I hadn't said it to tweak her, but I quickly recognized that I had.

"Is Harmony why you're here?" Her body was so taut now I could almost feel the magic strumming off her.

A few feet away Bubbe murmured something I couldn't hear. The tension flowing through Mel lessened but only slightly.

"It's just a question, Mel." The words came out soft and sad. Since Mel had left the tribe, there had been a gap between us, but now it seemed to have widened to a chasm. Standing there next to women I'd loved, who had supported me through some of the worst times in my life, I felt very alone.

Mel closed her eyes and balled her hands into fists. When she opened her lids, I could see some of my sadness reflected back at me in her gaze.

"We know. We know why you're here." Then she opened her mouth and expelled a gale-force wind. For the second time in days I flew backward—this time smashing into a wall.

Chapter 8

Bern thumped into the wall beside me.

My second collision with something solid and ungiving in a week did my back no good. I grunted and closed my eyes.

If Mel was using her energy to hold me to the wall, at least she wasn't doing something else—like drawing a knife to cut out my heart. Which didn't mean someone else couldn't do that part, but I didn't think either of the females in the room would, at least not without a bit more provocation on my part. Plus with Mel's wind blowing as strongly as it was, they couldn't get close enough to me to even try.

So I didn't struggle; I waited.

After only seconds the wind ceased and I landed hard

on my feet. Bern did too, but she didn't stop. She hurtled herself across the room toward my loving best friend.

This time Bubbe stepped in. She made a motion with her arm, like she was throwing a bowling ball into the warrior's path. Bern tripped and fell face forward onto her hands and knees. Bubbe, mumbling, made another motion with her hands, this time creating an arch.

Bern leapt to her feet, but I knew no aid would come from her now. It took her a second to realize it, though. Over and over she pummeled her body against the invisible barrier the priestess had created around her.

Bubbe sighed in my direction. "You wish her to damage herself so?"

I turned to the trapped warrior. "Bern. Leave."

She had staggered backward and was preparing to charge Bubbe's invisible wall again. When I spoke, she stopped and stared at me, looking, I knew, for some sign I wanted her to do something other than what I had said.

I shook my head. "Go outside."

Exhaling a breath big enough to make her chest and shoulders visibly move, she folded her arms over her body and waited.

Bubbe waved her hands and she was free.

"The babies too. Sunshine would be good for them." The priestess gestured to the carriers.

"No, leave them. That is why Zery is here after all." Mel walked over and took Dana's child from her arms. "Isn't that right, Zery? You're here looking for a baby."

"How . . . ?" My eyes narrowed. "You're working with the sons . . ." Thea had reminded me that Mel had left the tribe, and I'd known she had been traveling with Peter. But I hadn't thought she would have so completely slipped to the other side that she would know even before I arrived why I was here.

"Dana told you his name, right?" She bounced the infant and tapped a finger on his nose. "Pisto. Do you think your lieutenant would approve?" She looked at me then, her eyes filled with mockery.

We both knew the answer. Pisto had wanted no part of her sister's son. Naming him for her would have only angered my volatile lieutenant, but I knew Dana had chosen the name with only the best intentions.

"Mel," Bubbe barked, apparently thinking the same thing I had and not wanting it to be said in front of Dana.

Her eyes misty, the young hearth-keeper waved her hand. "Don't worry. I know Pisto wouldn't have approved of me giving him her name, but I loved her and want to remember her. And I want him to know about her, too."

Looking horrified, Mel darted a glance at me.

I tilted my head to the side. Mel had always been a little brash. It wasn't a trait she'd had to worry about too much when just living with her tough-skinned family, but Dana was different. She was one of the few Amazons I would honestly term sensitive—a trait that had enraged Pisto more than once.

Dana held out her arms, and a shamefaced Mel slipped baby Pisto into them. Looking humbled, Mel jerked her head toward her mother's workout room. "We can talk in there."

I followed her, my head high.

She waited for me by the door. Once we were both inside, she closed it behind us. It was a good-sized room filled with workout benches and weights. There was a plastic half barrel filled with medicine balls and a couple of staffs too.

The staffs were the only weapons in sight, but I knew if Mel planned to attack me it would be with magic any-way—if she intended to hurt me, at least. Her talents might be growing as a warrior, but I could still beat her . . . I hoped.

I glanced at my friend wondering how strong she had become, what being the daughter of a son meant exactly. How dangerous, if she was siding with the sons, was she?

She leaned her hip against a weight machine and stud-ied me. "How? How can we be this far apart?"

"You tell me."

We stood watching each other for a beat of twelve, neither understanding what the other was thinking.

Finally she pushed away from the machine and began to pace. "Peter told me what happened. I didn't believe him at first . . ." She stopped. "Or maybe it's that I didn't want to. I've always known you loved the tribe more than anything, but I trusted . . ." She placed her hands on a stack of weights and stared down at them. Then without warning, she looked up. "Do you really think this baby is a threat? That there is no choice but to kill him?"

"Kill? Him?" *What was she talking about?* I frowned. "Someone's been lying to you. I'm here to save the baby, to take her from the sons. They stole her from her mother. We don't know why." I waited for dawning to hit her, for the anger to come.

She laughed. "And you believe that?"

"The high council—"

"Fuck the high council." She slammed her hands onto the weights. "They don't even exist."

I stiffened. It had been a while since anyone had talked to me like that, in fact, no one except Mel, her family, and my mother ever had. I measured my words. "Of course they exist."

"Just because they have existed doesn't mean they do now."

"We . . . our new priestess just spoke to them. It's how we learned of the baby." Someone had been lying to my friend, the sons I guessed, to get her on their side for some reason.

"She may have spoken with someone, someone who *was* on the high council . . . but they aren't now because the high council has split. The members aren't meeting."

Split? She was speaking gibberish.

I spoke slowly. "The council has not split. The high council is the Amazons. It always has been."

She leaned forward; magic snapped around her. Even as talentless as I was in that area, I could feel it, like electricity. The hairs on my arms, legs, even inside my nose, stood, but I didn't back away.

"You can't believe the council is the Amazons. You are not that stupid," she muttered.

I ground my jaws together. "You've gotten brave in the last few months."

She laughed. "No, I just realized what's important, and what's really worth fighting for. And the council isn't it."

"The Amazons—"

"Aren't the council. The council was created to serve the tribe, not the other way around. Somewhere, somehow that got messed up. You can't follow them blindly. You need to think, Zery—for yourself."

I pulled back. "But we are the council; we give them our power when they accept the role."

"Do you give them your brain, your soul, your heart? Where does it stop? Have you thought about what killing that baby would mean? It isn't about one child—horrific as even that act would be. It's about all of our children. Dana's baby—he's the son of a son, and not just any son . . . the one who was strong enough to murder three Amazons and stake out one of their queens."

Me. I was that queen.

I opened my mouth to tell her again *she* was wrong—that I wasn't looking for the baby to kill her . . . *that it was a her,* not the *he* Mel seemed to think.

But she looked past me and kept talking. "My son. What about him? He's second generation. They're already watching Harmony; don't think I don't know that. If they find my son before I do, who will be ordered to kill him? You? Would you?" Her eyes were on me now and I discovered I couldn't meet them.

Something was curling around inside my heart, squeezing, making me want to run. Something she was saying rang true.

The Amazons had killed their infant sons before, and now after we had discovered the Amazon sons had gathered together, that they had powers and one had already used those powers against us . . . it made sense some might want to return to the old ways, especially if the male child was second generation, the son of a son.

"And Harmony, what about her? Yes, she's a girl . . . but if she doesn't agree with the council, doesn't want to play the role they lay out for her, if she stays with me . . . how long before they want her eliminated too?" Mel stepped closer and forced me to look at her. "What about that? Have you thought of all that? Do you know what you will do when they point at my child or Dana's or someone else's you know, maybe love?"

Despite the sick feeling her words were creating in my gut, I had to try and convince her what she was saying wasn't true. "I don't know what you are talking about. The baby I'm looking for is a girl and we don't want to kill her, we want to . . ." I paused. I didn't know what the council had planned for the child because no one had told me . . . because without knowing, I'd raced ahead and done my damnedest to do their bidding.

Mel leaned forward, her face grim. "It's a he, Zery. A

son of a son and a high council member. The rest of the council doesn't want to save him, they want to kill him. I know. I've talked to his mother. I've seen the child."

And like that, my world crashed around me. I don't know how I knew she was speaking the truth . . . No, that wasn't right, I knew because it was Mel, because despite all of our fallouts I trusted her.

I took a step back. Thea . . . the knife . . . the slit in my thumb . . . the blade had been sharp enough to cut it. I'd missed it, somehow, but it made sense. Thea had known this council's plan and hadn't told me. She'd been using me to find the child so she could do as the council asked . . . so she could kill him.

I wasn't a queen; I was a tool.

The realization was like a physical blow, and I couldn't stand next to Mel now, couldn't look at her.

A piece of me was dying and the only thing I could do was run.

I left Bern at Mel's. I needed to be alone and I didn't know what waited for her back at camp. I didn't know what waited for either of us, but this felt like my fight.

After being forced to see the truth, I'd walked from the room in a fog. I knew from the outside I'd appeared to be under control. I always appeared under control, but inside, my knees were buckling and my heart was thrashing around inside my chest.

I'd walked through those damn babies without looking

down. If I'd thought they were watching me when I entered, when I'd left, the feeling had been one hundred times worse. They weren't just watching, they were judging.

And I came up lacking, severely lacking.

The Jeep's engine roared as I barreled down the highway. I zipped past two semis and a car full of teenagers before thinking to glance down at the speedometer—eighty-five. I tapped on the brake.

Amazons didn't speed. Speeding invited troopers to stop you, which led to questions. We avoided questions.

When the vehicle was back under sixty-five, I shoved my back against the seat and tried to think.

But I couldn't—or I was thinking too much. Images from my life as queen and my life as Mel's friend swirled through my head. Images of Bern and Lao: Thea asking Bern to give up her *givnomai,* Lao telling the girls to put down the bowl.

All of them part of the tribe.

None of them completely seeing things the same way.

When did that happen? When did we stop all agreeing?

Then I thought of Bubbe. Before my birth, she had fought the high council, gone against the old ways and stopped Amazons from killing and maiming their sons. After that we had simply deserted them, left them for humans to find and adopt.

But since then the high council had grown, not in size but power. They had fought every change since all the harder until there had been no change, no independent thought at all.

My job as queen had always been to follow blindly, like a sheep.

I slammed my fist into the steering wheel.

Like a sheep.

Damn the wolverine son for seeing that when I couldn't.

Angry with myself and my tribe, I pulled off at a rest stop just past the Illinois border. I parked in the area for semis. I wasn't in the mood to deal with mothers and toddlers or old people walking their dogs. Truckers tended to mind their own business; I liked that.

Actually, there was only one semi in the lot. I parked as far away from it as I could and got out to do my business and walk a bit.

My mind was a swirl. Thea had talked with someone from the council. I believed that. What I didn't know for sure was if she knew that someone wanted the child killed. I suspected she did—suspected she'd taken the child to the woods to do the job herself.

But the council . . . they were still out there. Mel had said the council had split. That didn't mean the council was gone . . . it meant there were two now.

Which meant I had a choice of which one to listen to or, as Mel had suggested, the choice to listen to no one at all, to think for myself.

It was strange to realize I hadn't been doing that all along.

So which was it? After the shock of realizing I'd been manipulated wore off, did I understand why some of the council might want the child dead? He was the son of a son and a high council member. The potential power in that combination was unsettling.

But he was also just that . . . potential. He was an infant; he had done nothing good or bad. Who were we to condemn him?

The choice was mine. I could return to Madison and go hang around Mel. I could wait for Peter outside her shop and follow him wherever he went. Then I could force him to tell me what he knew.

I could find the baby if I really wanted to. I knew that.

But did I?

A car pulled into the lot behind me, but I ignored it, choosing instead to change direction and walk toward the empty playground that stood about sixty feet from the rest area building.

It was windy and warm. A swing moved in the breeze and a bit of dirt made its way into my eye. I was rubbing it out when I got struck from behind.

"Ready to leave the flock?" A rough male voice whispered in my ear as I hit the ground.

I flung back one elbow and was rewarded with a pain-filled grunt. I pressed my advantage by slamming my head backward, into, I hoped, my assailant's nose.

The grip on me loosened and I sprang to my feet.

My fairy godfather rose to his feet, blood streaming from his nose. "The sheep kicks," he commented.

"Baa," I replied, then circled to the left.

I needed this fight. I was even willing to risk human notice to have it.

He grinned and circled too. "Have a nice day in Madison?" he asked.

"Lovely," I replied.

"Heard you stopped by an old friend's."

I rushed forward, pivoting as I kicked. My foot hit him in the chest. He let out an *umph* of air and staggered backward.

"Nice," he murmured. He moved in quickly, swinging with his left fist. I ducked, but not fast enough. His closed hand made contact with my cheek. I could feel the flesh begin to swell.

He jumped back. "Oops. I hit a girl."

"Good thing this girl"—I spun again, this time dropping low, going for the backs of his knees with my extended leg; he tumbled backward onto his ass—"hits back." I finished, moving in to kick him again, this time in the head.

He grabbed me by the ankle and twisted. Pain shot through my recently reinjured back. I fell onto the ground beside him and he rolled over on top of me.

"You know, fun as it is, I didn't come here to fight." He was breathing hard; blood and sweat streamed down his face. Pea gravel that had been poured onto the playground to protect toddlers who tumbled off the slide bit into my backside.

"Really, why did you come?" I locked one arm around his, shoved the other into his chin, and rotated my body, flipping us over as I did. On top, I knee-kicked him in the groin, then pulled back my fist to sock him again in the nose.

"What? Whoa!" A new voice boomed over us. "He bothering you, lady? Someone call the cops!" A trucker approximately six feet tall and almost as wide leaned over us. "Heard some noise. Thought it was some kids scrapping . . . Don't you worry. I'll hold him till the cops can get here." He grabbed me and the son and hauled both of us to our feet.

Adrenaline raced through me and my breath came in quick puffs. Across the trucker's wide body the son stared at me, his dark eyes almost glowing. Neither of us had been ready for the fight to end, but unless we wanted to take out the trucker, we had no choice.

Of course, I also didn't want to stick around and talk to the cops.

Apparently the son didn't either. After one last dark glance at me, he jerked his arm free of the trucker's grasp and sprinted for the parking lot.

"Hey, you. Someone stop him!" the trucker yelled and lumbered after him.

I took the opportunity to run myself, in the opposite direction. My business with the son wasn't over; I was tired of having him follow me around. And no matter what I decided to do with the high council's orders, that was going to stop. But I couldn't stop it now. The best I could do was get away before the trucker went through with his civic duty and called in the human authorities.

I circled around the restrooms, drawing curious stares from a couple getting out of a small RV. The man stared openly at me until the woman elbowed him in the gut. Fussing at each other, they continued walking and disappeared inside the building.

I cut across the grass and headed back to my car. The trucker was nowhere in sight, and there were now three cars parked in the semi area, making it impossible to say whether the son was still around or not.

I guessed, however, that he had left in whatever vehicle he'd arrived in.

I slipped into the Jeep and steered it toward the interstate, pulling the seat belt across me as I did. I'd gone maybe four miles and begun to relax when I caught sight of movement in the rearview mirror. Movement *inside* the Jeep.

Chapter 9

A boot-clad foot appeared over the top of the back bench seat. I recognized it instantly—the son. I kept my hands on the wheel, maintained my speed, and basically didn't react at all, but my mind was spinning. We were in a stretch with no exits, making my only option to pull over onto the shoulder, but that wasn't the wisest choice either.

Some busybody Good Samaritan would surely spot us and either stop or dial 911.

At that moment I wished more than anything I had a talent for magic. Unfortunately, I needed direct physical contact with the son to do him any harm—or did I? His leg followed his foot. I waited until he was straddling the seat and then I slammed on the brakes.

The Jeep fishtailed, swerving sideways across two

lanes. The seat belt cut into my shoulder and jerked me backward. The son flew forward, his body twisting, his legs hitting the roof before the rest of him collided with the passenger seat and he fell to the floor. Smoke curled around us, five years of tire tread left on the road.

A horn sounded behind me, long, hard, and angry. A pickup truck pulling a horse trailer barreled toward us. I punched the gas and shot the Jeep onto the shoulder. Once there, I slammed the vehicle into park, unsnapped my belt, and threw myself over the seat and onto the son.

I socked him in the jaw. He groaned. I hit him again and pulled back my arm for another swing. This time he reached up and grabbed my wrist.

"I told you I wasn't here to fight."

I twisted my arm, trying to break his hold. His eyes glimmered. "Back down or I shift. Do you really want to be stuck in a closed car with a forty-pound pissed-off wolverine? And trust me, I'm getting mighty pissed off."

His threat didn't bother me, but truth be told I was getting curious. I pulled back and sat on the edge of the middle seat, but I kept my attention on him, my body tense and ready to spring. Still on the floor, he stretched out his legs and studied me. After a second he held out one hand. "Truce?"

I ignored the overture, choosing to stare back at him instead. I was curious what he wanted if it wasn't to kill me, but I couldn't begin to think of a question. Then I had it. "How long have you been watching me and why?"

He studied me for a second, then gestured toward the front seat. "Why don't we get going before state patrol decides to check and see what the ten feet of skid marks you left back there are about?"

I must not have looked all that eager. He added, "You drive; I'll talk. We've still got an hour or more, plenty of time to get to know each other as well as you like." His voice lowered on the last.

I wasn't all that keen on being trapped in a car with him, but on the other hand, if he was with me, I knew what he was doing and he was right, sooner or later a trooper would wander along. I climbed into the front seat, placing my foot firmly on his gut in the process.

He didn't comment, didn't even grab my foot, just let out a slight grunt. Once I was in place, he wedged his body through the opening between the seats and levered his long frame in the space allowed between seat and dash.

"You could have come through the door," I said.

"And risk you peeling out over my foot? I don't think so." With another grunt he pulled on the seat adjustment and sent the thing whizzing backward.

I didn't bother responding. He was right; I would have. After checking my side mirror, I pulled back onto the interstate. When I glanced back at my uninvited guest, he was lounged against the passenger door looking annoyingly pleased with himself.

"Well?" I snapped.

He raised both brows.

"Talk." I whipped the Jeep into the left lane to pass a convoy of semis before a man in a sedan wearing a business suit and chatting on his phone could cut me off.

The son waited for me to get back in the right-hand lane. I frowned at him. "I can stop again."

"In the same manner? I don't know if your tires can take it."

I put on my turn signal.

He held up one hand. "Fine. I'm Jack Parker, your neighbor of five years and an Amazon son."

Sounded like a confession, like you'd hear at some twelve-step program. I waited to see if another confession was coming, but his lips were firmly closed.

"Five years?" I thought back to where I had been, *what* I had been five years ago. Two days ago I would have said exactly where I was now—but today's events had made me realize that wasn't true.

"Five years. That's when we got organized enough to assign sons to the safe camps," he explained.

"So all the safe camps have sons watching them?" This was information the council, if they still existed, would want to know.

He shrugged. "Of course. Don't think it will help you, though. The sons assigned to the camps are good. You won't find them unless they want to be found."

I glanced at him. "I found you."

"Not at your camp. I showed myself to you there. I didn't have to."

"You did if you wanted to steal the baby."

"*Save.* We saved the baby."

I concentrated on the road for a minute. I wasn't ready to talk about the baby just yet. I had to decide what I was going to do about my assignment, but not at this exact moment.

"So, you've been watching us. Why?"

He twisted in his seat, sinking down a little and playing with a pen he'd picked up from the floor. He flipped it over the knuckles of his right hand so quickly the motion was nothing but a blur.

"I was told to."

"Ha." I shook my head. "Who's the sheep?"

His fingers stilled. "I was told to, but I was given all the information. Then I thought about what I was doing, knew the consequences and believed in the cause."

"I believe in the cause." Not his cause, but the cause of the Amazons.

"Really. Tell me what you believe. Tell me what you want for your tribe."

What did I want? Survival, strength, happiness . . . I shifted my hands on the steering wheel. "I'm not the one who's supposed to be talking; you are. Tell me how you got the baby, what else you know."

He held up the pen and waved it back and forth like a *no you don't* finger. "Bossy, aren't you? Of course, I knew that."

I suppressed a growl.

"The condor you saw. He knows the mother."

I let that compute.

"So she gave him her baby?" I asked. It was possible; not all Amazon mothers were as "motherly" as Mel. "Does he have the child now?" I was avoiding stating the baby's sex. I had been told it was a girl, but Mel claimed it was a boy. I'd like to hear this son confirm one or the other before offering it myself.

He smiled. "He may. Let's talk about you and the Amazons."

"You can't beat us," I replied.

He quirked his head. "Who said we want to beat you?"

"I'm sorry. I misunderstood the bite on my leg—what was that?"

"I didn't start that fight."

"You did, you—"

"Saved the baby. I know, we've covered that."

Not really. But maybe it was time we did. "Why?" I asked. Attacking us like they had, two against two, had been a risk.

A shadow passed behind his eyes. "Because we know what the Amazons have planned for him."

Him. He'd said it. "The baby is a boy? How do I know that?"

He frowned. "Why would I lie about that? He's a son, Mateo . . . the condor's . . . son. The mother is on your high council. When she learned some of the council members planned to kill her child, to send some kind of message to the rest of the tribe, she contacted Mateo."

"What message?" I asked.

The pen stilled. "That the Amazons are the same baby-killing bitches they've always been?"

I tensed, but didn't react. "If that were true, you wouldn't be sitting in this car."

He laughed. "One short two-hundred-year or so break. What? I'm supposed to give the Amazons an award? I don't think so."

"I wasn't asked to kill the baby, only to retrieve him." I didn't mention that I had been told the child was a girl. It would only strengthen the son's case that the council had planned to have the baby killed.

"Would you have?" he asked.

I jerked, startled by his question.

"It's a simple question, Zery. If the council had told you the baby was the son of a son and a high-council member. If they had told you they wanted him dead. Would you have killed him?"

I stared at the road in front of me . . . black, straight, and unending. I didn't know how to answer him. I hadn't questioned when I was told to take the child . . . what would I have done if I'd been told to kill him?

A chill passed over me. I felt sick.

"What will you do with him?" I asked.

"I don't know. He's Mateo's son. I assume he'll raise him."

"And the mother?"

"I haven't asked."

A sort of truce between us, we fell silent for a while. I

watched the road disappear beneath the car. Maybe they were wrong. Maybe the council didn't want to kill the child; maybe they just wanted to make sure he wasn't raised by the sons.

The sons were dangerous. They were, if they chose to be, a threat. The child did have the potential to be powerful.

Did we want that power being raised in the hands of our enemy?

But then that would mean Amazons keeping their sons, raising them alongside their daughters. That would mean the end of who and what we were.

More confused than ever, I gripped the wheel and wished I was back at the camp sparring with Areto, not sitting here being forced to face that this baby signified a lot more than just his own tiny life.

Jack tapped the pen against the heel of his hand. "All babies are important. All life is important. Do you believe that?"

Finally I answered, "Amazon life." It was the simple answer, pat.

He sat silent for a second, then he replied, "I don't believe you."

"You should." Amazons lived too long. Saw too much death. It didn't pay for us to value any life besides our own.

"Because humans come and go?" he asked.

I nodded. Came and went. Been there, done that.

"Who?"

The questions were going somewhere I didn't like, somewhere I didn't want to go.

"You ever been in love, Zery?"

I reached for the radio, to turn it on. He grabbed my hand. "Tell me your secret and I'll tell you mine."

I glanced at him. "All of yours?"

His fingers were warm on my skin. I wanted to pull back but didn't let myself.

He tilted his head. "Most. As long as it doesn't endanger anyone I love." His eyes flickered.

I swallowed. Why not tell him my story? It had happened a lifetime ago; it wasn't important, not anymore. The girl it happened to didn't even exist anymore. Give him this, make him think I trusted him, and he'd give me more. I pulled my fingers away from the radio knob. He let me.

"Once," I replied. "I was young and stupid . . . sixteen. A baby in Amazon years. We were living in Arkansas and my friend Mel was in California. I was all alone, or felt that way.

"It was hot that year, really hot, and before most people had air-conditioning. I spent my days swimming in the local springs, and I met a boy. Mother was too busy doing whatever she was doing to pay attention to me, and I was too old for the hearth-keepers to manage—to keep me on track with the warrior training my mother thought I was doing.

"He was young too, and even more stupid. He started

gambling—there was a lot of gambling in Hot Springs then, and prostitution and bootlegging. The place had it all. Made for an exciting time." I wiped sweat off my palms onto the steering wheel. I hadn't told this story in a long time, not since I'd told Mel . . . seventy-three years ago.

"What happened?"

I didn't look at him. I felt silly telling the tale; it was so long ago . . . didn't matter.

I licked my lips. "We went out and gambled, even though we knew we'd gone over our limits. When they pushed us to pay, we ran. It was fun, a rush—until they started shooting."

I looked at him then, could feel the deadness in my own eyes. "It isn't like they show in the movies; isn't glamorous at all. Bullets hurt, and the noise . . ." I bit the inside of my cheek. "I got him into the car and got us away. We'd both been hit, but I'm an Amazon. I heal fast. He wasn't and he didn't."

The son was quiet for a second, then, "And after seventy-plus years, you still have the scars."

Surprise and suspicion shook me out of the cloud that had settled around me. "How'd you know?" I reached across my body and touched the scars hidden under my shirt where the bullets had gone through my side.

His gaze dropped to my hand, then moved back to my face. "Not those, the other ones, the ones you hide from everyone, even yourself."

I put my eyes back on the road. "Tell me about the guns," I bit out.

"What guns?"

"The ones in your cabin."

"The cabin you blew up?"

"I did not blow up your cabin. You know who blew up your cabin."

"Really? You?"

I'd wanted to change the subject away from me, but this conversation was beginning to feel like a tennis match, and I was almost overcome by a desire to smash the ball back over the net—to flatten it, actually.

"I told you a secret. One I haven't told anyone for a long time. Now it's your turn. Tell me about the guns."

He inhaled with long exaggerated patience. "I don't know anything about any guns—at least not at my cabin."

It was my turn to breathe, and struggle to remain calm. "When we went to your cabin . . . *before* you blew it up and tried to kill me . . . I looked inside the window. There were guns, most in boxes. What were they for? What do the sons plan to do with them?"

He leaned back. "Guns? Really? In my cabin?" His expression was studied innocence. Then he raised his hands. "Sorry. A guy has to make a living."

"By selling guns?"

He shrugged. "That's so much worse than stealing and conning?"

"A picked pocket never killed anyone."

"Maybe, maybe not. Do you research your victims? Know that they don't need that last dollar to feed their families? Pay for some medication?" He leaned back against the door, looking superior. "Don't judge me, Zery. In a moral battle, right now you are going to lose."

He twisted his lips to the side, thinking. "Actually, though, I'm surprised they were still there. That *whoever*"—he glanced at me—"blew up my cabin didn't take them first."

"You're insinuating we would take them?" I laughed. "Amazons don't do guns, don't do technology in general."

"Yeah, I know. Rather stupid of you, actually."

We passed a sign saying an exit was coming up in one mile. I got into the right-hand lane.

My passenger had worn out his use. It was time to get rid of him.

"I'm sorry. I didn't mean to offend." His expression said he did, or at least didn't regret doing so.

"I can see that. What I can't see is how driving you back to my camp will be of any benefit to me."

He placed a hand on my forearm. Since I was driving, I didn't jerk away, just waited, tense.

"Sorry. I'm being honest; just maybe not as serious as I need to be. Go ahead. Pull over. Maybe it's time we had a real talk."

A real talk . . . made me wonder what spilling my guts before had been.

I took the next exit. At a deserted roadside park, I stopped the Jeep, and without speaking we both got out.

We took up positions on opposite sides of a bird-dropping-adorned picnic table.

He leaned forward, placing his forearms on the table as he did. The sleeve of his T-shirt pulled up, revealing the bottom half of his wolverine tattoo. I made a concentrated effort not to stare at it. My fingers curved toward my palm; I wanted to lean across the table and touch the animal—see if I could feel the difference between his *givnomai* and mine, feel why his gave him the power to shift and mine didn't.

"Maybe you'll feel more comfortable if I tell you a little more about myself. As I said, I'm Jack Parker. I'm one hundred and twenty years old and I've known I was a son since I was twenty-two and shifted for the first time."

My eyes widened. "But your tattoo—?" I thought the tattoo gave the sons the power to shift, but if the shift came first . . .

He lifted his sleeve, completely revealing the wolverine. It was the first time I'd seen it clearly and up close. It was colored exactly like he was when in the animal's form and looked just as intimidating with its lips curled and its teeth clearly visible. My fingers twitched; I hid them under the table. He gave me an appraising look. I had the uncomfortable feeling he knew of my disturbing need to touch his art.

"Got it when I was eighteen. I had no idea the guy who volunteered to give me a free tattoo was a son. Didn't know sons existed." He turned to the side and leaned toward me. "Go ahead."

I looked past him, as if his suggestion was insulting.

He smiled and pulled down his sleeve. "The offer," he whispered, "is always open."

I ignored the tingle that went from my fingers down to my toes—at least enough to keep a look of bored impatience on my face.

He patted his arm where the wolverine was now hidden under his shirt, then continued. "The night I shifted five sons revealed themselves to me—got pretty torn up in the process too." He caught my gaze. "Them, not me, nothing like a frightened wolverine who doesn't have enough sense to know he's a wolverine. Bad news."

"Why make you one, then? Whoever gave you the art had the choice, right?" I tried not to look too interested, but I couldn't help myself, I was. The sons were little more than myth to us, and a new one at that. To have one sit down and reveal so much . . . it was seductive. I stiffened, realizing that sometime during the conversation I'd relaxed, let down my guard.

Aware now, I looked around and checked to make sure there was no one or thing in sight. A squirrel skittered up a tree; grabbed my attention.

Jack laughed. "Not one of mine."

I shot a stare at him. "How do I know? How do you know?"

He shrugged. "Just do. It's the magic; I can feel it. I'm surprised you can't."

I paused. "All the time or just when they shift?"

He studied me for a second. "I think that's something you should figure out on your own."

For a moment I thought he was going to do it then, change into his wolverine form, but he just smiled and patted the table with his flattened palm. "In answer to your question, I asked for a wolverine. The artist didn't prompt me or give me choices, just asked of all the animals in the world which one appealed to me, which one I'd want to know better."

"And you picked a comic-book character. Too bad you weren't a fan of Spider-Man."

"Think you would have crushed me?"

"Right under my boot."

The air between us grew tense; I could feel energy bouncing between us. Anger. Impatience. Then he laughed.

"Doesn't work that way, and you know it. I didn't pick a wolverine out of a comic; comics didn't exist yet. I simply was meant to be a wolverine or I wouldn't have chosen him."

I still wished he'd picked a spider, with my feelings for the arachnid, there would have been dual pleasure in stomping him out of existence. But he hadn't and I was stuck with him as he was.

"So," I prompted, "the sons found you and what? You started working for them?"

"Not for them. It's not a job."

"What is it?" They weren't Amazons. They didn't have our history, weren't a tribe with a high council.

"It's . . ." He frowned and shook his head. "It's who I am, my history."

I snorted. "What history? You said it yourself, you didn't even know you were a son until you were twenty-two. What kind of history is that?"

He scowled. "You're a snob. Did you know that?"

A snob? I drove a ten-year-old Jeep I didn't even own and shared a house with, at times, twelve women. I had very little besides my underwear that belonged totally to me. Even it at times got mixed in with others in the wash and wound up on another body.

Reading my expression, he added, "Or maybe the term is *elitist*. You think Amazons are the only beings worthy of walking this earth. The rest of us are just annoyances in your oh-so-grand existence."

He made it sound, well, bad. I narrowed my eyes. "I haven't seen a lot of evidence to the contrary."

"Of course not. You don't mingle with anyone else, not unless you are setting them up to steal from them."

"And sons don't steal? What about the car you left behind at the rest stop? I'm thinking if it was yours, you wouldn't have abandoned it so freely."

He acknowledged my observation with a tilt of his head. "True, but I don't just see humans as something put here to prop up my position in the world." He stopped then and smiled like he'd just made some new discovery. "That's it; that's how you do it. You only allow yourselves to see humans as tools; you don't get to know them, not as people."

"I did, once."

"And look how that turned out . . ." He laughed. "You, my queen, are a mess."

Angry, I placed my palms on the lip of the table and straightened my arms. "I'm not your queen."

"No, you're not."

The energy was back . . . thick, angry, and throbbing.

Chapter 10

I stood, my hands fisted. I had my belt buckle knife and the belt itself, but my anger was more basic than that. I needed to pummel something or someone with my bare fists.

Jack, however, didn't stand. He just sat at the table and glowered.

I waited, my feet braced.

He bit the inside of his cheek and stared. "You can't have it both ways. You can't deny the sons and expect us to recognize your authority. You have no authority with us."

I flexed my hands. His refusal to engage physically was frustrating; it made me feel awkward standing there, waiting to fight an enemy who refused to fight back.

I spun and paced toward the Jeep.

"Don't you want to know the rest? Don't you want to know what I know about the Amazons?"

I stopped and turned slowly, gravel grinding under my foot. Taking a cue from Jack, I gritted my teeth, tamped down my anger, and sat.

He stared at me for a moment. I could see I'd misjudged. He was angry also. It simmered in his dark eyes, not just anger but a threat too. Like he was one straw away from losing control and wanted me to know it.

Squaring my shoulders, I lifted my chin and let him know I met his challenge. "What do you know, or think you know, about the Amazons?"

He flattened his hands. "More than I want to."

The anger pulsed between us for another second, then seemed to sputter and die. He huffed out a breath and glanced down. When he looked back up, the darker emotion was gone, replaced by resolve. "As I said, we have sons outside all of the Amazon safe camps. We have sons watching as many Amazons as we can—including the high council."

Not believing him, I smiled. "Really? The high council? And how exactly are you watching all these other Amazons? You follow them from town to town? You don't think Amazons would notice if the same tattooed guy showed up everywhere they did?"

"Amazons are like whales, geese . . . all migrating animals. You've been doing the same things forever. You travel the same routes. Work the same jobs." He lifted a shoulder with arrogant ease. "You're predictable. We don't have to follow you around. You come to us, over and over."

I moved my jaw to the side.

He leaned forward. "You work at carnivals. We work at carnivals. You visit fairs. We set up fairs. Everywhere you are; so are we."

It was a struggle not to let emotion show. We were watched, everywhere . . . for how long? "The farmer's market?" I asked.

He nodded. "Someone direct you to your spot today? Buy some tomatoes? It's really not that hard."

My first thought was that I'd have to tell Lao, that we'd have to find some other way to make money. Then I saw how Jack was watching me, the knowing expression on his face.

There was no other way. There was no avoiding them.

"What about the high council?" I asked. Honestly, I didn't even know where they met. The group wasn't like a safe camp. They didn't live all together, and the location of their meetings changed from time to time. I assumed they went to various state campgrounds, but honestly didn't know. As far as I knew, only the high-council members themselves did.

He tapped the pads of each of his fingers against the tabletop, one after the other. Made me wonder what he'd done with his pen—if he was missing it.

"What if I told you the high council knew about us, was working with us?"

"I'd say you were a liar."

"How many Amazons are on the council, Zery?"

I could see he knew the answer. I didn't bother answering.

"Twelve, right? And to get on the council you have to be what? Weak? Nonopinionated? Not an Amazon?" One corner of his mouth lifted. "You think they all get along? All agree? You think just because you hear the 'final' decision that there wasn't talk of doing something different before that?"

To be honest, I hadn't thought about it at all. "The final decision is all that matters," I said, my voice calm, bordering on bored.

"Really? You think that?"

I didn't like the way he was watching me, didn't like what his slightly amused expression meant.

"I do," I replied, keeping my face straight, confident.

"So the members who disagree with the majority, who think killing that baby is the wrong choice, they don't matter."

My mind stuttered.

"Majority wins, might makes right, and the other Amazons, those who didn't win, have no value at all?"

"I didn't say they didn't have value." Of course they did; they were still Amazons.

He tapped his fingers again, just the middle ones this time. "You ever been in the minority, Zery?"

"There is no minority in the tribe. We all believe the same thing; it's what keeps us strong."

"Not anymore."

I wasn't sure what he was saying . . . believing the same thing didn't keep us strong or that we didn't all believe the same thing. But I had already faced that, realized we were all individuals. I just hadn't worked it out to the next step, that if we disagreed on the little things, we might disagree on the big ones too. The ones that might split not just the council, but the tribe.

"Maybe all the Amazons don't agree. Maybe some think working with the sons is smarter, better for the tribe, than trying to fight us. You're the Indians, Zery, and we're the white flood. We aren't going away."

I snorted. "Like working with whites helped the Indians. I'd rather die my way than have everything I stand for and believe in stripped away from me."

"Yes, you are definitely Geronimo rather than Washakie. Most Amazons are, but what makes you think the enemy is only outside the Amazons? What makes you think the sons are the sole threat? As I said, we've watched you, we know about you—things you don't even know about yourselves."

"You're saying there are Amazons who want to damage the rest of us? Why?"

"Not damage. Change."

"You want us to change."

"True, but we aren't the only ones. And we don't even want you to change that much. We just want the tribe to acknowledge us, to work with us—to realize they don't need to kill and maim their own children to stay safe."

A pain began to pound inside my head, right behind

my eyes. What he was saying didn't make sense, or maybe it made too much sense.

I stood. I was done with the conversation. I was ready to go home where things made sense. I'd call the council from there and tell them everything. See what was true.

And I wasn't taking the son with me.

He must have sensed it. He didn't follow me. When I reached the Jeep, I looked back. He'd pulled a phone from somewhere and was talking into it. He had a cell. Of course he did. And another son would be here soon, picking him up and most likely dropping him off where he could spy on me again.

I should have stayed, or left and sneaked back, but I didn't. I got in my vehicle and left.

I knew it wouldn't be the last I'd see of Jack, knew it wouldn't be the last chance to kill him or for him to kill me.

I pulled into the safe camp around one. I knew immediately something was wrong—or different, at least.

Two of the birders were sitting in lawn chairs in the front yard. Squatting beside them was Areto. As I approached, I noticed they were holding a small box, the same type of electronic device the women in the woods had used, and they were showing it to Areto.

"You just enter the address like this." One of the birders, a middle-aged blonde dressed in denim shorts, white tennis shoes, and a peach tank top punched something into the box. "It's really handy when there is road construction. I used it all the way from Nashville."

I realized then the woman had a Southern accent. As I walked toward them, she looked up and smiled.

I didn't return the gesture.

"What's happening?" I directed the question to Areto, who stood and took a step away from the two humans, but the woman sitting in the second chair, a brunette maybe ten years older than the blonde, answered.

"We got lost. Thea went inside to get the keys to drive us back to our car."

Again I looked at Areto. "They couldn't walk?"

"That wouldn't be very polite, now would it?" Thea stood on the porch, a key chain dangling from one finger. She hadn't changed in the few hours since I'd seen her last night, but knowing there was a possibility she had hidden the council's plans for the baby from me, I looked at her differently.

"Why would we need to be polite?" Manners were for humans. We treated each other with respect—that was real, manners weren't. Besides, assuming someone needed your help was an insult. I glanced at the two women. They both seemed able-bodied. There was no reason they couldn't go the way they'd come.

I said as much to Thea.

The women looked at each other, their shock at my outspoken behavior clear.

Thea gestured for me to step to the side, out of the two humans' hearing. Tired, confused, and not at all in the mood for a discussion, I considered ignoring her request but grudgingly moved the few feet she'd indicated.

"They wandered up a few minutes ago. They're connected to the one Bern found." Her voice low, Thea kept her focus on the pair still chatting mindlessly from the lawn chairs. "They said they went on a walk, looking for some bird—"

"An owl," I interrupted, wondering when she was going to get to the part that explained why we had rolled out the welcome mat.

"An owl," she repeated. "Apparently this owl was important to the dead woman. They wanted to get pictures of him, prove he nested here in honor of her."

"So they came on our property and you welcomed them." I didn't put any judgment into the words. I thought they spoke for themselves. My last order had been to run the birders off, not pull out the lawn furniture and brew some ice tea.

"They got lost and they wound up here." Her eyes flared. "Their friend was found dead. Apparently, the police believe the accident scenario, for now. But if we act unfriendly, that could change."

"They bought the accident?" This was, at least, good news. "How do you know?"

Thea slanted a look toward the two women.

I let air hiss from between my lips. Fine. Maybe chatting with them a bit had its uses, but that use was over. I said as much to Thea.

She held up a ring of keys in response.

I started to object. Not being antagonistic didn't mean we had to play chauffeur either, but I thought better of it. If Thea drove them, we'd know they were gone. I did, however, remind her of our original plan, making it clear I didn't want the birders to think they could drop by for coffee and cake . . . or traipse around our woods, period.

The priestess didn't reply, but as she walked off to get the birders packed up and off, I felt she'd gotten the message. I waited, thinking she'd hand off the keys to Areto or call for someone else, but she didn't. Instead she waved the women toward a compact that belonged to Sare and took off.

Surprised by her choice, I frowned, but quickly decided it fit with my needs better anyway. As my potential lieutenant, I needed to talk to Areto. Thea's news that the police had found the body and considered the death accidental was reassuring, but I still wanted to hear more about what had happened. Lao's comments earlier had made me wonder a few things. I hoped talking to Areto would either reveal more or alleviate my concerns.

My call to the high council would have to wait.

I gestured to the warrior. She followed me into the kitchen. It was empty and would stay that way for a while. The farmer's market stayed open until two, then the hearth-keepers would have to clean up and drive back here. Dinner would be late or self-serve, which meant cold something grabbed from the refrigerator. But even that was a ways off for most of the tribe.

While Areto pulled out a chair, I went to rummage in the refrigerator for a late lunch for myself. I found cold chicken and potatoes. After dumping them onto a plate, I carried it back to the table.

She watched me as I picked up a leg and bit into it. "How was your trip?"

It was a strangely polite and somewhat distant question. I chewed the meat, then answered, "Fine."

She glanced to the side.

The suspicions that Lao's comments had created sprang to life. I took another bite of chicken, then asked, "What happened this morning?"

She sat with her back straight and her eyes facing forward, like a robot. Her posture made me realize I'd been wrong before. The length and color of her hair aside, she was nothing like Mel. There was always fire in my friend; frequently it was misdirected or not directed at all, but it was always there.

"We did as you said. We took the birder's body to the remains of the cabin. Lao came too. She had us prop the body against an old tractor, made it look like the woman had been messing with it. Then she turned on the engine and worked the cord on her binoculars so it got caught in the belt. The cord pulled tight. We left with it still running."

I waited for her to say something else, some opinion on moving the body, or my leaving and taking Bern, or on the birders I'd found in the front yard . . . anything, but she gave me nothing. She just waited.

Suddenly her lack of opinion, or at least inclination to keep it to herself, bothered me. Just days earlier I would have said that is what I wanted in a lieutenant, but now I wasn't sure.

I set the chicken leg down on my plate. "Areto, what did you think about it?"

She blinked. "About what?"

"Moving the body. Making it look like she died somewhere other than where she did."

A line deepened on her forehead. "It's what you told us to do."

"What if I hadn't?"

"But you did."

"But if I'd said to do something different? What if I'd had Bern take responsibility? Asked her to have her *givnomai* covered, then say she'd killed the birder. Would you have agreed with that?"

She didn't hesitate. "Yes."

"Because?"

"You're queen."

"And that's enough? You'll do what I ask because I'm queen?"

Confusion and a little wariness shone from her eyes. She nodded.

"What if I wasn't? What if the high council announced a different queen? Would you follow her too?"

Again, not so much as a breath before her reply. "Of course."

I wiped my fingers on my shorts, thinking and not liking my own thoughts. I looked at my would-be lieutenant again. "What if I asked you to kill someone? Someone who as far as you knew had done nothing wrong, just in my opinion held the potential. Would you do that?"

There was a flicker this time and for a second I tensed, expectant.

Then, "Of course."

Of course.

I looked at her again, hoping I'd see something that would change the sick feeling twisting in my gut, making me regret my lunch.

She sat waiting, ready to do as I said, whatever I said. But there was no fire inside her, no life.

No, she wasn't like Mel. She was like me, a blind follower, a sheep.

Chapter 11

I put in another call to Kale before moving back out into the sunshine.

In the meantime I'd done what I could do and my bit of self-discovery didn't seem that grim. Maybe I had been a sheep, but it didn't mean being one hadn't served the tribe well. Areto following my orders served the tribe well . . . it was all about the leadership. If the right Amazons were in the top positions, following them had to be okay.

So as far as the baby, I just needed to talk to someone. There was every possibility the sons were lying and had convinced Mel of those lies. When the council called back, I'd know. Until then there was no reason to stew.

With my conscience clear, I headed toward the barn. I hadn't ridden in days and not only did the horses need exercise, I needed the peace that came with galloping across a field. I could indulge that need and work in some practice throwing spears from horseback for our upcoming performance at the state fair while waiting for my call.

As I stepped onto the gravel that separated the yard from the barn area, Thea pulled back down the drive. She parked under a big maple, hopped out, and strode toward me.

"I've found the child."

The sugar cubes I'd brought for the horses fell onto the ground.

"She's in Madison." She placed two fingers in her mouth and blew, a move that resulted in a sharp whistle.

The warriors immediately appeared from the barn and Areto from the house. Sare, who had been sitting under a tree carving fetishes, brushed dirt off the seat of her shorts and moved toward us too.

Thea glanced at the approaching Amazons, then addressed me. "The bird son took her to your friend. Did you see them?"

My mind played back the scene in the basement like an old movie reel, jumpy and scratchy. Had I seen the baby? One looked just like another to me, but the bird son? I knew I hadn't seen him. Of course, I had seen Jack, not at Mel's but soon after.

I shook my head.

Areto walked up, followed closely by Sare. The warriors had already taken up a position a few feet away. I was surprised that none of them had stepped closer or lined up beside me. As it was, they could have as easily been flanking Thea as me. She had signaled for them, but, still, their choice of position was odd.

I forced myself not to look at them, not to let any sign of my confusion show. Instead, I answered Thea. "I didn't see them, but Bern stayed behind. I can have her check it out." Thinking we were done, I bent to pick up the sugar cubes.

"That will only alert them that we know she is there. In fact, your trip and leaving Bern there may have already endangered our success. We should go tonight."

"And do what?" I'd picked up the cubes and held them in my loosely closed hand.

Thea glanced at the others and then back at me. "Attack, of course. Get the baby back and bring her here."

I shook my arm, felt the cubes rattle inside my fist like beans in a maraca. "No. Not yet." I turned toward the barn.

Thea reached out, placing a hand on my shoulder to stop me.

I stiffened. It was instinct when anyone touched me, but in this circumstance being watched by the warriors and artisan of the camp, I particularly didn't want to be touched, especially by Thea. I stepped to the side and spun, causing her hand to drop and bringing me back to facing her.

"There is no reason to wait."

I could feel eyes on us, but when I glanced at the warriors their gazes dropped.

Thea stepped closer and stage-whispered in my ear,

"It was one thing to run last night, to leave those here to clean up. I understand your past, that you can't afford a second run-in with the human police so soon after your arrest last fall, but to add to the crime of losing the child by not going after her now, how can you justify that?"

Two of the warriors shifted their feet.

My fingers tightened on the treats in my hand. The cubes cut into my skin. I didn't know where to start with her outrageous claims. That I ran? That I was denying a charge?

But I was queen. I didn't have to explain.

Instead, I moved the cubes into my other hand and wiped the left-behind bits of sugar off my palm and onto my shorts. "How exactly did you learn where the baby is? How do we know she is there at all?" I used the feminine because Thea had. I didn't want to alert her I might not believe everything I had been told . . . not yet.

Emotion flickered behind her eyes. Annoyance, I guessed.

"We tracked the . . . son."

I had been feigning interest, really only concerned with reminding her I was in charge, but her response surprised me. "We?"

She opened her mouth, then closed it with a smile. "I hired someone. I know it isn't normal, but we needed someone with experience researching."

"A detective?" I frowned. "What did you tell this detective? What job did you give him?" I was concerned now. Amazons all had created pasts. You couldn't live to be five hundred in the human world. The fact that we did required some creative paperwork—or a complete avoidance of paperwork. Both of which a detective could easily spot.

"Not a detective . . . friends."

"Friends? Amazons?"

"Friends to the Amazons." She waved her hand, as if waving away any other questions. "The point is, I know where the child is, but the son could move her. We need to go tonight."

This time I was more direct. "No."

Her eyes flickered. "No? What about the high council?"

"I'll talk to them."

"I already have."

"I'll talk to them again." My temper was slipping. I wasn't used to being challenged, and despite my concern that the Amazons were becoming sheep, I didn't like this obvious proof that Thea was not among that group—at least where following my command was concerned.

Thea pulled in a breath, a patient *I can't believe I have to say this* breath. "There is no reason or time to talk to them again. We have to go tonight."

Then as if that settled everything, she gestured to Areto, and my would-be lieutenant hurried over. I took a step back, surprised and for perhaps the first time in my life, unsure. Somewhere, somehow I had lost control.

It was, however, a momentary setback. I glanced down at the sugar cubes in my hand, staring at them blindly as my mind whirled. Unless the high council said otherwise,

I was queen. Thea, no matter how she presented herself or what her magical abilities, wasn't.

And right now I didn't even know if the high council still existed.

I dropped the cubes on the ground. "We will do nothing until I have talked to the council." I stared at Areto, let my gaze bore into her. It took longer than it should have, seconds when it should have been immediate, but her eyes flickered and her head dropped . . . she nodded.

Having made my point, I turned, paced back toward the house, and hoped to hell my call was returned soon.

It was, two hours later.

I answered on the third ring. I had the phone in my hand on the first ring, but I waited until two more peals had passed before pushing the button to connect. The call felt more important than it was, I told myself. It was just a call, like a thousand others I had participated in in the past.

The future of the Amazons wasn't riding on this; my future wasn't riding on this.

"Zery?"

"Kale?" I asked. I didn't speak with my contact enough to recognize her voice.

"Away. This is Padia. Why did you call?"

I hesitated. To question her again would be to question her authority, but to not question her . . . it reeked of sheep. Still, breaking one hundred years of training was a hard thing to do in one step. "I wanted to know what we are to do with the baby."

Her tone sharpened. "Do you have the baby?"

I hesitated. "We captured her from the sons three days ago."

"Three days?" There was a pause; I could hear her thinking, judging.

"Yes, I called, but no one called back." I paused. "Where did you say Kale is?"

"Don't worry about Kale. Give the child to . . . Thea. She knows what to do."

I stared at the wall. I was sitting in a small sitting room, off the dining area. A fold-out couch was crammed in one corner, a bureau in the other. It was where Bern had slept before I'd left her in Madison.

"I'm queen. I should know what the plan is for the infant."

There was silence, then . . . "Give the child to Thea."

There was a spot on the wall. I hadn't noticed it before even though it looked old and had probably been there for two decades. I stood and placed my palm over it, then pulled my hand back and stared at it again.

"It's true." The stain was still there, still as obvious. How had I missed it all this time?

"What, Zery? What's true?" Padia's voice had an edge now, held a challenge.

I turned my back on the wall and the stain. "Sorry. I wasn't talking to you. Someone walked in, asked me a question."

There was tension on the other end of the line; I could feel it vibrate. "Good. So you understand what you are to do." Each word was an order: short, terse.

My fingers were tight around the phone; my wrist began to ache from my grip. "I understand." I understood way too much. "One last question. The council, have they met recently?"

Silence for a second, then . . . "The council isn't your worry. Giving the infant to Thea is. Tell her to call me, after."

After. One word and it was all the answer I needed. More than I wanted to know.

"Zery, the tribe has to stay strong. Don't question what you don't understand."

Be a sheep. That was my job. Being queen had never felt so demeaning.

I knew it was a farce then. That everything, every bit of pride I'd had in my elevated position, was a lie. The son Jack was right. I was nothing . . . not to him, not to anyone. I might as well have been a human in a dead-end job tightening whatever cog I'd been assigned to tighten.

"Zery?"

I snapped out of my daze, but not the fog that now seemed to engulf me. "Yes."

"I think I need to talk to Thea. Can you get her?"

Of course I could. That was what I did—follow orders. I carried the phone into the yard and handed it to our new high priestess; then I walked into the woods.

I knew Jack was watching. I knew he would find me.

* * *

If the son was watching, he didn't show himself. I wandered along the meandering path for half an hour, waiting. For what, I didn't know. If he showed, what would I do?

Tell him he was right—the council did plan to kill the baby?

I'd lied to Padia, by omission at least. She thought we had the child. Of course, after she spoke with Thea she would know differently. What was the punishment for a queen who lied to the council?

I had no idea.

Just as I had no idea what I was going to do when I returned to camp and found the Amazons, my Amazons, planning their attack on Mel.

I stopped by the obelisk. Someone had been here recently. There were leaves from a plant I didn't recognize strewn on the ground. The birders, I assumed. What they had been doing I couldn't imagine, but it wasn't important, not right now.

I placed both hands on the cold stone and closed my eyes while I prayed to Artemis. She was a moon goddess, but she didn't sleep. I had to believe she was near, near enough to guide me.

I needed guidance and I had no one else to go to to find it. At one time I would have gone to Mel, but she had moved on. Yes, she would still talk to me, but she had left the Amazons. What kind of advice could she give me, who couldn't imagine life without the tribe?

And that I realized was what this was coming down to. Go along with what I knew the council had planned, as I assumed Thea was doing, or walk away and leave my entire life behind.

A pain, worse than any I'd felt in the last few days, shot through me.

Leaving might not have been easy for Mel, but for me? It was unimaginable. It would be easier to pick up a sword and hack off my own arm. That would hurt less.

So I drew on every bit of faith I could muster and let my desperation show . . . bared myself to the goddess I had taken for granted and prayed she'd look in on me now.

Something rustled in the trees. My hands still on the stone, I opened my eyes. A hound sat five feet away at the edge of the forest. Hounds were one of Artemis's animals, and we had a number of them back at camp.

While I didn't recognize this one, there were strays in the area—it was how most of the dogs at camp came to us. A year ago I would have had no reason to be wary of the creature, but the sons had changed that. In fact, the son who had killed the teens last fall had shifted into a dog. He'd been in his dog form when he learned my *givnomai* and used it against me.

So I had every reason not to trust this creature, or at best, to brush his appearance aside, but I didn't.

I took him as a sign, which probably showed how desperate I'd become.

He watched me from the cover of the brambles for a bit, neither nervous nor aggressive. Not even, I realized, curious—more patient. Like he was waiting for me to come to some conclusion or finish what I was doing, but since I was doing nothing, I continued standing there, waiting too.

After a second, he sat.

It was then I started to feel silly. I lowered my hands and took a step toward the creature, still half expecting him to disappear in a puff of smoke before I got too close.

Instead, he whimpered. Another step and I could see him more clearly, more of him. Enough to realize he wasn't a he at all, but a she, and *she* had recently given birth.

Which made sense. Pregnant dogs, or dogs in heat, are frequently dumped on rural roads by humans too weak to do what needs to be done if they are not prepared to care for the creatures. They let nature take care of the ugly tasks they lacked the guts for.

Disgusted and prepared for the worst . . . to find the bitch had been starved and beaten, I kept my demeanor mild as I continued to approach. I had no food on me, but I hoped presenting a calm energy would gain her trust so I could at least assess her condition.

Before I got close enough to touch her, she stood and turned to move deeper into the woods. I followed. She went off the path. The underbrush was thick. Briars slapped against my legs and what was probably poison ivy tickled my ankles, but for whatever reason it seemed important I continue.

Maybe I just needed it to be important.

Finally, at the base of an oak, she stopped and the whining increased, but this time it wasn't coming from her. Hidden in a bed of leaves were three tiny bodies. They were white with black spots and speckles and they were squirming. At least two of them were; the third was still, heartbreakingly still.

I dropped onto my knees beside them. Ignoring the two who shoved with their feet and noses for their mother's attention, I scooped up the third, a boy. He screamed when I did, a horrible shrill peep that made my jaws tighten and my heart leap.

His muzzle was black, like he'd stuck it into something he shouldn't have, but I knew he hadn't performed such mischief. He was only hours old and his body was cool . . . almost cold.

I had no idea how to care for the pup, how to save him and, truth be told, no reason to, but suddenly I had to. I pulled up my close-fitting shirt and tucked him inside. With him snuggled against my bare skin, I picked the other two squirming pups up too—one in each hand. Like their brother, the girls screamed, but theirs was more a shriek of outrage than distress. I ignored it and with their mother on my heels, began the trek back to the safe camp.

When I got there I discovered my world had changed for good.

Chapter 12

The Amazons were outside the house, even the hearth-keepers, who had apparently just returned from Madison. The bed of the truck was still loaded with leftover produce and empty boxes. The warriors along with Sare were, as I'd expected, talking with Thea. What I hadn't expected, however, was how they were sitting . . . cross-legged in a circle . . . or the small fire in the center that someone had started.

The scene brought me to a halt.

It looked casual, but I knew better. Amazons didn't gather around a fire like that in the middle of the day, not when there was work to be done.

This fire wasn't casual. It was planned, a formal act by, I guessed, Thea to do something . . . something she obviously didn't want revealed while I was around.

But I was around now, and I was queen.

Time to act like one and regain my tribe.

As I glanced toward the hearth-keepers, Lao stepped forward and held out both hands. I dropped a puppy into each, then reached inside my shirt for the third. Without comment, the elder hearth-keeper tucked the first two into an empty basket and slipped the third into the top of her shirt, squeezed into her cleavage. Then she nodded toward the circle.

"No good," she murmured.

As I turned toward the circle, Bern stepped out from behind the truck. She held a staff in each hand. She didn't say anything, just tossed me one.

I'd asked her to stay in Madison and she'd disobeyed.

She was a bad Amazon, a worse sheep, and an ideal lieutenant.

I tossed the staff to gauge its weight and balance, then approached the rest of my tribe. When they didn't look up, I knew things were worse than I'd suspected.

I placed the end of my staff into the dirt about an inch from where Thea sat.

With a sigh, she stood. "Zery, I'm glad you are back." Behind her the circle of Amazons kept their focus on the fire. I shifted my own onto Thea and waited.

She looked calm, sad even, but I knew it was an act. I knew whatever she was about to tell me thrilled her to the core of her manipulative soul. She practically hummed with excitement.

"I'm afraid the high council is concerned with how you have handled their latest assignment."

I kept my face motionless, outwardly as calm as she and twice as confident, but inside, my heart was thumping.

"They were distressed when I told them you lost the baby that night—"

That night? She had called them that night? Of course, she had her own phone. She could be making more calls than Ma Bell and I would have no idea.

"Then, of course, when you refused to protect the tribe from possible exposure—"

"By sacrificing one of our own?" I let my skepticism show.

"And ran to protect yourself—"

"Protect myself." I twisted my lips to the side and nodded. Things were beginning to fall into place, Areto's discomfort when we talked, for one. I exhaled through my nose, my nostrils flaring. Thea's act would have been comical if I'd had a sense of humor.

"Then being in the same room as the baby and doing nothing . . ." The priestess shook her head. "How could they overlook that?"

My back stiffened. I replied, my words low and soft, "I didn't say I was in the same room."

She tilted her head. "But you were, weren't you?"

I held her gaze, but my mind was whirling. Had the baby been among those in the plastic seats? Had Mel known that? I smiled. I was lucky she didn't blast me to little bits.

Thea lowered her head. "Is something funny?"

My smile widened. "Everything. In fact, it's hysterical." I was hysterical. I had to be or I wouldn't be about to say what I was about to say. "We aren't killing the child. There is no reason to."

Thea shook her head again, but she didn't correct my words, didn't deny that our mission had been to kill the baby. "Zery, the high council has spoken and we have drawn the fire. Now, before witnesses and this ceremonial fire, I revoke your position of Amazon queen." She took a breath; there was a glimmer in her eye. I had the distinct feeling I was seeing the real Thea for the very first time. Then the glimmer was gone and she was back to her polite facade. She waved her hand toward the group. "You are welcome to stay at the camp, but only if you follow the high council's directives. I do, however, hope you will stay."

Oh, yes. I was sure she did.

I didn't look at the group; whether I had their support or not wouldn't change what I was about to do. "What are you, Thea? Are you a sheep or are you a wolf? Because I know one thing you aren't. You aren't an Amazon; not as I see Amazons. Not as Amazons should be." I twisted the staff in the dirt and leaned into her space. "So, tell me, are you a blind follower, or are you doing all this for some other reason? For some gain of your own?"

There was another flicker; this time strong enough I

knew to duck. Her hand flew out as she grabbed for my staff, but I jerked the weapon behind my head. With my knees bent, I shifted so it fell behind me, the free end dropping into my other hand.

The ground beneath me moved. I had seen Thea in the woods with the sons, but I still wasn't sure of her powers, wasn't sure exactly what a battle with her might bring.

Something pushed up against the sole of my foot.

I stood and spun, using the strength of my legs to add speed and strength to my swing as I aimed the staff directly at her head.

Rocks erupted from the ground around me. They were small, none bigger than my fist, but one hit the end of the staff, knocking it off its trajectory.

Thea yelled and the Amazons stood. I realized then who had been given my title, who the new Amazon queen was.

Thea, a high priestess taking the role of queen. It was unheard of.

Warriors I had worked beside, Areto who I had trusted, faced off against me.

They weren't armed. Weapons weren't part of a ceremonial fire, but there were four of them, only one of me, and they were well-trained. I had taken care of that myself.

I braced my legs, my staff held out in front of me. I could fight them, I had no choice really, but the odds were also good that I would lose eventually. Still, I'd made my decision, made a stand, and there was no going back.

Areto approached first. I knew her strengths, but I knew her weaknesses too and I had every intention of using them against her. From somewhere a staff appeared. Probably my own left just inside the front door.

I concentrated on that thought, used it to focus my anger as Areto raised the weapon against me. My training, my weapon . . . my tribe. Thea wouldn't take them from me, not easily.

Areto attacked first. She swung downward; I stepped into her blow, raising my staff from below as I did and smacking it into her groin. It was easy. She had obviously spent more time directing than training. An oversight on my part, I realized, but one that would serve me well now.

Without pausing or giving her time to react, I slid my staff forward and grabbed her hand—the one wrapped around her weapon. Keeping her elbow locked, I used her straight arm and my staff to force her to the ground. I held her, pinned, but I was unsure what to do next.

I could have grabbed her by the neck, twisted and left her broken on the ground, but that wasn't my goal. Despite her blind following of Thea, I didn't bear her any ill will—but I had no intention of dying myself either. I seized her by the back of the head and smacked her forehead into the ground.

As I did, two more warriors stepped forward. My staff was under Areto's body. I leapt to my feet, pulling the staff free as I moved.

Areto remained on the ground, but the others kept coming. I spun and twirled the staff at the same time, going for intimidation more than an offensive attack. I was known for my skill with the weapon and just witnessing how easily I had downed Areto, I hoped the others would back off. Skilled or not, I had no desire to fight them two or even three at a time.

Behind me a truck roared to life, reminding me of the hearth-keepers and Bern. They had been on my side, or it had felt that way, when I approached the circle, but that was before they had heard the high council's rule.

There was no hope of them following me . . . a traitor . . . now.

Which meant the vehicle revving its motor wasn't the cavalry, but the last wave of soldiers coming to finish me off.

How do you defeat a charging bull? Divert or avoid.

I pivoted quickly on one foot to get a three-hundred-sixty-degree view of what was happening around me, to see where I was being challenged from.

Lao was behind the wheel of the truck. Tess, the young hearth-keeper, was in the back, clinging to the side of the bed. Bern stood a few feet away, her staff gripped tightly in her hands and a look of deep indecision on her face.

I caught her gaze briefly as I moved. She lowered her head and charged. I still wasn't sure who she was rushing—me or the other Amazons—and I didn't have time to worry about it. The two warriors who had moved toward me had found weapons too. One jerked Areto's staff from under her body and the other caught a sword Sare, who had raced into the house and back out, tossed at her. Thea stood to the side smiling.

It was the smile that sent me over the edge. I didn't want to fight my warriors; I wanted to fight the priestess who thought she could take my place.

I held my staff in both hands perpendicular to my body, bent my knees into a squat, and rolled head to feet. The warriors didn't see the move coming. They thrashed at the spot where I had been, then cursed.

I rolled three times before popping back onto my feet squarely in front of Thea.

Her attention was still on whatever was happening behind me. "Kill her!" she yelled.

Focused on my intended target, I didn't pause to think who she meant or what might be happening behind me. I lifted my staff and prepared to smash it into the side of her skull.

She looked back at me before I had the chance. She lifted her hand and a knife flew from the ground into her palm. My heart skipped, but I pushed my shock aside. She'd revealed a power, one I had never seen before, but she was also armed now, and the blade in her hand was my most immediate threat.

She lunged toward me. I sidestepped, lifting my staff as I did and whipping the far end to strike her across the eyes. As the force sent her backward, I lashed the staff behind me and swung again, this time targeting the back of her knees. She fell and I pounced forward, intending to pin her and end this farce, but her hand lifted and the knife she held flew toward me—not thrown by the strength of her arm. I had her in a position where that was impossible. The blade was sped and guided by something I couldn't see . . . or perhaps I could . . . Thea's eyes were focused like lasers and her lips moved in some unending chant. She was calling on some power I had never seen before, doing something I didn't even realize was possible. She was moving objects with her mind.

I darted to the left, but the blade struck my thigh. It was short, probably only six inches long from tip to guard, but it still hurt . . . more than it should have.

With the knife sticking out of my body, I recognized it: a kitchen knife probably in the items brought back from the market by the hearth-keepers. I grimaced and reached up to grab the handle, to pull it free. Under my hand it began to twist, as if some invisible being held the handle too and was trying to twirl the blade sheathed in my thigh.

Thea stared at the knife, her face dispassionate but her intention clear. With my left hand I lifted my staff and smashed it across her face. Then, my chest heaving, I dropped the staff onto the dirt.

The chanting stopped. The twisting stopped. I jerked the blade free and stood over the high council's chosen queen. If I plunged the blade into her heart while she was queen, there would be no going back. I would be like Mel, cut off from the tribe forever. Except Mel was happy with her decision; she would never ask to come back.

How would I feel?

The knife's handle was slippery from my blood or sweat. I wasn't sure which.

Thea's head was turned to the side; she didn't know she was about to die.

I started to squat; my lips were dry and my hand shook, but I knew I could do it. Knew she would continue to fight me, to lie to my own tribe about me. There was no choice. My time with the Amazons was over; my life as I knew it was over. Why not take the person who took it from me out too?

The knife gripped tightly in my hand, I lifted my arm.

A grunting snarl caused my head to raise. Jack in his wolverine form dashed toward me. I barely had time to register what was happening before he struck me in the chest. I fell backward, the knife still in my hand. Around me a full battle erupted.

Bern spun and jabbed with her staff, holding off the warriors who had first rushed me. The hearth-keepers' truck was parked beside the fracas, the doors open and the engine running. Sare, armed with a short knife she used when carving totems, was fighting with Lao. The hearth-keeper, armed only with the hard plastic lid of a cooler, swung double-handed and smacked the artisan in the side of the head.

When Lao saw me, she motioned to Tess. The younger hearth-keeper jumped behind the wheel and gunned the engine.

I realized then we were leaving, or at least the others were planning to leave.

But leaving meant giving up, deserting the camp that had been my home for over ten years.

I couldn't do it.

I shoved Jack off of my chest and stood. Immediately the son was beside me, naked and in his human form.

He grabbed me by the arm. "Don't be an idiot. The battle is bigger than this." He motioned to the Amazons still fighting. "We need you. Your tribe needs you."

My tribe. Were they my tribe? They didn't seem to think so.

I stared at him, denying the angry tears I could feel forming at the back of my eyes. I blinked and shut down the response. I had never cried in my life; I wasn't going to do so now.

Back under control, I glanced at the two Amazons still fighting with me, for me. Lao, a hearth-keeper well past her prime, and Bern, an outcast warrior. Then there was the wet-behind-the-ears hearth-keeper shaking like a newborn rabbit in the truck.

My own personal army of misfit toys.

Jack leaned close, until his lips were pressed against my ear. "Sheep go to slaughter. Don't be a goddamn sheep anymore, Zery."

I jerked my arm free, picked up my staff, and jumped into the fray. Taking unfair advantage of the warriors' focus on Bern, I smacked one in the back of the head with my staff. As the other stumbled, unsure what to do, I gestured for Tess and the truck. She roared into the middle of the fight. Bern and I jumped into the back, jerking Lao in after us, and Tess hit the gas.

The mother dog had been curled up on an old feed sack in the corner with her two healthy puppies. She belly crawled closer and I stroked her head as Tess wheeled the vehicle in a sharp U-turn.

In seconds we were thundering down the thin drive. Behind us Jack held up one hand, then shifted. In his wolverine form, he gave a last snapping growl at Sare, who still held her blade, and dashed into the woods.

My hand stroking the dog's head, I stared blindly at the disappearing house.

I had done what I thought I never would. I had left the tribe.

Chapter 13

As the truck turned onto the highway, I think we all realized we had nowhere to go. Tess yelled at us through the open sliding window.

"Where to?"

The puppy I'd been afraid was dying poked his head over her shoulder. He looked weak, but still alive.

All eyes turned to me.

There was really only one answer. "Madison."

Tess's eyes met Lao's in the rearview mirror, but the older hearth-keeper just nodded her head. "Back to Madison, but I think we may have a stop to make first." She looked at me. "Is that right?" She tapped on the truck with her palm.

I realized then what she was saying. We couldn't drive

to Madison sitting in a truck bed. We needed a new, bigger vehicle—or at least a second vehicle.

After a brief discussion, we opted for the second.

We pulled into a truck stop and let Lao out. It hadn't taken much talk to decide Bern and I stood out too much for the job.

But who would suspect a woman who appeared to be in her sixties of boosting a car?

We kept busy by driving down the road a bit and lifting a set of plates off a sedan parked behind a garage. The thing was smashed in completely on the passenger's side, but the plates were perfectly fine, and since the shop was already closed for the day and would stay closed tomorrow, Sunday, we had until Monday before anyone noticed—if they noticed then.

With the plates dusted off and ready to install, we drove to our meeting place, a country cemetery visited by more cows than people.

Lao drove up in a dark blue two-door. The back was loaded with boxes.

Standing next to the vehicle, Lao said, "Salesman. Looks like a company car."

I nodded. Jack had been wrong about us . . . at least the Amazons under my command. We did think about how our stealing affected our victims. Didn't mean we never hurt someone, but we weren't totally callous about others either. If we could choose between leaving a family stranded at a truck stop and a lone salesman? No contest.

"What's he selling?" Hopefully it was nothing that would bring too much heat down on us.

Bern reached in the backseat and ripped into a box. "Looks like toys." She pulled out a squishy frog that lit up when you squeezed his stomach.

"Oh." Lao gestured for Bern to grab a plastic bag sitting on the car's floor. The warrior pulled out a can of evaporated milk and an eyedropper.

"In case the mama won't feed him," Lao explained.

Loaded down with the puppy, toy, milk, and eyedropper, Bern went to sit in the shade while Lao changed the vehicle's plates.

When the plates were changed, we divided up again—Bern and Tess in the truck, Lao and myself with the dogs in the car.

Lao drove. We left the stolen car's plates behind, but we kept the toys. Eventually we'd sell them.

When you live like we do, you learn to appreciate even the smallest opportunity to make a buck. And today, with our future so unknown, we had to embrace those opportunities even more.

It was late by the time we got off I-90, not dark yet, but getting close. The exit for Mel's place was about a five-minute drive. I closed my eyes and tried not to think about what I was going to say to her this time.

The parking lot had quite a few cars in it. It was Saturday night, what I guessed was a popular time for humans to get tattoos. Deciding an audience might be just the thing to get Mel to accept my reappearance without reaching for power first thing, I led my ragtag group to the front of the old schoolhouse and up the stairs that led to the shop.

Mel's office manager, Mandy, met us with a surprised stare.

"You're the—"

"Self-defense group. That's right. We're wondering if Mel would be willing to rent us some space again." Last fall the tribe had posed as a self-defense group while living in Mel's gym and hunting the killer who had turned out to be a son.

"I'll ask . . ." As the unsure words came out of her mouth, she spotted the puppy poking his head out of Tess's shirt. Much oohing and aahing ensued, attracting the attention of three college-age girls who had been studying the shop's flash.

With Mandy busy, I strolled through the door that separated the tattoo area from reception. Mel had three artists who worked for her, four if you counted her mother, Cleo. I didn't think Mel did, though. Cleo was a warrior and thus not big on sitting in one place and doing intricate work. Her other employees included Janet, a middle-aged lesbian, and Cheryl, divorced mother of three. Her remaining employee was the son, Peter Arpada. Mel had hired him before she knew he was a son, but she hadn't fired him after. And now apparently they'd been traveling together. I still wasn't sure how I felt about that.

There were two rooms for tattooing. The biggest, the one I had entered, had three stations. Cheryl and Janet were both busy with clients. The third was empty. I didn't know if Peter or Cleo normally used the seat. I was hoping Cleo. I trusted her.

She had at many times been more of a mother to me than my own.

From here you could see into the smaller room too. There were two stations there. A client, an older man in his fifties, sat at one, but there was no sign of an artist.

Janet turned from her customer to grab some gauze and spotted me. "Mel's in back, getting gloves." She nodded to a door at the back of the connected room, a room I knew from previous visits was used to store its supplies and sterilizing equipment.

"How about Cleo?" I asked, staying casual.

"Basement."

I turned on my heel and strolled back out the door. In reception, I cocked my head at Bern and Lao. Tess seemed to be paying attention too. As a group we filed back out.

While Lao and Tess went to check on the rest of the dogs, Bern and I returned to the basement. I didn't realize I was tense until I stepped into the main room and saw it was empty—no babies this evening.

The door to Cleo's workout room was open. Feeling back in my element for the first time in days, I strode through the door.

And ran smack-dab into my biggest nightmare.

My mother, Scy Kostovska . . . and she was holding a baby.

I suddenly had a very sick feeling.

She looked shocked and almost as horrified to see me. "Zery." She dropped to a squat and quickly tucked the baby into one of those plastic seats. After pulling the seat's safety bar down over his head and snapping it in place, she stood and faced me, her face morphing into the picture of a warm welcome.

"What kind of shit are you getting ready to dump on me?" I asked.

My mother was not warm. If I wasn't standing in front of her, obvious evidence that it wasn't true, I'd say she was the type to eat her own young.

"Who's the baby?" I asked. There was a ticking noise starting in my head, like a bomb growing closer to explosion. I didn't want to think what I was thinking, didn't want to deal with a potentially confusing new discovery.

She glanced at the seat like she'd just noticed it. "Just a baby. I'm watching him for Dana. She does that, you know, watches other people's children."

I tried to believe her. I wanted to believe her. But the coincidence was too big—a high council member had given birth to the baby I'd been ordered to find . . . Mel had claimed to know the mother. Now I find a high council member, my mother, who had no reason to be here, in Madison, with a baby in Mel's basement. The conclusion was obvious.

I stared down at the child. Chubby cheeks, dark hair . . . not enough for me to say yea or nay, but then I saw the cow . . . the flat cow Tess had been holding at camp. I realized then I hadn't seen the seat or the stuffed cow since. Jack must have sneaked into the yard and stolen them too.

We'd gone to Walmart thinking he'd need supplies without even realizing he'd already done a little shopping in our yard.

Damn him.

And damn my mother.

I turned my attention to her. "He's yours isn't he? You're the council member."

She looked like she was going to argue for a moment, then seemed to remember herself. She squared her shoulders. "Yes. He's mine."

I stared at the seat and the wiggling body inside it. "I have a brother. A brother I've been ordered to capture so he can be killed. How nice."

My mother stood with her hands on her hips—angry but not alarmed. She thought she could beat me. Who was I kidding? She was on the high council. Of course she could beat me.

But then I'd come here to tell Mel I'd defied orders. There was no reason for my mother to beat me, challenge me, even. We were on the same side, or should have been.

The infant made some gurgling noise. Our mother didn't look down, but I saw her twitch. She noticed; she cared.

For some reason that hurt.

"You defied the council for him," I stated. She had never defied anything or anyone for me. I had never come first; I'd been an afterthought, someone who followed her around, got in her way.

"I had to," she replied.

I laughed. "You've never done anything because 'you had to.' Don't pull that now."

Her eyes flared, more emotion than she'd shown me my entire childhood.

"The council wants him killed, you know."

She tilted her head. "I heard."

I tapped a finger against my leg. She wasn't playing the game, not how I wanted her to. Of course, I didn't even know exactly how that was. Frustrated and pissed off, at her, the Amazons, and myself, I spun and left the room.

She followed me, pulling the door closed behind her.

That at least was somewhat satisfying. That at least said she was a little concerned over what I might do.

"He's your brother, Zery."

I looked back. "Half, I'm assuming. Unless there's something else you need to tell me." This baby was the son of a son. If he and I shared a father . . .

She shook her head. "No. You're right *half* brother."

I licked my lips. For a second I'd thought . . . I shook my head. I wasn't the daughter of a son. No reason to think about what that revelation might have meant.

"So, half brother, and the son of a son. Is that part true? Did you sleep with a son, Mother?"

"I wouldn't be the first or, I'm sure, the last." She looked at me strangely then.

For some unknown reason my mind jumped to Jack. I growled. "Was it on purpose? Did you do it to have some kind of superbaby?" A baby who could grow up to be everything she wanted him or her to be?

"Why would I do that?"

It wasn't an answer, but then again maybe it was.

"What happened at the high council?" I asked. "When they found out."

She did the damn head-tilt thing again, to one side and then the other, as if deliberating if I could handle her response. "You got your orders. You know."

Actually, I didn't. I had been kept in the dark more than anyone, but I didn't want to admit it to her.

"But you are on the high council. Was there a discussion? Was there a vote?"

She crossed her arms over her chest. "Do you care, Zery? Does it matter? Is there anything I can tell you that will make you see my side?"

I'd already seen her side, but I wanted her to explain it to me. Wanted her to try and convince me. I'd say beg me, but that would be like waiting for a hyena to roll over and ask for a belly rub.

"Try me," I responded.

She sighed, although from her it sounded more like an exasperated huff. "The high council is split, but not evenly. Of the twelve members of the council, three feel strongly that we should return to the old ways, kill our sons. Three feel strongly we shouldn't and the rest are spineless, indecisive wastes of time."

Now this was the mother I knew and genetics dictated I love.

I answered drily, "So, you went to great lengths to woo the middle to your side."

Anger flared in her eyes. "They chose to vote with fear rather than strength. I reminded them we are Amazons. We have nothing to fear. Yes, one son surprised and attacked us when we didn't know about the threat, but we do now. We are prepared or can be if we get to know the sons better. The more we learn of them, the stronger we will be."

"And the babies? Where do they fit into this? Are you planning on turning them over to the sons to raise?"

She glanced back at the door. "That was an issue. Of those who agreed we should meet with the sons and learn more about them, we were split on what to do with male children. None of us wanted to return to maiming or killing, but some wanted to keep the boys and raise them with their sisters. Some felt only Amazons could or should be raised as Amazons."

"So even in your splinter group you couldn't agree." The revelation reminded me why having a certain element of sheep could be good. If everyone was trying to lead the flock, the flock had no solid direction in which to go.

"Which side were you on?" I asked.

"Turn over to the sons," she replied.

A bit of tension left my body. In this, at least, she was the same.

"But . . ." She grimaced. "I'd never spent this much time with a child I meant to give away before."

A nerve near my mouth jerked. She'd never spent much time with a child period, at least certainly not me.

"The longer I care for him the more I think . . ." She held up a hand. "But right now that isn't the issue. What about you, Zery? What side are you on? Do you plan to kill your brother?"

Did I? I had decided I didn't right after I found the dog, before I faced off against Thea, before I tossed away a lifetime of work and establishing myself as a leading queen, one who might someday herself be looked at for a position on the high council.

How ironic was it that now I knew my mother was involved I wished desperately I could stand on the opposite side? I toyed with the idea for a second. The temptation to tell her I was against her was tantalizing. She'd always had the power; now was my chance to change that.

But I couldn't.

"No. I don't," I replied.

Her eyes rounded, telling me I'd surprised her as much today as she had surprised me. That at least brought some reward.

"I questioned the council's order and a new queen has been appointed to my camp." The words were like sand in my mouth.

Her eyes were wary. "You're here to . . . ?"

I bit the inside of my cheek. Why was I here, really? To help? To lead some kind of heroic battle for what was right? Or just because I had nowhere else to go?

I stared past her, lost and unsure. I'd never been unsure. Right and wrong had always been clear. My world had always been black and white. How did it become so gray?

"The gym is open." Mel appeared around the corner. She must have come down the front steps. I couldn't see them from my current position. So I didn't know how long she had been standing there, hidden, listening.

She had her red Wisconsin Badgers cap on along with a white V-necked tee, denim shorts, and hiking boots. Even with the snake bracelet both she and her mother wore, she looked very human, not in the least bit threatening.

She cocked her head, her gaze shooting past my mother and on to me. "Mandy said the self-defense group was back and looking to rent space. How many are with you?"

I gestured to Bern, who had been standing quietly by the side door that led outside. "Plus two more, hearthkeepers."

Surprise flickered behind Mel's hazel eyes, but she didn't comment on my lack of companions, or the fact that hearth-keepers wouldn't be anyone's first choice in a battle, unless it was a cook-off.

At least, that is what I had thought just a week ago.

Recently I'd seen a side to Lao I'd never realized a hearth-keeper possessed. Maybe Tess had more to offer too.

Mel nodded. "Plenty of room if you don't mind sharing." She tilted her head toward my mother. "Your mom is staying there too." She zeroed in on Bern, who had taken up position by the side door that led outside. "Let's find the others and get you settled."

She walked past me on the way to the door. I wrapped my fingers around her bicep. "Thanks."

A hardness shone from her eyes. "Don't thank me. I haven't said how long you can stay yet." Then she kept moving. Bern followed and in thirty seconds I was alone with my mother again.

I stared at the woman who had given birth to me. Then I moved to follow my friend. My mother's voice stopped me. "If you don't say why you're here, she won't let you stay long."

I turned back. "You and Mel get close?"

She lifted one side of her mouth in an imitation of a smile, then gestured with her head toward the workout room where we had left the baby. "We have something in common."

Of course, they both had sons from a son. Mel was looking for hers. She'd only found out about her grandmother's deception last fall. She'd been looking for him, or as far as I knew she had. I hadn't heard that she had found him yet—and I was fairly certain I would have. Even in the unplugged world of the Amazons, that kind of news would have made it back to me.

My mother was still watching me, waiting.

I let out a frustrated grunt. "My camp turned against me, all but the three I mentioned. I'm not sure what that means, where that leaves me."

She frowned. "What do you mean, 'where that leaves you?' Where could it leave you?"

"I lost my position of queen. It was stripped from me."

She shook her head like I'd said something she couldn't quite believe. "Says who? And what made you queen anyway?"

"The council . . . or . . ." Thea had said it. There was a possibility she was lying. Confused, I pressed my fingers to my forehead.

"What council? I'm on the council and no one asked my opinion."

"But you left."

"Did I? That's news to me."

"You had to; the council voted to kill the . . . *your* baby. And you haven't . . . he's still—" The conversation was uncomfortable. I was uncomfortable.

She walked toward me, her face grim. "I'm still an Amazon, I'm still a warrior, and I'm still on the high council. Do you honestly think I'd walk away from any of that? What about you, daughter? What are you?"

Dana walking into the room with a baby in each arm gave me a good exit point. I left the basement through the side door without answering.

Darkness had fallen while I was having my mother/daughter chat, but Mel's outdoor lights had clicked on. I got as far as the walkway between the main building and the old gym/cafeteria where we would be staying before being stopped by another surprise.

Jack.

He was leaning against the door that opened into the old cafeteria part of the building, right across the walk from the outside stairwell I'd just climbed up, out of the main building's basement.

I thought about walking past him, but didn't. I knew he wouldn't let me easily and I was tired of fighting—something I'd never imagined I'd be.

I stopped in front of him, my arms crossed over my chest.

"You left," he said.

He'd been there. He'd seen me. I didn't have to tell him what had happened.

"I wasn't sure you would."

I shrugged. My mother's words were still ringing in my ears: *What about you, daughter? What are you?*

Jack seemed to sense what I was thinking . . . feeling . . . He pushed himself away from the wall and into my space. "What's wrong with you?" His eyes were hard and dark, filled with fire.

I stared back at him knowing my own were dead. My fire had gone out. I didn't know if I could ever get it back.

He leaned even closer, until his nose almost touched mine. "Don't tell me I was right the first time. Don't tell me, you *are* just a sheep."

When I didn't reply, he cursed. His hands opened and

closed at his sides. I could tell he wanted to grapple something . . . me, I guessed.

I watched dispassionately. The Amazons didn't want me. I wasn't queen. I had no pony in this race.

When he spun back, I could see the wolverine inside him staring out at me. "I get through to you and you give up? Is that it?" He took a step back toward me, back in my space, but this time he went further. He pushed me against the building.

With one hand on each of my shoulders he held me there, pinned to the wooden siding.

"So, tell me. One little slap of reality and you fold up? Give up? Is all your fight gone? Exactly how far down did you let them beat you?"

He spit the words out, ugly and harsh.

"If you're that easy to defeat, I guess they were right. You aren't a queen." He bent his elbows and propelled himself away from me.

I let him get as far as the walk before I picked up a cantaloupe-sized stone that doubled as a doorstop and flung it at his head.

Chapter 14

He spun so quickly, I didn't see the movement, but I saw him duck, saw his hand shoot above his head, and I saw his grin when he caught the cannonball of rock in his bare hand. "The queen is back."

I didn't share his joviality. I jumped and kicked, aiming for his head. He dropped the rock and plowed forward, his head going between my legs. With me straddling his shoulder, he stood. Momentum sent me falling backward. I would have tumbled to the ground except he held me by one calf. I dangled with my back to his, my hair brushing the ground.

I cursed, then used every bit of abdominal strength I had to pull myself back up. I grabbed him by the hair and jerked, then dropped my weight forward. I landed palms down in a handstand that I quickly converted to a flip. Four feet away, I faced him.

The grin was back.

I growled, and he rushed me.

He was fast, preternaturally fast. I was too, but nothing compared him. I tried, but was unable to move out of his path. He slammed into me, knocking me onto the ground.

His full body weight pressing me into the earth, he stared down at me. "If we work together, you can get everything you want."

My heart pounded against my breastbone. "You think?" I asked.

He dipped his face lower, so his lips barely brushed mine. "I know."

I didn't move; my mind was whirling. My training said to toss him off, to wipe the wearisome smile off his face, but another part of me, a part I'd forgotten existed, couldn't move, not without doing something that would give away thoughts I didn't want to be having, shouldn't be having.

He was a *son*. Whether I thought killing Amazon infant sons was wrong or not, I didn't approve of what my mother had done, and I didn't want to follow in her footsteps.

His lips brushed mine again, and I caught a whiff of the scent I'd noticed that first time in the woods, earthy and masculine, dangerous and alluring. And this time it was *very* alluring. There was no denying it.

When his lips brushed mine a third time, I leaned up and captured his mouth with mine.

Adrenaline rushed through me. He tasted of mint, not the fake taste of toothpaste, but the real zing of mint grown wild in the woods. His chin was covered in stubble. It rasped over my skin, hurt and excited me at the same time.

His hand moved from the ground beside me to my arms. His hands, the same hands that had grabbed me so roughly before, softened.

I softened too, pressure releasing from me like air from a deflating beach ball. Then as his hands roamed past my arms onto my stomach, pushed up the thin tee I wore, new pressure began to build.

"Excuse us." Two older women wearing stretchy shorts and knee socks stumbled to a stop beside us. At least I assumed they were older, based on their shoes and clothing from the waist down. From my angle on the ground that was all I could see.

Their feet, clad in some kind of practical-looking thick-soled tennis shoes, shuffled to the side. Probably two of Bubbe's clients.

"Should we . . . ?" one asked.

The other made some kind of hushing noise, then, "Never mind us. We'll be going on our way. Just act like you never saw us."

The other argued, but only briefly and so low I couldn't truly make out the words, not that I wanted to. I was completely and totally humiliated—not because I'd been caught acting like an animal in heat by humans, but that I'd been playing the role with the son at all.

I shoved him off me and scrambled to my feet.

He stayed on the ground, watching me, his expression unreadable and his body language relaxed—as if lying sprawled out blocking the sidewalk and the entrances to two buildings was perfectly normal. I spun with every intention of stalking off. A whisper of movement told me he'd stood, but not in time to stop him from grabbing me around the waist.

"You're shy. Who knew?"

I threw back my elbow, aiming for his gut. With a laugh, he stepped to the side, his arm slipping from my body as he did.

I got maybe ten feet, even with the front of Mel's main building, before the blast sounded. The ground moved, or seemed to. A tremor traveled from the earth into my feet and up my legs. And the noise . . . a blast that made me want to clap my hands over my ears . . . there was no mistaking it, not after living through the explosion of Jack's cabin.

Something had blown.

I took off in a run around the front of Mel's shop, praying as I did that the blast hadn't been inside the structure, that Mel, her family . . . my family . . . were safe.

Smoke billowed from the other side of Mel's shop—outside her shop. I kept moving, dashing over the sidewalk and onto the grass. Before I rounded the second corner I caught sight of the fire . . . a line of holly bushes that separated Mel's property from her neighbor's was blazing.

Heat crackled and smoke tore at my lungs, but I plowed ahead. On the side of the building was a spigot with a hose. Unable to think of any better plan at the moment, I followed the example of the idiot humans I'd seen outside Jack's cabin and turned the tiny stream of water onto the bushes.

Yells came from the front yard. The occupants of Mel's shop and home flowed out. In seconds the tiny side yard was filled with bodies. Bern moved into view, a blanket in her arms. She held it up for me to douse with the hose, then marched into what looked like the middle of the flames. Jack was there too, but he stood apart. He seemed almost unaware of the chaos that had broken out around him. His brow was furrowed and his gaze was on the ground.

Thinking he'd lost it under the pressure, I ignored him.

Overhead, a window flew up, and Mel yelled to watch out. Water began to shoot from the open window like a hole had been punched in a dam. The water coming from my hose sputtered and stopped.

I dropped it and stared, amazed at my friend's skill. Beside me, Bubbe stomped into view. She held her hands above her head. The spray of water became less diverse, like it was flowing through an invisible channel the old priestess held somewhere above her head. Working to direct Mel's flood onto the trees, she twisted in place like a human water sprinkler except slow and flinging hundreds of gallons of water with each jerk of her body.

The water combined with the fire, creating clouds of steam that clung to us all. My hair fell to my shoulders in heavy clumps and my shirt stuck to my skin.

The rest of the group fared no better. Mandy's and Cheryl's faces seemed to melt as their makeup ran down their cheeks. And even the men who'd been awaiting tattoos seemed to have wilted and weakened. But we all continued doing what we could, throwing dirt and stamping on falling sparks.

All except Jack.

Suddenly, he looked up . . . at me. Some kind of realization glowed in his eyes, and without saying a word he dashed around the back of the building.

I pushed a sad-looking Mandy out of my way and followed.

I heard Jack's growl—the unnatural sound of a wolverine pissed off to the point of exploding. I didn't know until I turned the second corner, taking me back to the sidewalk that ran between Mel's shop and the gym, that he was still in his human form.

Almost directly under one of Mel's giant floodlights, he stood, legs apart, hands at his sides but his fingers spread, stiff. Anger radiated from him.

When I came up beside him, I saw why.

Babies, two of them tucked into their little plastic

seats, sat on the ground where only minutes earlier I'd lain beneath Jack. Beside them were the two women who had walked up on us—I recognized their shoes and shorts. And in their hands were guns—handguns, ugly black squared-off looking things.

"No reason for anyone to get hurt. Just stay where you are," one called. Her voice was steady, as was the gun in her hand. Her eyes shifted in her face, looking from Jack to me, to someone I couldn't see, hidden in the stairwell.

There was movement, a blond head appeared. My mother. Of course. She placed her fingers on the concrete top of the stairwell.

I knew her plan. I jumped forward, drawing the attention of the two armed women.

The gun clicked. My heart skipped, but I dropped and rolled forward. The gun exploded and I landed back on my feet, still ten feet from the women. One of them grabbed a baby carrier, the other froze. I could see the panic in her eyes, could see the gun shaking in her hand.

I relaxed; she'd panicked. We'd won.

But as her gaze darted over me, she raised the gun again. Her friend, the carrier's handle slipped over one arm, did the same. Two pairs of eyes, two guns, both pointed at me.

I froze, determined to drop at the first twitch of their fingers, determined to outmaneuver not one but two bullets.

Behind me my mother screamed, a war cry—anger, hate, and determination flying from her lungs.

The women jerked. The guns moved and then exploded. The women's faces pulled as they stared down at the guns in their hands, then back up at me, shocked. I turned, moving as if through water, slow and surreal. My mother stood on top of the stairwell, her arms out and her mouth open.

I'd never seen her look so fierce, so full of strength and power. I realized in that split second how much I loved her, how much I needed her now that I'd lost everything else.

Then the bullets hit and nothing happened. She didn't move; her face didn't change. Nothing. For a split second I thought she was safe . . .

Then she took a step back. Two round splotches of blood grew on her chest and her gaze shot to me. Surprise and hurt, not physical pain, but loss. My lips parted; I took a step toward her.

And she fell backward into the stairwell.

She made no other sound, no yelp of pain, no curse of anger, nothing.

"No!" I spun, determined to knock the two women back to whatever hell had created them.

One of them, the one with the baby, lifted her gun again. I could hear Jack yelling, maybe he'd been yelling all along, but all I could see was my mother's killers and all I could think about was reaching them, destroying them.

Overhead something shrieked. I didn't look up, couldn't.

There was another click; somewhere in my brain I recognized it as the sound that came right before the gun fired. I could see the woman holding the baby now. I focused on her. Her eyes were blue and watery. Her hair was gray and tucked behind her ears. She wore tiny pearl earrings and today she was going to die.

There was another shriek, louder, closer.

Something big and dark dropped from the sky . . . the bird from the woods. Its talons extended, it tore at my intended target's face and hair.

She screamed and dropped both the baby and the gun. The gun fired as it hit the ground, but the bullet went wild, lodging into the brick wall of Mel's shop.

The second woman paused, then dropped her gun and ran away from us toward the front of the building. At an old maple she stopped and picked something up off the ground. Not sure what was happening, I raced toward her. She glanced at me, but I didn't think she saw me. Then she glanced back at where the other woman battled with the bird, where the babies lay on the ground.

Her thumb hovered over the box.

I spun and yelled, but Jack had already started moving, as had the bird. They both raced toward the baby seats. Jack got there first, grabbing both by the handles as he ran toward me.

There was a click, this one softer and less metallic, and the space between the two buildings exploded.

I stood straight up, my arms over my head, and cursed.

Something smashed into me from the side. An *ooof* of pain and expelled breath left my body, and I was slammed onto my back. My face was covered by something both soft and scratchy; I couldn't breathe. I kicked out. Whatever had been covering me moved.

Dirt clouded the air blocking my view of anything but shapes. On all fours, I held my hand over my mouth and nose and peered at the world through squinted eyes. Something rustled nearby, then wings flapped, loud and close . . . the bird. I felt the air move as he took off. The dirt seemed to clear some too, enough that I could see Mel's outside lights again and Jack. He stood fifteen feet away, his face streaming with sweat, his arms shaking and a baby carrier in each hand.

I scrambled to my feet, trying not to cough, and searched the area around us for the two women.

"They're gone. She blew something." Jack, his face ashen, glanced to where the woman with the tiny box had stood, then in almost the same movement slanted his head toward the stairwell where I had seen my mother fall—or what had been the stairwell. It was now filled with rubble.

I moved toward it, my legs stretching as long as they could, devouring the ground as quickly as they could.

Bern was there beside me. I didn't know where she'd come from. I hadn't seen her approach. But I didn't question her appearance. I just grabbed a piece of broken concrete and tossed it off the pile. Bern did the same.

As I lay my hand on a second segment, a man appeared, his walnut-brown body naked. He dove in, grabbing chunks in both hands and tossing them onto the ground behind us.

Soon the grass was strewn with debris.

"Was she . . . is she?" I mumbled to myself, unable to comprehend that the mother I'd seen only as a super-Amazon lie trapped beneath pounds of stone.

A siren sounded; it was close.

"Humans to the rescue," the naked man muttered.

Jack jumped forward and grabbed him by one shoulder. Jack's fingers were pale against the other man's darker skin. "We'll take care of this. You have to leave. You're illegal as far as they're concerned, and naked. It will just cause new questions. Go to Makis's. I'll call you, let you know what's happening."

The man ignored him, kept tossing hunks of concrete, but with an increased fervor, an almost crazed energy.

Jack grabbed him again, by the arm this time, pulling him around. "Leave. You'll just create more questions."

The man cursed. He was older than Jack, had gray at the temples of his close-cropped hair and lines by his eyes. His body was sinewy, like a long-distance runner or maybe a swimmer, and his shoulders were unusually broad for his slim hips.

He opened his mouth in one long stretch, like the famous painting *The Scream* and a screech ripped from his lungs. Then before I could jerk or respond in any way, he was gone and the giant bird stood in his place.

He turned his neck and stared at me. His feathers

were inky black except for a white ruff that ringed his throat. His eyes were brown but with a reddish tinge that made me shiver, or maybe it was the expression in the eyes, the pure unadulterated dislike pointed directly at me.

The sirens grew louder, and not far away a fire truck honked its horn, trying to clear cars from its path.

"Go!" Jack pointed to the sky.

With a last shriek the giant bird shot into the night.

I moved into his place, tossing rocks with shaking hands.

As firemen and paramedics flowed onto the property, I kept tossing. I heard people muttering behind me.

"Her mother's under there."

"Call someone."

But no one tried to stop me and when two firemen dressed in bright yellow stepped beside me to help, I didn't stop them.

We found her ten minutes later. She wasn't breathing and hadn't been since the first bullet hit.

I was down inside the stairwell by then, my legs up to my knees covered in dust and broken bricks. I stared at my mother's too-pale face. I didn't need the fireman to tell me she was dead; I knew it. She'd never looked like that, never been lacking in the confident swagger that emanated from her like light from a halogen bulb.

My heart slowed. Someone was talking to me . . . Mel standing behind me, her hand on my shoulder. I couldn't hear what she said. The fireman said something too. He yelled and gestured.

Mel disappeared. Someone grabbed me under the arms and pulled me from the debris. I could feel it slipping over my bare legs, the rough concrete bits scratching my skin. My heels bounced as my body moved. All I could do was stare down at that face and think how what I was seeing couldn't be true.

Amazons lived for hundreds of years . . . hundreds. And my mother, as much as she angered me, wasn't supposed to be dead.

She wasn't.

But she was.

Chapter 15

After they found my mother's body, more humans had crowded onto Mel's property. There were firemen, paramedics, cops, and neighbors. People everywhere.

The babies were fine. Jack had handed them off to Mandy before pulling me from the stairwell.

He'd dragged me as far as the paramedics would let him. Only about eight feet from where my mother's body lay, he propped me up against the base of the old school and kneeled down beside me.

"Get mad, Zery. Getting mad will get you through this." Then he squeezed my hand and stepped to the side.

Mel and a paramedic took his place. The paramedic asked me a lot of useless questions and tried to get me to agree to get in an ambulance and go to a nearby hospital.

I refused. Actually, I didn't even bother refusing. I stood instead.

Jack was right. This wasn't the time to mourn. This was the time to be pissed.

And I was. More pissed than I ever remembered being in my life.

I looked at Mel. "They shot her." Humans, older women, like the birders who I'd run off my property, like the one Bern had found dead. Who were they? And why were they targeting the Amazons? Why had they been here?

Mel glanced at the human male who was still trying to press a stethoscope to my chest. I shoved him. He stumbled back and fell onto the ground.

Two policemen moved in. Mel stepped between them and me, or tried to; one of the cops pushed her to the side.

My hands opening and closing at my sides, I stepped forward.

As my foot moved, dirt swirled from the stairs in a minitornado. It shot over the ground, descending over me and the officers. Coughing, I stepped back. The cops did too. And, just as suddenly, the tornado lifted. It rose above our heads, then with a puff it was gone. Dirt rained down over us.

"What the . . . ?" One of the policemen raised his hand to shield his eyes. The other, caught in a coughing fit violent enough to make him double over, waved for me to move back.

Bubbe stood behind them, her lips pursed and disapproval in her eyes. Beside her was Mel's mother, Cleo. The older warrior mouthed "stay" in warning.

My world clicked back into place. The pain wasn't gone and neither was the anger, but seeing Mel's family, knowing they would both support me and punish me if I stepped out of line, reminded me of who I was and why I had to be strong and in control—why I had to be queen.

Things moved fast after that. The police broke the crowd into small groups, sending gawkers on their way while trying to corral those of us actually involved. I saw Bern in the back of the crowd beyond the front of the gym and motioned for her to leave.

A police officer approached her, and after a last glance at me she shook her head, denying she'd witnessed anything. He waved her toward the street behind us and she stalked off.

She wouldn't go far; I knew that. But the fewer of us involved even slightly from the police's point of view in this mess the better.

The police never got around to questioning me. I'm not sure why, but I suspected Bubbe had a hand in it. While the police were occupied clearing out the crowd, she'd walked in a wide circle around me and Jack, murmuring.

As the two officers who'd tried to question me earlier finished their crowd duties, a new group of police arrived. The first two turned as if to point at me, then stopped and stared at each other instead. They glanced at me again, then shook their heads.

I wasn't sure if they couldn't see me anymore or just didn't remember me, but either worked. I squatted down on the dirt next to Jack and waited for the human part of this drama to play out.

"What happened? Where did the women go?" I asked, my voice low. I wasn't sure how strong whatever spell Bubbe had woven was. I didn't want to do anything to draw attention to myself, at least not as long as it appeared Mel and her family had the situation under control.

"They got spooked. They didn't know what they were dealing with."

Amazons. They didn't know they were dealing with Amazons, but if that was true, why were they here at all? I didn't recognize either of them, but they looked like the birders. There had to be a connection.

The thought was there and then it was gone. The police were photographing my mother's body where it lay in the stairwell.

"She shouldn't be dead," I murmured. Two humans against two Amazons and a son. How had we lost?

"We accomplished what she wanted. They didn't get your brother or Pisto."

His words held little comfort for me. My mother, who had survived fights with legendary warriors, had been felled by two gray-haired women with guns.

I stared at Jack for a second, my anger shifting to him. He sold guns, could have sold the ones those women used . . .

He laid his hand on my knee. His skin was warm, almost burning. "She chose to draw their fire."

Still angry, I glared. "Why?"

"Why did you charge them in the first place?"

Because it was what I did. I hadn't made a conscious choice; I'd just done it.

I licked my lips and shifted my attention to my mother's body, now removed from the rubble. A man and a woman squatted next to her, examining her. They had found the gunshot wound.

I looked back at Jack. "Who were they? Do you know them? Did you sell them their guns?"

Shock showed on his face; he shook his head. "No. I didn't—know them or sell to them."

I let that set in, waited to see if my anger lessened. Finally it did. He was on my side. Because of my past, I might not agree with how he made his money, but it didn't mean he was responsible for my mother's death.

I nodded, letting him know I accepted his answer.

He nodded his too. We were in agreement, focused on the same puzzle. "Do you know them?"

"Maybe." I told him about the birders and the two women I'd found at the safe camp when I'd returned from Madison.

I stared at him, willing him to see an answer I didn't. "Why would two old human birders, if they even were part of the group I confronted, try and steal babies here?"

"Revenge?"

"Because they think I killed the birder Bern found?" My nunchakus had been used to kill her. Another birder could have found her first, seen the weapon, and recognized it as mine, but then why not go to the police? Why follow me to Mel's and take two infants? It made no sense.

Unless, while roaming our woods, they had heard something? Did they know more about the Amazons than they should? Had they heard the baby was in Madison and realized he was important to us? Did they plan to use him to get us to do something for them?

It was as logical an answer as anything else I could come up with.

"The babies . . ." Jack began, but I stopped listening.

I'd been so focused on why the birders were here, I hadn't thought of what might have happened before, how they got the children in the first place. I'd also forgotten my mother wasn't the only mother who would fight to the death for her child.

Forgetting I was keeping a low profile, I jumped to my feet. "Dana. Where's Dana?"

Mel raced toward me. "Keep still. We're almost done with them." She nodded back over her shoulder. The police were questioning Bubbe now. It was obvious from the expression of strained patience on the officers' faces it wasn't going well.

"The"—I hesitated for a second, not sure what to call them—"birders . . . women had two babies. One was Pisto, wasn't it?" I asked.

"Yes. He's with Mandy."

I nodded; that was part of my concern. I hadn't seen Dana. I'd lost my lieutenant last fall; if I lost her sister too . . . "Is she okay? Was she with them?" I tried to sound calm and in control but knew by the understanding expression on Mel's face that I'd failed.

"Dana wasn't here. She took Lao to a neighbor's. We trade produce with them. She heard the explosion, though—everyone did." Mel grimaced.

Tonight's happenings were going to cause a lot of problems for my friend. She tried hard to blend with humans. Attention like her shop was getting tonight would not be welcomed. But she seemed mostly unflustered by it. She smoothed her hands over her shorts, getting more dirt on them than she removed. "You said birders. Who are they?"

"I don't know. I'm not even sure they are birders, but the coincidence . . ." I told her the same story I'd told Jack minutes earlier.

"Could they be Amazons?" she asked.

I shook my head. "No." There was nothing about the women that said Amazon. "But . . ." I explained my theory that they might think Bern or I were involved in the other woman's death, that they might have followed us.

"But why take the babies?"

I shook my head. "I have no idea."

"Opportunity?" Jack suggested.

"They came into the basement and found the babies unattended and took them thinking they'd make good bargaining chips?" Mel asked.

"And the rest was just coincidence? The fire and explosion outside too?" It seemed too much to me.

"No." Jack again. "I don't believe in coincidence. The explosion was planned. They wanted us to be doing something else. It's why I came around here in the first place.

"Blowing up a line of trees . . ." He snorted. "Who would do that?"

"Teenagers, according to the police. Apparently there's been a group of them vandalizing fences and businesses lately." Mel's face was devoid of expression.

"And I guess these teenagers may have gotten scared and shot when Zery's mother came out of the basement?" Jack asked.

Mel shrugged. "Not an accusation I would make."

"And if they find a suspect?"

She smiled. "I don't think they will get their man."

"Why not describe the real shooters? We've decided they can't be Amazons." Jack's suggestion. I knew the answer.

Mel looked at me. Jack did too.

"Because we don't want them arrested." We wanted them dead.

Mel's eyes flickered. I wasn't sure what my friend who had left the tribe a decade earlier was thinking. The old Mel would understand, the new one? I didn't know, but she hadn't told the police about the women. For now I'd take that as a sign she was on my side.

She twisted her lips to the side. "We do need to find them. They weren't hurt, were they?"

"The one, maybe. The bird attacked her. The other . . . I don't think so." Either way, both had managed to escape and quickly.

"We could check the hospitals," she offered, but she didn't sound convinced and I wasn't either. If I had just set a line of trees on fire and shot someone, I wouldn't be heading to the hospital unless absolutely necessary. And I didn't think either of the women were that hurt, if at all. Still . . . "When Lao gets back with Dana, I can send her. She will blend better than the rest of us."

With that avenue, unlikely as it was, covered we returned to our conversation.

"Maybe we just need to break this down more," Mel suggested. "Zery, what happened exactly, when you ran around here? *Why'd* you run around here?" There was a groove between Mel's eyes. I could see she was working as hard as I was to make sense out of what had happened.

I glanced at Jack.

He shifted his jaw to the side. "The sons have watched the Amazons for a long time now. We know how you think."

Despite the fact we seemed to be working together at the moment, I didn't appreciate his view that the Amazons could be so easily pegged.

"That told you to catapult around the building?" I asked my voice dry.

He nodded. "There was no obvious reason to set that fire, or to sound the explosion. No real damage was done. No one was hurt. So why do it?"

Mel released a noise from the back of her throat. "To divert our attention."

Jack and I had already had this conversation. I tapped

my toe, impatient for us to move on to something that would bring my mother's killers into arm's reach.

Jack touched the tip of his nose. "What was here someone wanted?"

"The baby." Me this time. "But we've been over that. Unless they heard us talking and knew the baby was important to us, there was no real reason to target him."

He shrugged. "I didn't know your birders would be here. I was just thinking of what wasn't where we were."

He looked at Mel. "Do you know how they got the babies? That might tell us something. Would they have been hidden somewhere, or could they have just stumbled over them?"

Mel rolled her lips into her mouth. "Scy, Dana, or Bubbe was with them all the time, but Dana, as I said, was gone, and when she heard the explosion, Bubbe came up to help me."

Leaving my mother alone. But my mother should have been enough. Two humans shouldn't have been able to get past her.

Mel continued, "Bubbe said the babies were asleep when she left, alone with Scy in Mother's workout room."

"So they got the babies away from my mother somehow."

Mel nodded, looking unsettled. "Or lured her out and stole them while she was gone."

I looked at Jack. We had seen the birders. We let them go past us. We could have stopped them, stopped everything.

He moved his head slightly, telling me there was no reason to explain that, that it didn't change the outcome.

I bit back the confession, but it boiled and churned inside my stomach, mixed with the rest of the guilt stewing there.

"When I came around the corner, my mother was in the stairwell. The birders warned her to stay put, but she didn't."

Mel smiled. "She was a warrior."

"And a mother." I'd seen Mel when she thought someone had killed her son. I'd thought the crazed emotion that had overtaken her was a Mel thing, but now I realized my mother had felt it too. It made me uncomfortable, wondering if I'd misjudged her all along. I'd never had to balance being on the high council with raising a future queen. Maybe she'd cared for me more than I knew.

Or maybe I just wanted to believe that now that she was gone.

"What happened then? Did you see where the birders went? If there was anyone else with them?" Mel asked.

I shook my head. The dirt had provided a perfect cover for their getaway.

"This was not all some strange coincidence. We have to assume they wanted the babies. That this was all planned."

My lips thinned as I pondered my next move.

I wanted to revenge my mother's death, but every moment the high council's rule to kill infant sons stood, a baby might die. Which would my mother think was more important?

I forced my mind to focus, to push emotion aside. The answer was obvious; my mother had died trying to save two infants. If I let even one die now, it would be an insult to everything she'd been trying to accomplish.

Somehow I had to do what my mother had failed to do. I had to change the high council's rule.

And then I'd kill the bitches who took her life.

Chapter 16

As soon as the decision firmed in my head, I began moving forward. Mel grabbed me.

"You can't leave."

"My mother is dead. There's no reason for me to stay here."

"What about your brother?" she asked.

I blinked, confused for a moment. Then realization hit me . . . the baby. My mother had been caring for him. Would that responsibility fall to me now? I stiffened. A child wasn't in my plans, never had been.

"His father will take him." Jack watched us, his eyes moving back and forth in his face.

His father . . . I looked at Jack. "The man helping . . . with the concrete." Jack had told me the bird was the baby's father, but somehow once I'd put my mother into the picture, I'd forgotten him.

He nodded. "He met Scy a few years ago. She didn't know he was a son at first."

"But she did before she got pregnant." No one had said it, but I knew it was true. My mother had wanted her children to be strong . . . the strongest. She had wanted it for me and she would want it for this child too. What better way than to give him a son as a father?

Jack's gaze dropped for a second, but then rose. "I don't know when she found out. Mateo hasn't told me."

Mateo. He didn't like me; it was obvious from how he looked at me. It made me wonder what my mother had told him about me. . . . Then I remembered he knew me not as my mother's daughter but as the queen who had hunted and, he thought, tried to kill his child.

I stared at Jack, unsure how I felt about turning the baby my mother had been so determined to save over to a son who hated me. I shouldn't care. If asked, it's what I would have said was the best solution . . . give our male children to the sons who wanted them . . . but now faced with it . . . it felt wrong.

I pressed the pads of my fingers into the heels of my hands. I couldn't afford to quibble about it now. Even if I knew word one about caring for an infant, I couldn't do what I had to do with a baby strapped to my back. Maybe my mother could have, but I wasn't her.

I accepted Jack's proposal with silence and looked back at Mel.

"My mother's position on the high council is open. She couldn't convince them that things need to change, but maybe someone else can."

"You would try to get on the council?" There was reservation in Mel's voice. I knew what she was thinking—the council was the enemy—but according to what my mother had told me, they weren't.

But I wasn't a queen. I wasn't sure where I stood with the Amazons right now. To think of joining the council was ludicrous.

That didn't mean, however, that I couldn't try to open their eyes to the fact that the sons weren't their only enemy. It might be enough to convince them killing infants wouldn't keep them safe from attack.

I returned my focus to Jack. "Will you help me find the birders?"

Confusion flitted across Mel's face. "I thought—"

But Jack held my gaze. "I will."

He knew what I was asking. I didn't know how he knew when Mel didn't, but that didn't matter right now, what did is that he'd agreed to be my ally. He'd agreed to fight my enemy.

The Amazons, some at least, would respect that. Another plus in my case to not demonize the sons.

I shifted my attention back to Mel. "I need Bubbe to tell me where the council meets." Years ago, years before Mel had left the tribe, Bubbe had been on the high council, and even if they didn't meet in the same place, I'd never met a priestess more powerful than my friend's grandmother. She could find the council; if she had to ask Artemis herself, she could find them.

Mel's face was grim. It was obvious she didn't agree with what I planned to do. I wasn't sure why—if it was her general hatred of the council or her lack of faith in me. It didn't matter. I had already made my decision.

"You won't get ten feet from where you stand. You move out of this circle and Bubbe's ward will be broken. It's anchored to you, but it won't move with you. The police will remember who you are and why they wanted to talk to you, and they won't look kindly on you leaving without doing it."

Behind Jack, two men lifted my mother's body and placed it in a dark zippered bag. My throat tightened.

"Get Bubbe. She can hurry them on their way."

Mel's lips were pressed into such a flat line now that I could barely see them. Finally she spat out, "They tried to kill her, Mel. Your mother didn't tell you everything. She didn't want you to know, she wanted you to keep your love of the damned tribe, but the council tried to kill her. She had to leave, they were going to kill her son *and* her if she didn't."

Mel's revelation should have surprised me, but it didn't. I'd already accepted that I didn't know the tribe like I thought I did. . . .

But the tribe was still the tribe, and I still loved them enough I was willing to die to protect them, even from themselves.

* * *

The police continued to measure and photograph. Then the media showed up. Shootings weren't common in Madison. It was a blessing, though. It drew the police's attention and made it easy for me to step away—even without Bubbe's help.

Back inside Mel's shop, we gathered and discussed our plan.

Jack called the bird son, my half brother's father and my mother's lover. He was at an art shop owned by Makis, the son confined to a wheelchair, but immediately agreed to return to take charge of the baby. Jack went to get him so he could arrive in his human form, clothed. He left the baby with us. I insisted. I was willing for the bird man to watch him, but I wasn't handing him over totally. Not yet.

When I made this clear, Mel shook her head.

"He's his father," she said. "He would give his life to protect him."

"And a son," I replied. This new partnership was too unfamiliar. Besides, my mother had given her life, but that hadn't been enough to save her son. He'd have been lost if Jack, Mateo, and I hadn't been there.

"Makis is a son," she countered. "And I trust him." She didn't, I noticed, mention Peter.

"You may. I don't." In fact, I trusted Makis least of all.

He was higher ranking and older than the other men. He was also Harmony's, Mel's daughter, grandfather— just another of the little surprises we'd discovered last fall. Based on his handicap alone, Makis had more reason than anyone to hate us.

Makis, however, wasn't in town. He was with Harmony and Peter in Michigan. When Mel returned, she had returned alone.

"You let her stay with just them?" Mel was the definition of protective. I was shocked she would trust anyone, much less two sons, alone with her child.

At my question Bubbe, rummaging through a drawer in the kitchen, grunted.

Mel placed a heavy stare on her grandmother, then answered. "Makis *is* her grandfather." Despite the strong look she'd shot Bubbe, I could see uncertainty in her eyes. She glanced to the side. "She has relatives."

"Relatives? Sons?" Amazons didn't recognize family outside their direct line. We didn't keep track of things like cousins or aunts. They had no more importance in our lives than any other member of our family clan. I knew there were Amazons in the lion clan who shared a grandmother with me, but I didn't give them any thought. I certainly wouldn't go out of my way to visit them.

"Harmony's father had other children—two, both boys. They live in Michigan with an uncle."

"And you let her stay there with them." My mind was reeling. "What if they don't bring her back?"

Bubbe jerked a phone book out of the drawer and slammed it down onto the countertop.

Mel's eyes flashed. "They will." Then she relaxed a bit.

"She called last night. They went to Mackinac and rented horses. She's having fun."

A snort from Bubbe interrupted my response. As Mel narrowed her eyes and glared at her grandmother, I stepped away from the conversation. Harmony was out of the picture, which was good. One less child of a son to worry about.

As much as I didn't understand Mel's reasoning for letting her go off with the men, at least we didn't have to worry about the Amazons deciding Harmony was a threat.

A tiny snort of my own escaped. How things had changed. I was actually glad an Amazon teen was with the sons and afraid my tribe might decide she was a threat that needed to be destroyed.

While I waited for the tension between Mel and her grandmother to settle, I approached the members of my camp, or the few who had thrown their loyalty to me over Thea and the high council.

Lao and Tess sat next to Dana, who was cooing and stroking tiny Pisto's back. She hadn't put him down since she and Lao had returned and she'd learned the birders had tried to steal not only my mother's baby, but her own. Even now Dana's voice cracked and her eyes when they met mine appeared manic, reconfirming my suspicion that a hearth-keeper could be just as determined and dangerous as a warrior.

Bern stood to one side, not far from my half brother who was asleep in his seat. The warrior was as silent as always. She hadn't said a word to me since I'd asked her to leave earlier, but she watched all of us with the patience and intensity of a guard dog awaiting an order to attack.

I appreciated her coiled aggression. I felt the same. I couldn't wait to get on with facing the high council, and after that, my mother's killers.

Bubbe moved toward the stairs, a disposable wand-type lighter in her hand. "I build the fire to find the council," she murmured. She scowled at Mel as she passed.

Mel shook her head and stared at the wall.

Content their disagreement wasn't going to get in the way of finding the council, I pulled out a chair at the table and sat down. Tess poured a cup of coffee and slid it toward me.

I sipped and I waited, as did everyone else. Silence fell around us; even Dana quit her cooing; only the sound of her son sucking on a pacifier offered any disturbance.

In an hour Bubbe was back. And I could tell by the expression on her face, what she had to say wasn't going to be good.

"The high council is no more." Bubbe punctuated her words by slamming the end of a short staff onto the wood floor. Then she turned and stalked from the room.

Not knowing what else to do, the rest of us followed her, babies in tow. No one felt safe leaving them behind.

She walked down the front stairs and down the hill that led to Mel's front lawn.

The schoolhouse was set on an acre of land, most of it in the front of the building. While the area around the school was crowded with the main building, the old gym/cafeteria, and a number of large trees, this area was flat and open with a clear view of Monroe Street.

At four in the morning the street was quiet, but Bubbe went about setting a ward to hide us anyway. Once we had sat in the traditional crescent-moon shape, she circled us, chanting. Back at the moon's tip, she stopped and took a seat herself.

I glanced around the group, realizing this was most likely the first Amazon circle a male had ever attended. Yes, they were infants and didn't understand a word that was being said, but it was still huge.

Bubbe held her staff to the side, one hand wrapped around it. "I reached out to the council, felt for their energy." She dug the end of the staff into the earth. "It was broken . . . fractured."

I frowned. "Perhaps because my mother—"

"No." She slammed the staff down. "It is more than that. Their power. It is broken." She held the staff in front of her. There was a crack, and the thing split into two pieces.

Mel's eyes found mine. Resolve was there. She'd already known this.

I curled my fingers into the grass beneath my thighs and repeated what my mother had told me, how the council had been divided on what to do about the sons, how the other group had managed to pull those in the middle to their side for the vote.

Still holding the two halves of the staff, Bubbe nodded. "It is more than that. I sensed . . ." She looked up at the moon and murmured something low that I couldn't hear.

We waited for her to finish her murmuring and go on.

Finally she looked back. "Another goddess. It is not just the sons over which they argue. It is the goddess herself."

The goddess? "But . . ." But the goddess was Artemis. I looked up too. The moon was still in the sky and only five days past being full.

"Some have deserted Artemis." Bubbe dropped the pieces of the staff. They rolled across the ground.

The others stared at them, afraid and uncertain.

While I wouldn't admit it out loud, I was afraid and uncertain too.

I'd never imagined any of this could happen. The sons, my mother's death, the council taking my position as queen, but to learn some had left Artemis?

Artemis was everything to us. Our safe camps were built on her places of power. Our ceremonies were held at night under the moon. I bore her crescent on the back of my neck. Everything we held dear, everything that made us Amazons, involved Artemis in some way. How could any desert her?

But as much as I wanted to, I couldn't doubt Bubbe. I

trusted her, as a person and a priestess. She had no reason to lie, and she wouldn't, couldn't, make a mistake like this.

But what did it mean—to the tribe and me?

I scrambled for a question that would make the answer clear.

"What goddess?" Maybe if I knew this I would understand, but I doubted it. There were many goddesses, but none I could think of who matched the essence of the Amazons like Artemis.

Bubbe pressed her lips together, making her look, despite the difference in years, like her granddaughter Mel. "I don't know. My tie is to Artemis. I cannot see the other."

"How . . ." I struggled, trying to think how this would affect us. "Our talents, they come from the goddess . . . Artemis." It was a statement, one I thought was true, but I'd thought so many other things were true too. Now I couldn't take anything for granted.

Bubbe sighed. The corners of her mouth edged down, pulled by disapproval. "We are the daughters of Ares and Otrera, a god and our first queen. Our long life, your strength, they come from them."

Long life and strength. That wasn't much, not when compared to all the other talents the Amazons held.

"All of our talents are part of who we are," she added.

I relaxed, then stiffened. While I found comfort in the idea that our talents were part of us, that no matter what happened we would retain them, it also meant the other Amazons, the ones who had deserted Artemis, would hold those skills too.

"However . . ." Bubbe ran her fingers down the leather thong that hung from her neck and grasped the tiny stone wolf that dangled from it. "While we are born with our talents, our worship of the goddess enhances them—especially our magical talents."

I smiled. "So these Amazons who have deserted Artemis, they will have lost some of their skills." It was good news, the best news.

Bubbe's hand closed more tightly over the wolf. She held her breath and for a moment I thought she wasn't going to answer. Then she placed the stone against her lips and kissed it. With it still held in front of her, she replied, "But their new goddess will bring them more."

"More? More than the Amazons?"

Bubbe's lips lifted on the sides, a shade of a smile, but still the wire that had started to weave around my heart loosened a tad. She opened her fingers and the wolf thumped into place over her heart. "More, perhaps is wrong . . . different, like the goddess they choose. Each goddess, she has different skills from the next. Artemis strengthens our magic, our use of the wild forces of nature. She looks down on us during childbirth, and helps us to hunt. She attracts us to the woods, and gives us the strength and skills of her chosen animals." Bubbe's fingers flitted over the stone wolf. "But another goddess, she would have skills too. If she accepts the worship of these

Amazons, she could bestow her skills, like Artemis has bestowed hers upon us."

"What kind of skills . . . stronger skills?"

Bubbe lifted one shoulder. "I tell you what I know. It depends on the goddess and how she receives these Amazons."

I clenched my jaw, uncertain again. "What about Artemis? Could they have her talents too?"

Bubbe smiled, a full smile this time. "Artemis, she is a jealous goddess. She would not like to share."

I sat quiet for a moment, letting this new information sink in. Finally I looked up. "What now? How do we know who is following Artemis?"

How do you identify your enemy when she looks just like you, is you?

Chapter 17

We talked another hour or so but got nowhere. Bubbe
had no more idea than I did of what to do next. As the
morning sun began to creep up on the horizon, we split
up. Mel left to research other goddesses. Lao and Tess
went to start breakfast so Dana could get some sleep.

I ordered Bern to take a nap too.

I was sure Bern could survive without sleep, but while
things were calm I wanted her to take the opportunity to
get some.

Our future was uncertain, and I needed everyone in
my circle strong.

We were officially in war mode. We would sleep by
rotation and be on constant alert.

I plodded toward the gym/cafeteria building myself,

not sure what I planned to do. I was exhausted yet at the same time fairly sure I wouldn't be able to sleep.

Cleo had already made it clear she and Bubbe would be up for the next few hours, as would Mel. I could take this turn to sleep, or I could sit and stew and hope some solution came to me.

As my feet pulled their way through the long grass that covered the hillside, I knew which one I would do.

I didn't even bother going all the way to the gym. I lay down in the grass and stared at the sky. The day was going to be warm. At maybe five in the morning it was already approaching seventy degrees. I jerked off my T-shirt, lay back down, and enjoyed the feel of the cool grass against my bare shoulders. The jog bra I wore had a high neck to cover my *givnomai*. So if one of Mel's customers came by, it was decent while still being cool. The sky was a ruddy pink now, and the birds were in full swing, chirping and fighting for whatever territory they thought of as theirs.

It was peaceful—the most peaceful place I could remember being in for quite some time.

My eyes were closed and my brain had just started to settle when I heard someone approaching from behind. I shot forward into a somersault, landed on my feet, and turned immediately.

Jack stood a few feet from where I had lain, his hands shoved deep into the pockets of his camouflage pants.

"Mateo is going to have to sleep in the gym with you and your camp if you won't let him take Andres home."

"Andres?"

He pulled his hands from his pockets, then shoved them back in. "Your brother."

Right. The baby . . . Andres. I wasn't sure I liked knowing his name; it made him more real.

"So what's the plan?" He took a few steps down the hill.

"Did you talk to anyone?" I asked. I wasn't sure how much I wanted to tell Jack, should tell him. My loyalties were a tangled-up ball of yarn right now.

"No." He stopped and stared down at me. I could see he was waiting, knew what I said or did now was going to set a tone for where we went from here.

I glanced up at the sky. The moon was barely visible now. Maybe it would be one of those strange days where you can see the moon, even when the sun was at its highest. I took it as a sign.

I gestured for Jack to sit, then I told him everything Bubbe had told us. When I was done, I sat down beside him. The silence that settled between us felt right, comfortable. We were both lost in our thoughts, but we were lost in them together. I wanted to stretch out again, to share the peace of lying on that hillside with him, but I knew I couldn't.

This wasn't the time to relax; this was the time to act. But how?

Mel walking up behind us brought part of my answer.

She dropped a stack of papers onto my lap. "I don't know that there are answers there, but maybe some clues.

I printed out descriptions of thirty of the most popular goddesses."

The papers felt like it; they weighed a ton. I carefully picked them up and thumbed through them. My eyes quickly blurred.

She smiled. "I know." She kneeled and took a place on the grass beside me. I was flanked now, her on one side, Jack on the other.

"But if we do notice something strange . . . a power we've never seen before or something . . . we have something to reference."

I stared at the stack of paper. Amazons were not scholars. As an Amazon destined to be a queen, I'd been taught more than most, but by modern human educational standards I'd probably have barely graduated high school . . . unless the school gave credits for wrestling or sword fighting.

The thought of reading these papers made my head ache.

"Too bad Harmony isn't here," Mel murmured. "She'd love diving into this."

Her face turned sad. If I'd been a different kind of person I would have reached for her hand, but that wasn't me and Mel knew it. It would have just made us both uncomfortable.

As it was, Jack reached over and grabbed the papers. "Let me. I studied Greek mythology in college."

I looked at him, surprised. "You went to college?"

He grinned, a slow sexy slide of his lips over those

impossibly white teeth. "When I was fifty. The sons don't have the same antimingling beliefs the Amazons do. I figured a little education would be good."

"What did you major in?" Mel asked.

He rolled the papers into a scroll shape, or tried to. They were too thick and sprung back out flat. He slapped them against his palm. "I didn't graduate, just took classes, whatever interested me. Mythology did."

"What else?" I asked, realizing how little I knew about my self-named godfather.

"Usual things: girls, athletics . . . explosives."

"Like the birders used?" I asked, instantly alert.

He lifted a shoulder. "Somewhat. What they did wasn't fancy. I could have done it."

I turned, my hand forming a fist as it rose.

He grabbed me around the wrist.

"I said I could have, not that I did. Anyone with an Internet connection can build a bomb these days."

"How about the supplies? You know where they got those?" I asked. He still held my wrist. I didn't pull away; I just waited, tense.

"I'm a gun dealer, not a terrorist. There is a difference."

"Then why'd you study explosives?" My voice vibrated.

His, however, was calm. "That came after. It's why I left college. There was a war going on in Europe. I left to join it." He dropped his hold on my arm and stood. "It was a long time ago. Things have changed, but I thought you'd like to know I had some knowledge in that area too, that if needed we could match them explosive to explosive."

Explosives and guns. I couldn't see using either. In fact, I bristled at the thought.

Mel stood too. She angled her body so she was between us. "Are we on the same side, or not?" she asked.

Still seated, I stared up at them.

Were we? Did we all want the same thing here? Guns and explosives were two things I knew nothing about, didn't want to have to know anything about.

"I don't know. Maybe we should ask." I bounced the question back to my best friend. "What is your goal in all of this?"

Hurt and a bit of anger showed on Mel's face. "I don't care about the tribe. You know that. But I care that they want to kill children. I care about that a lot."

I believed her, but then I'd already known Mel's motivation. I looked at Jack.

He tapped a finger against the sheaf of paper he held. I suspected he was weighing whether he should answer my question at all. Finally he did. "I don't want any children killed either. And I want the tribe to survive. You may not believe me, but I care about the tribe, not"—he added as I opened my mouth to disagree—"in the same way you do. More like an ecologist cares about an endangered species. Amazons are rare and old; they are part of the world, a part I think should continue to exist." His finger quit moving. "But that doesn't mean I don't think they shouldn't change; they should. And I'd like to be a part of both things—the save and the change."

I weighed whether being put in the same class as an endangered animal pissed me off or not. Deciding there were plenty of other things to piss me off, I let it lie.

"Close enough." I stated and stood. Neither of them had missions that would get in the way of what I wanted . . . the tribe together, strong and not operating out of a place of ignorant fear.

Jack flipped through the papers again. The sheets made a rippling noise and I caught snippets of pictures of various goddesses as he did—one regal, crowned, and holding a scepter; one fanciful, with a rainbow arching from one palm to the other; and even one I might have mistaken for a human's angel, with wings. There were others, but as I watched the pages flip past, they blurred into one.

Then I saw Artemis and something clicked into place.

My contact on the high council. I hadn't spoken with her since before Thea arrived and we got the order to steal Andres.

I looked at Mel. "If I have a name, can Bubbe find her?"

Mel jutted out her jaw, thinking. "It's easier with her *telios* and *gívnomai*. Do you know them?"

"Not her *gívnomai*, but her *telios*. Is that enough?"

There were twelve members of the council, a representative of each clan. There were also currently four warriors on the council; I knew each of them by name and which clan they were from.

Looking uncertain, she replied, "We can talk to Bubbe. I never know what the old reprobate can do for sure."

With that uncertain offer, I headed up the hill toward the school. I guessed my contact's disappearance meant she was on the losing side, my side now. She could help identify the rest of the council. And with that knowledge we'd be able to learn who was behind the split.

I stared down at my foot, hidden in the long grass. The same grass that earlier had been cool and reassuring now seemed to grasp at my legs, to let go with an unwilling whisper as I pulled my shoe free. Tamping the disturbing feeling down, I swallowed and kept walking.

We would figure this out. We would stop whoever was trying to split the Amazons in two.

If I could find my contact, that is.

And if she was alive.

We left Jack at the sidewalk that connected the school to the gym. He raised his hand holding the papers. "I'll read up."

With the basement stairwell closed, we went in the front and then down the main steps. Bubbe's space, where she ran her business, was off the main room, near the outside door that was now inoperable.

The priestess was inside and she was alone. She was sitting on the floor, her legs crossed and her red skirt pulled up almost to her waist. Her legs were bare and pale with firm muscles that didn't match the age of her face. It made me wonder if she did something to make herself look older to others.

Humans tended to underestimate the elderly. Bubbe wasn't beyond taking advantage of that.

As Mel often pointed out, Bubbe wasn't above taking advantage of much.

The old priestess spread a pile of dirt over the floor in a circle in front of her and without looking up, asked, "What did your Internet tell you?"

Mel growled, and I guessed this was yet another sticking point between them. But then she answered, "Too much. Jack is looking it over."

Bubbe snorted, then picked up the stone image of a panther and placed it on the edge of the dirt. There was a pile of similar stones, each carved into the shape of one of the Amazon *telioses* sitting beside her. One by one, she placed each into the shape of a crescent moon. When she was done, she looked up. "You have a job for me? One you cannot do yourself?"

Annoyance flickered over Mel's face, making it obvious her grandmother was prodding her in a way I couldn't see.

"Zery has a name. She wondered if you could locate someone based on that."

"She wondered? And you could not tell her?"

Mel's jaw hardened. Afraid the two of them would let their personal issues get them off track, I stepped in.

"She's a past queen and on the high council. Until a few weeks ago she was my contact."

Bubbe's gaze stayed on her granddaughter for a few breaths, then with a sigh she turned it on to me. "You are not to reveal the name of your contact. You know that."

I had the unexplainable urge to squirm, not all that differently than I had when I was six and was caught playing with Mel in her grandmother's workroom. But I was too old to allow her to intimidate me now, or at least to let her see she intimidated me.

I lowered my chin, stayed strong. "The council is broken. The rules don't hold."

"If you respect the tribe, the rules must hold."

"Like the rule to kill Andres?" I asked. "You can't pick and choose."

She rubbed the pads of her middle finger and thumb together. Again I had the feeling she could reach out with some power I couldn't see and swat me to my knees.

I braced my legs and stared her down.

She smiled. "Come. Whisper in my ear."

Beside me, Mel murmured with strained patience in her voice, "You passed the test. Artemis knows what it was, but you passed."

Pretending not to have heard, I knelt beside Bubbe and did as she had asked.

"The *telios*?" she said.

I opened my mouth, but she shook her head. "Touch. Move into the center."

Feeling completely out of my element, I plucked a boar from the line and carefully placed him in the middle. I started to pull back then, to stand and give the priestess room, but she grabbed my hand and held it tightly in her own.

Then she started to chant, low, fast, and in Russian. I didn't understand a word of what she was saying.

The dirt rose from the ground, darted back and forth, thickening in spots, then thinning—fleeting images, or what almost was an image before flattening out into nothing but dust. It swirled and boiled, rose up and spread out . . . then with no warning, it fell.

The boar was still sitting in the middle. All the fetishes were sitting where Bubbe had placed them, but the dirt had formed a shape, one that looked familiar but that I couldn't quite place.

Bubbe held her hand out over the crescent and muttered. When she looked up, her eyes were worried.

"She is here." Her finger jabbed toward the center of the shape, shoving away dirt to reveal the concrete floor beneath it.

I stared, trying to see what she was telling me.

"Here." She jabbed again.

I frowned, then I saw it. The dirt had formed the shape of the North American continent and her finger was right of the center, where I guessed Wisconsin, perhaps the northern part of Illinois would lie.

I gasped.

"She's here."

Chapter 18

I wasn't sure what my high council contact being in the area meant, if it meant anything. Like any Amazon, she could be traveling through for the upcoming fair, visiting relatives . . . lost.

Or she could have come looking for my mother, or me.

If she was looking for my mother, she would be at Mel's. If she was looking for me . . . ?

The safe camp.

I went to wake Bern.

I slept on the way down, as did Mel. There were two cars' worth of us. Everyone except Dana, Mateo, and Bubbe came, and the babies . . . we left them at Mel's.

Leaving Bubbe behind was a tough decision, but we

couldn't trust the babies with just a son and a hearth-keeper, even if that hearth-keeper had a mother lion's ferociousness when it came to protecting her child. And, to be honest, I had no idea what, besides shifting into a massive bird, Mateo's skills were.

Weighing everything, it made sense to leave Bubbe with them. Heading back to Illinois, we had three warriors, two hearth-keepers, a son, and Mel, who while classified as an artisan I knew had strong warrior and priestess skills too. It was a strange group, but one I trusted for the job—even Jack.

Oh, and we also brought the dogs. Bubbe had insisted.

We pulled into Jack's driveway around nine thirty.

There was nothing left of the cabin, at least nothing that could be used as shelter, but with access to the safe camp through the woods, it seemed like a good place to set as our base of operation.

We did, however, need some shelter besides our cars if we were going to stay here for long. And, since we had to assume no one at the safe camp was on our side, we needed a place we could stay hidden as much as possible.

Jack suggested we check his neighbors. Apparently one of the reasons he liked the location was that his closest neighbor, the man we'd seen getting his mail, spent most of the summer in northern Wisconsin and most of the winter in Texas. Remembering the camping trailer I'd seen parked in the drive during my last visit, I sent Lao and Tess to check out the house.

They were back in under ten minutes with good news.

"Looks like they've cleared out. Water and electricity are on, but the fridge is empty." Lao placed her hands on her hips and rocked back on her heels. "There's phone service too, if we want to use it. Long distance would show on their bill."

"Is there a computer?" Mel asked.

Lao nodded. "Don't know much about 'em, but one's there."

Happy with the news, we hid our vehicles inside the neighbor's detached three-car garage and moved ourselves into their house.

It was small, two bedrooms and two baths with a wide back porch that looked out over the woods. The furnishings were nice. There were redwood lawn chairs and two rockers on the back porch—a hot tub too. Seemed like a place you would go on vacation to, not from.

But we weren't on vacation.

There was a fence also, a partial one that shielded most of the property from anyone who casually approached from the main road and a deep freeze filled with what appeared to be venison in the garage.

After we'd walked around the house and the property one more time to make sure no one was home and there was no sign that anyone had been hired to watch the place, we met in the small living room.

We quickly decided our best course of action. We would send Mel's mother Cleo to the camp. Between her and Mel, Cleo was less likely to be known to anyone at the house. Also, she would blend in more easily. Besides, I could tell the idea of trying to blend gave my friend twitches, and I didn't need Mel's true personality and thoughts on all things Amazon coming out.

So Cleo would arrive in the stolen car, claiming to be arriving early for the fair. Bern, Lao, and Tess would stay hidden for now at the house.

Mel, Jack, and I would approach through the woods.

We had no set goal at the moment, except to see what was going on and to check for some sign my high council contact had been near.

We agreed to meet in three hours at the obelisk. It would be afternoon by then, not a time any Amazons should be worshipping the goddess.

Assuming they still worshipped Artemis.

If they didn't? Well, I had no idea when, where, or how they might choose to worship. We might be walking into a crowd of goddess worshipers I had no chance of recognizing.

I didn't dwell on the possibility too much.

I took another nap instead. Bern was on watch, and I needed to be at my best. I knew whatever happened, I wasn't going to be welcomed back at camp with open arms.

I had to be prepared to fight.

As we walked through the woods, my body tensed. I felt like a stranger here, walking a path I'd traveled daily for over a decade.

I resented the high council and whomever the Amazons were who had drifted for making me an outsider. I even, if I was honest, resented the safe camp members who hadn't questioned this false high council's orders. But that was unfair. I had followed their orders blindly too . . . or tried to . . . would have if Jack and Mateo hadn't jumped in to stop me.

How could I be angry at others for doing what I had done myself?

My place here, however, my goal, was to prove I wasn't an outsider, that my view of what the Amazons were and should be was the best one. If I had a high-council member by my side who knew the council had split and that some had even left Artemis, I could convince the others at the camp that the high council who had ordered my dismissal wasn't valid.

From there we could tell others, expose the false Amazons among us and keep them from burrowing deeper into our hearts.

I had brought my staff with me. Shifting it a bit in my hands calmed me. I longed to stretch and run through a few exercises to relieve even more of the built-up tension, but there hadn't been time. The nap had felt more important.

Jack walked directly behind me wearing only pants—no shirt or shoes. I assumed he wanted to be free to shift without having to worry about escaping his clothes, but I hadn't asked. Mel was behind him, no weapons, but armed with her magic.

As we approached the obelisk, I heard a voice. It was female and familiar but I couldn't place it. She seemed to be singing.

Motioning for Jack and Mel to stay hidden, I stepped into the clearing.

A woman stood in front of the obelisk. Her back was to me, but based on her height and impressive physique, it was easy to guess she was an Amazon. The sword shoved into the ground not far away added weight to my guess.

The sun shone down brightly, glistened off her shoulder-length hair. She wore no adornment that I could see except a wide leather wristband. It was only a few shades darker than her skin, which visible in athletic shorts and tank, was tanned. She looked like someone who worked outside during the day . . . like a hearth-keeper . . . or a warrior.

The sword made me guess the latter.

My missing high-council contact was a warrior.

"Kale?" I offered, my voice low so I wouldn't startle her.

Her shoulders pulled back and her head tilted. She turned slowly. As she did, she dropped something . . . a metal flask. The lid had been off, and clear liquid spilled onto the ground.

She was facing me now. I'd never met Kale, but she was much as I'd imagined her. Fierce, strong, and in control.

She stared at me for a moment, her eyes narrowing.

Then she glanced down at her hand and I saw what she held . . . a gun, black, square and ugly, just like the ones the birders had held.

The gun began to rise.

A hand hit me square in the back and I flew forward, just as the bullet zipped through the space where I had stood.

"Shit." Mel leaped toward me, pulling in a breath as she did.

My staff perpendicular to my body, I log-rolled across the ground out of her reach.

Kale had seen me, shot at me.

I wouldn't let Mel take a bullet meant for me.

I'd lost my mother. I would not lose Mel.

Three feet and I ran out of cleared space. I folded my body forward and somersaulted to a stand. As my feet hit the ground, I broke into a run. My staff dug into the earth and I vaulted, my feet aimed at Kale's head.

She turned again and my gaze locked onto the gun— once again pointed at me. Better me than Mel.

A battle cry split from my lungs. I kicked, the sole of my foot jamming into her forehead. The gun fired again.

My mind searched for the pain but came back empty. I landed four feet past where she had stood and spun.

She was lying prone on the ground. Jack in his wolverine form was over her, his jaws around her neck. Her fingers twitched; her lips moved.

"Wait," I yelled.

Both Kale and Jack froze.

I could see the craziness in Jack's eyes, the lust for her blood. I didn't know what happened to the sons when they shifted—how much of the animal they truly became, but I knew as I stared into Jack's wolverine eyes that he want to kill, wanted to taste blood more than he wanted anything at that moment in time.

I lifted my staff so it was angled across my body and took a step forward.

Mel stood where I'd left her. She blew the breath she'd held into her closed fist. "I'm not sure he can, Zery." She shook her hand as if something alive was concealed in those closed fingers. And I suspected it was, or close enough . . . a tiny tornado buzzing with whatever energy Mel had blown into it.

"Zery," Kale muttered. Her eyes shifted in her face. She blinked. "Zery," she repeated, softer. Then she glanced to the side, toward the woods.

Dread, thick like tar, settled over me. My staff still held ready, I sidestepped across the clearing.

At first, with my eyes not yet adjusted from the bright light of the clearing, I saw nothing, then hidden in the shadows I saw a hump, like a fallen log . . . or . . . I moved closer, close enough I could see the lump wasn't a tree or anything else that had grown naturally here in Artemis's woods.

It was a body.

My jaw tight, I started to kneel, then I saw the second one.

* * *

"Don't kill her," I yelled—an order, one I hoped Jack would respect. I placed my foot on the closest body and pushed. It flopped over. The face of the birder who'd pushed the button and blown up the stairwell stared up at me.

The glassiness of her eyes told me she was dead, almost as much as the round bullet hole in her forehead.

"What is it?" Mel, close behind me now.

I held one hand to the side, blocking her from coming closer.

"The birders. The women who tried to take the babies. They're dead. Shot." Mel paused. It was a tangible pause, one I felt as much as saw. She opened her hand and the tiny tornado spun down into the ground. Dead leaves rustled up from the floor of the forest, broke into tiny pieces, and scattered over the dead woman's face.

Moving past me, Mel pulled the second birder over and onto her back. She was shot too, in the chest. It was bloody and gory and everything I'd dreamed it would be . . . except I'd planned on delivering the blow.

"She shot them," Mel said.

"Looks that way." I turned and trudged to the clearing.

Jack still had Kale pinned. Neither had moved. Which was strange. An Amazon warrior didn't lie in place and wait to be killed . . . and a warrior on the high council? I would expect her to do what I'd never been able to do myself . . . defeat the wolverine son so thoroughly that there would be no denying Amazons were the stronger sex . . . had no need of a fairy godfather.

Disgusted, I kicked the pistol that lay less than a foot away from the fallen high-council member deep into the woods, in the direction of the bodies.

Then I twisted my staff and jammed it into the center of her back. In an advantageous position if the need to battle arose, I gestured for Jack to back off.

His lip curled and the ugly growling bark I'd come to recognize followed, but after only one such complaint, he loosened his jaws and shuffled backward.

The air around him grew fuzzy, like someone had rubbed Vaseline over a camera lens. Knowing what was happening, I waited, and just as quickly as it had begun the spot lengthened, the air cleared, and a naked Jack replaced the wolverine.

His lip raised revealing teeth. "She shot at you."

I stepped away from the fallen queen and spun my staff so it was directed at the son. "Dead, she can't tell us anything."

Kale was my only hope of convincing the Amazons that the basic premise of the high council and the trust we had placed in them had been violated.

He growled again, but turned and stalked to where his pants lay in a pile near the edge of the clearing.

Kale didn't move. I watched her with one eye as I walked to the sword shoved halfway to its hilt into the earth. I jerked the weapon out; a boar was engraved on its blade, answering any doubts I might have had as to her identity. I walked back and pushed the Amazon over with my foot, just as I'd pushed the dead birder.

Kale's body moved in the same manner, lifeless, with no fight. She could have been dead, if it weren't for the up and down movement of her chest and the slight humming noise coming from her throat.

I pressed the tip of the sword against the base of her neck until a bead of blood appeared. When I got no reaction, I pressed harder.

"Where is the rest of the council, Kale?"

She blinked, and the fog lifted. I realized then it wasn't a hum I heard, but a chant, a low repetition of words I couldn't make out.

Her lips dry, her voice cracking, she rasped, "What happened? Where is—" She grabbed the sword with her bare hand and pushed it away.

The tip tore at her skin as she did, leaving a long ugly line of blood and ragged tissue. Then she bent her knees, raised her hips, and propelled her body to a stand.

Ready for another attack, I spun.

Except, she didn't . . . she staggered, backward then sideways like a drunken middle-aged man surprised to find he couldn't hold his liquor like he had in his youth.

Her hair fell forward over her face. When she looked at me, strands still clung there, half-hiding her features. "What have you done to me?" Then her knees buckled and she fell forward onto the ground.

"Zery . . . ?" Mel behind me, warning in her voice.

Thinking she was afraid I would skewer the fallen council member where she lay, I lowered the sword to my side. "Don't worry, I won't—"

"No. Someone's coming. And not Mother, Bern, or any Amazon I'd guess."

I listened. There were voices, male, and the sound of bodies thrashing their way through the woods.

I retrieved my staff and tossed it to Mel. Then I bent and levered the fallen warrior's body onto my shoulder.

"What about the birders?" Jack asked.

"Leave them." And I jogged out of the clearing.

Chapter 19

We got maybe twenty feet away from the clearing before the owners of the voices closed in.

"What the hell is that thing?"

I stiffened. *The obelisk.* I looked at Mel.

She shook her head.

Still holding the sword and with the unconscious, bleeding warrior over my shoulder, I couldn't move closer, not without risking discovery.

But I also couldn't see or hear what I wanted.

Jack held up his hand and pointed for Mel and me to leave, then he shifted.

The air waved, then his pants crumpled, and out of the fallen material the black snout of a wolverine appeared. Without a glance at us, he crept through the underbrush.

It was smart. He could get close, and even if seen there

was little risk. They could shoot him, but unless he attacked one of them I doubted they would.

I still didn't want to leave. I still wanted to be there myself. I lifted my foot to edge closer.

Mel dropped the end of my staff in front of me.

I stared at the wooden rod, my emotions saying to shove the barrier aside, but my head saying she was right.

Finally I adjusted Kale's weight on my shoulder and turned back toward Jack's cabin.

I had my spies in place.

I had to trust that Cleo and Jack would bring me any information I needed.

Plus I had a warrior to interrogate . . . once I made sure she wasn't dead.

While I carried Kale inside, Lao laid towels on one of the beds to protect the linens from blood. Once the mattress was protected, I heaved my burden off my shoulder and laid her as gently as I could on the bed.

Lao went to work cleaning the wound where the sword tip had torn at her neck.

I left her alone, choosing to sit outside on the back porch and wait for Jack or Cleo to arrive. The dog wandered up. Someone had made a bed out of a cardboard box and set it on the porch. The smallest pup, the one that had barely been alive when I'd found him in the woods, whined.

I picked him up, mindlessly stroking him as I waited. By the time the chug of the stolen car's engine announced

Cleo's arrival, I was completely calm and for whatever reason feeling under control . . . like we were making progress.

The older warrior got out of the car and walked toward me.

Before I could ask her what she had learned, Jack's wolverine head poked out of the woods. His body soon followed. He stood at the edge of the forest, sniffing until I raised my hand giving the sign that all was fine here. Then he shifted.

While he pulled on his pants, which Mel had brought back and left lying on the ground, Cleo went to get Mel, Bern, and Lao, if she was able to leave Kale.

Soon Cleo, Bern, and Mel had appeared. Lao, Cleo said, wasn't yet willing to leave our houseguest alone. The five of us sat cross-legged in a circle on the grass. Tess sat on the porch fussing over the puppies.

The whole thing would have had a picnic feel if it wasn't for the lack of food and our topic of discussion.

"Who were they?" I asked, directing the question at Jack.

"Sheriff's department, I think. Someone called them."

We glanced at Cleo. She shook her head. "Could have been someone at the camp. The deputies arrived not long after I did. They seemed to be expecting them. The priestess, at least . . ." Her eyes wandered over Bern and me.

"How were things there?" I asked.

"Strange. Quiet." Cleo frowned. "As I said, they seemed to be waiting for something."

"Did anyone mention Kale?" I assumed since we'd found the high council member by the obelisk, she had come from the camp.

"No. No one really talked to me at all. I drove up, and they all just stared at the car. When I got out, the high priestess . . . Thea?"—she looked at me for confirmation—"came to talk to me. Asked where I was from, the last camp I'd visited, things like that. But it didn't feel like idle chitchat."

"You think she suspected something?" I asked.

"Maybe . . . or she just wasn't sure she wanted me there."

Not wanting an Amazon at a safe camp was unheard of. Being a stopping point for wandering Amazons was our entire purpose, and I knew the camp wasn't overfull. Four sleeping spaces had recently been vacated.

"But then the sheriff arrived."

I considered this: perhaps that was it. If Thea knew the sheriff was arriving, I'd understand how a new unknown warrior being thrown in the mix might not excite her, but how would she have known the sheriff was arriving—unless she had called them? And Amazons didn't call in human authorities . . . ever.

Jack jumped back into the conversation. "They found the bodies. It shook them up. I heard one of them say they'd been shot. I don't think they went there expecting to find anyone dead."

Which made me wonder what they had expected, why Thea had directed them toward the woods.

"Did any of the Amazons come with them, or show

up?" I asked. If human authorities had wanted to investigate in Artemis's woods while I was at the safe house, I would have done everything I could to stop them. As it was, I'd had a hard time not challenging their right to be there. Point being, if I'd been *forced* to pretend I was cooperating, I still would have tagged along after.

"No," replied Jack.

I glanced at Cleo. She shook her head. "They came to the camp and Thea talked to them. Then she directed them to the path."

"She directed them to the path? To the obelisk?"

Cleo nodded. Her jaw jutted out to one side.

"Did no one object?"

"No one."

I looked back at Jack. "What about the sheriffs? Did they say who they thought shot the women?"

"They thought they shot each other. They found two guns."

I'd only looked at one of the bodies, but whoever had shot her had either known what she was doing or made one hell of a lucky shot.

Jack continued, "After they talked a bit, they broke up and started searching the woods. One of the guns wasn't where they expected to find it, not if one of the dead women dropped it. I was afraid they'd find you."

The gun Kale had held, the one I'd kicked. "We left," I replied.

"And they haven't been by here?" he asked.

I shook my head. But he had a point. Eventually

someone would realize there were houses close to the obelisk that weren't the safe house. Even if they did think the two women killed each other, we needed to be prepared for the authorities to come calling.

"So how'd they know to come to the safe camp?" I asked, going back to my original question.

"I think someone from the camp called them, reported hearing two trespassers arguing. Whoever called said the pair had acted strangely and they were afraid to approach them to run them off."

"Do you think Kale shot them?" Mel asked, directing the question at me.

"She says she doesn't remember." Lao stepped onto the porch. "Doesn't seem to remember much. Aside from that I'd say she's hale and hearty, or should be." The hearth-keeper stared at me.

I only registered the first of Lao's words. I looked at Jack. "Any of the goddesses have the power to steal someone's memory?"

"You think someone at the camp is on the other side?" Mel dropped her hand from the head of the puppy I held.

I raked my fingers over the tiny dog's fur.

"I don't think we can discount the idea. . . . We can't discount anything."

Not long after Cleo had returned to the safe camp, Tess came to find me. I was still sitting out back in a rocker, this time waiting for Kale.

Tess wandered out looking shy and insecure. For the first time I noticed her chin-length hair was uncombed and her clothes were rumpled.

She walked to the end of the porch and wrapped her arms around the rough wood pillar.

I waited.

"I . . . I was thinking . . . Cleo, Mel's mother . . . she said no one would talk to her at camp." The young hearth-keeper slid one foot over the wooden porch floor. Her thick-soled sandal hit a rock and knocked it down into the long grass. "When I was there, people talked to me. I think they would again."

I frowned. "You want to go back?"

She straightened her arm, pushing her body away from the pillar. The position showed she was thin but muscular. Her arms had almost as much definition as mine.

The benefit of youth, or maybe the hearth-keepers' household tasks gave them more of a workout than I gave them credit for.

She continued, "Not *want*. I mean I understand what you are doing, how important it is. The fact that they wanted to kill that baby . . ." She shook her head, her mouth pulling down at the corners. "But I think I could go back. I think they would trust me. I could find out things Cleo can't. And you don't need me here. I sat with Kale for a while, but she's well now."

"You want to be a spy?" It was hard to imagine the soft-spoken hearth-keeper as an undercover agent.

She nodded, eager now. "I could tell them I didn't agree with you, that I missed being part of the tribe and hitched a ride back to camp. I don't think they'd suspect anything. They wouldn't think I'd be up to anything."

Her eyes were wide and innocent and her voice held a tremor. She was right, they wouldn't. I wouldn't.

"You could tell them we forced you to come," I added.

She smiled. "Yeah, kidnapped. That would be cool."

"By Bern?"

The silent warrior had just stepped onto the porch.

Tess laughed. "They'd believe that."

"Maybe in your escape you could have taken her down."

"Poisoned her eggs." The girl was grinning now.

"I like that."

She laughed and I even managed a smile. Bern grimaced.

Kale, led by an annoyed-looking Lao, appeared in the doorway. There were circles under the warrior's eyes and a long white strip of bandage taped to her throat. She looked like something you'd see on a slasher movie poster.

I gave Tess my blessing and asked Bern to walk her as far as the highway. The girl would send any information she learned back to us through Cleo. If for some reason we decided to pull Cleo or something happened where she needed to contact us directly, she would come through the woods.

Her arms crossed over her chest and her brows pulled together, Lao watched Tess and Bern disappear down the drive.

"You okay with that?" I asked her.

"Don't see the sense in it."

"She wants to do something."

"There's plenty of doing here—toilets to clean and Amazons to feed."

"You don't need her, though, do you?"

She snorted. "No. But I still don't like it." She shoved her hands into her pockets and whirled back toward the house.

Leaving Kale and me alone. Considering that the last time the council member had faced me with her eyes open she'd tried to kill me . . . and to be fair I had pierced her in the neck with a sword . . . it was natural we could only stare at each other with distrust at first.

Just as I thought the tension wouldn't pass, the mother dog tromped onto the porch. She shoved her nose into the box with her puppies. They kicked their feet and moved their snouts, vying for her attention. She pulled her head back out and stared at me—with what I interpreted as strained patience.

The stuffed cow that had been in Andres's baby seat was lying on the porch's wooden deck. It must have made its way in with our things and someone had put it in with the puppies.

I threw it out into yard; the mother gave one last glance at her puppies, then sailed off the porch after it.

Kale laughed. "She's recovered quickly. The pups can't be what? A week or so old?"

I let my hand fall toward the pile of puppies, enjoying

the feel of their pin sharp teeth on my skin. "Less than that. I found her in Artemis's woods; maybe she's part Amazon."

Kale nodded. "Must be." Then she collapsed into one of the porch's redwood chairs.

"What happened?" I asked. "Why'd you quit calling?"

When she looked up, there was confusion in her eyes. For a moment I thought she didn't remember our conversations, but then her emotions cleared. Still, she only stared back at me, seemed to be composing her thoughts.

Lao reappeared with a glass of cloudy green liquid and shoved it into her hand. Kale lifted it, the drink inside sloshing back and forth as she did. As she drank, a bit dripped onto her leather wristband. She wiped it off with her thumb.

"Lao said your mother is dead."

I inclined my head slightly.

"A waste." Her gaze was steady, assessing and unnerving.

Taking her comment as a form of condolence, I nodded. "What happened?" I asked.

She hesitated. "I'm not supposed to tell you anything, you know. High council business . . . what happens at the circle . . . we don't discuss it."

"The council is dead," I said it as bluntly as I could. I was past wasting my time honoring tradition for tradition's sake. Or letting someone take advantage of my regard for those traditions by not questioning something that needed to be questioned. "Ex-high priestess Saka"—

I didn't use Bubbe's first name because I didn't know it, and it felt strange to call her Bubbe to a council member—"tried to find them. You know what she said?"

Kale took a drink. Her eyes quiet, her body quiet, she looked at me over the top of her glass. "And she shouldn't have done that."

A growl loomed inside me, misplaced loyalty was not going to save the tribe, but before my annoyance grew too big to be contained, she sighed. "Yes, Tess told me. I don't know if I can believe it . . . another goddess. We never suspected that." She ran her thumb over her wristband, then looked up. "What can I tell you? What did your mother tell you?"

The growl evaporated. Finally I was going to get the answers I needed. I asked her to start wherever she thought the story started, didn't explain how little I'd learned from my mother, how little time we'd had for her to tell me anything.

She seemed hesitant, but finally she spoke. "I didn't suspect anything, not like you are saying. We disagreed on what to do about the sons, but that was nothing new. The council doesn't tend to agree on anything; unwilling compromise is about the best we can hope for."

She took another drink.

"But this time it went past that, got more intense, quickly. Valasca brought up the idea of going back to the old ways first. I was surprised, her being a hearth-keeper, but then I figured she was older and probably hadn't really agreed with the shift when it happened. For a while she seemed to be the only person who really felt that way, and it seemed like there was no rush on deciding. We did our normal thing, what feels like arguing for argument's sake. Until your mother got pregnant. Then things changed. Padia spoke up; she was for going back to the killing too. Soon Fariba joined her, and one by one they all seemed to follow—everyone but your mother and me."

Padia, the priestess who had called back when I'd tried to contact Kale, who had told Thea I was no longer queen. Things were beginning to fall into place.

"Mother said there were two groups, with the majority in the middle."

Kale swallowed. "She didn't know. They quit talking about it in front of her and I didn't want to tell her. The more determined they became, the more determined she became, and I knew she wasn't going to hand over that baby—no matter the ruling. I should have, though. They tricked her or tried to. Your mother took the baby and ran. She told me she was giving him to his father."

"And she did. That's who we stole him from."

"You stole him?" Her expression sharpened.

"Yes, but we lost him soon after. The sons stole him back . . ." I paused, thinking. "How did the council know where Mateo would be?"

"Mateo?"

"Andres's father . . . the baby's father."

"Oh . . . I don't know. Padia must have run some kind of spell that located him."

"So Padia is behind all this?" A priestess, it made sense.

Kale placed her hand over her eyes as if the early evening light bothered them. "Yes. I don't know why she was so adamant about killing your mother's child, but she was. . . . I don't think . . ." She shook her head and stared at the clumps of green floating in her glass. "What happened to me?" she murmured.

I waited for her to sort out whatever she was going through. "Do you remember anything else? Why you came to the safe camp? When? Do you think someone drugged you?" My mind went to the flask she had dropped when we first entered the clearing.

"Drugged? Could I have been?" she asked. She sat there frowning, seemed lost in her own thoughts. "Drugged . . . that would explain how—" She looked up. "I don't even know how I got here. I remember leaving the Northwest, knowing I needed to find you for some reason, or maybe it was your mother. That would make sense, that I was going to help her keep the baby from Padia, but . . ." Her words faded away. Uncertainty . . . insecurity . . . shone from her eyes. She stared down into the glass. There was only an inch or two of the green liquid left.

"How did I come to this?" she murmured.

My fingers dug into the stuffed cow in my lap. The dog, waiting for me to throw it again, looked up expectantly.

I wondered the same thing as Kale.

How had any of us come to this?

Chapter 20

The sheriff showed up a half hour later. I was still out with the dogs when Bern whistled the alert.

I plucked all three puppies from their box and slapped my leg to call the mother dog to my side. Then I walked quickly in the direction of the main road.

The car, a white sedan with a gold stripe down the side, pulled to the side of the road as I approached. An older man wearing a tan uniform rolled down his window.

"You live around here?" he asked.

I shook my head. "Not lately. My boyfriend owns the house, or what was a house, next door."

"Oh yeah, sorry about that." He cast his glance to the home behind me, then back at me, a question in his eyes.

I smiled. "Damn dog." I gestured to the mother dog

walking beside me. "She disappeared the night of the fire. Jack dropped me off so I could look for her. I found a little something extra."

He laughed. "Looks like you did at that."

I nodded to the runt. "You wouldn't want one, would you?"

He held up his hands. "Not me. Might want to tell your boyfriend he needs to get the bitch fixed, though. Or maybe this will teach him."

With a sigh, I replied, "Maybe."

After a few more questions, ending with me assuring him there was no one around Jack's property or his neighbor's house, he backed the car back out the way he'd come.

The bitch needed to be fixed.

He didn't know how true the statement was. And now, thanks to my conversation with Kale, I knew who the bitch was . . . I just needed to find her.

After the sheriff left, I went to find Mel. She was standing on the other side of the garage talking on her cell phone. Probably looking for privacy. I walked up and stood a couple feet behind her.

Her shoulders tightened, but she didn't turn. She didn't alter her tone, volume, or what she was saying either.

"No more tattoos."

Pause.

"I don't care."

Longer pause.

"Get Peter."

Short pause accented by Mel moving two short angry strides forward.

"Harmony—"

Her daughter must have hung up. Mel muttered a curse and stared at her phone. She started dialing.

I stepped around her, so we were facing. Her expression said to back off.

I didn't. "Is she looking at a full sleeve?"

Mel flicked her eyes upward.

"Neck tattoo, or maybe some kind of mask?"

"This isn't funny." She had lowered her phone, but I could tell by how she was holding it that she was one good breath away from blowing me off the continent so she could recall Harmony and restart their argument. Finally she sighed. "You asked how I could trust Makis with her? Well, I don't—not one hundred percent. I'm new to this too. It's not easy letting go. And I know more than anyone the power tattoos can have. What I don't know is everything about how the sons use them." She pressed the heel of her palm to her forehead. "She says it's purely decoration, on her ankle, but how do I know that?"

I tilted my head in a *do whatever you like* gesture. "If you call her and say no again, she's just going to want it more."

Mel's nostrils flared. I could see she didn't like my answer, but without replying, she shoved the phone into her pocket . . . hard.

Her arms crossed over her chest, she asked, "You just eavesdropping or did something happen?"

It was a little of both, but she knew that. I filled her in on both my conversation with Kale and the sheriff's visit.

"So you think Padia is the problem?"

"Or the hearth-keeper who brought it up first, but since Padia's the one who went after my mother and Andres, she's my guess."

"Unless she's just a minion."

I twisted my lips. I didn't like my theory being batted back at me. "Do you think we should start somewhere else?"

Her eyes sparked. She was laughing at me. "Would it matter?"

I ignored her question. "Can you find her?"

Her mouth opened and snapped closed.

"Bubbe found Kale."

This time when her eyes flashed, it wasn't with amusement. "I'm not Bubbe."

I waited. Mel knew I thought she underestimated herself. I'd always thought that, but in the years we were apart, before being reunited last fall, her talents had grown even more. I wouldn't have been surprised if she could out-priestess her legendary grandmother—not at all.

"I don't have the tools."

"What do you need? Totems?" I pulled the stone lion that hung from a leather cord over my head. "We should have, what? Four of them covered." Mel, Lao, Bern, and myself—none of us shared a clan. "We can get your mother to borrow the others from camp."

Mel stared at the lion, then turned on her heel without taking it. "Give me an hour."

I spent the hour getting in some fighting practice with Bern and Jack. The son had never used a weapon with me. I'd stupidly thought he couldn't.

I was wrong.

He decided to teach me a game he'd watched as a child. He stood fifteen feet away armed with twelve knives. My job was to dodge them as he threw.

Without warning, he began to throw . . . so quickly it seemed as if they were all thrown at once with no more than seconds between each.

I rolled. Three dug into the dirt where I'd been. I leapt to my feet, jumping in the same motion so my knees reached my chest. Two more zinged beneath me. I landed hard, but on my feet, and threw myself to the side as two more flew toward me. Five remained, and I was winded. I lunged for my staff; two more grazed my skin, one cutting a hole in my shorts.

Staff in hand, I bounded back to my feet and batted the last three, which were zipping toward my heart out of the air.

"You cheated," he said.

"And you didn't give full disclosure," I replied. Sweat dripped down my neck, soaking my workout top. I shifted the staff in front of me, unwilling to put it down. "What exactly is your talent?"

He walked to where three of the knives lay buried in the dirt and jerked them out. With his eyes on me he began to juggle—faster and faster until the flashing blades were nothing but one solid silver blur.

"Maybe you should ask what I did as a child. What my father did."

I moved the staff again, into a position where I could easily deflect another knife if needed . . . or try. "Clown?" I offered.

"Close. Carny. Worked the sideshows. My mother, my adoptive mother, was the living target."

"How sweet." I twirled the staff. "Why haven't I seen you use knives before?"

"Because . . ." The spinning blur slowed. He jerked his hands to the side and all three blades sank into the ground. "I didn't need to."

Bern stood to the side throughout the exchange, her expression unreadable. With his comment, she grunted and began gathering up the rest of the knives.

I tapped my staff against the side of my foot, unsure how or if to respond.

Mel stepping around the side of the house saved me from my dilemma.

"I'm ready." Two words and she was gone, back in the direction she'd come.

Still holding my staff, I walked past Jack. His voice followed me. "And I did offer to show you my talents. You just haven't taken me up on it." His voice sizzled with promise. My libido sizzled in return but, eyes focused on the corner Mel had disappeared behind, I kept walking.

Mel was sitting in the dirt between the detached garage and the house. In front of her was a small fire, surrounded by a ring of rocks. Beside her was a stack of papers.

As I got closer, I could see a *telíos* was drawn on each sheet. She handed them to me. "Do you know Padia's?"

I stiffened. I didn't, of course. I looked at Mel.

With a patient sigh, she said, "We can do it by process of elimination, but it will take longer."

We were able to cross off the four high council *telíoses* I knew were represented by warriors, but that still left eight.

Mel handed me the stack of papers.

"Put one under each rock, except the first that we're hoping is Padia's. Hand that one back to me."

I did as she asked, glancing at the fire as I did.

She stared at me. "Just because you think I should be able to do something or want me to be able to do something doesn't mean I can. Bubbe doesn't need the fire. I do . . ." She shook her head. "Even with the fire, I don't know if I can do what she did . . . there might be a delay, or I might get nothing at all."

I had faith in her. I pulled out the sheet with the hawk on it and handed it to her, then sat down, out of her way.

Like her grandmother, she chanted. Unlike her grandmother, it was in English, but it didn't matter. I couldn't follow her words. She fed the sheet I'd given her into the fire, and I concentrated on the smoke that streamed from its blaze.

It took six tries before we got a hit. Even then I wasn't sure at first if the spell was working. The smoke looked like what you'd expect from any fire, drifting with the slight breeze that blew along the alley formed by the house and garage. But the sixth time it began to snake, forming shapes I could almost, but not quite, identify.

I wanted to reach out and grab the dancing shapes, hold them so I could study them at leisure, but as quickly as one solidified, it would mist away.

Then the smoke thickened, so solid I swore I could pluck the shape from the fire. I went so far as to hold out my hand and felt the heat on my fingertips before my brain registered what I was seeing—an obelisk, a house, trees . . . The shapes continued to morph, but I'd seen enough. . . .

I looked at Mel.

She was staring back at me.

"She's here."

While Mel went about extinguishing the fire, I rocked back onto my heels.

Padia was at the safe camp. How long had she been there? Kale had been at the camp; at least I assumed she had been at the house before going to the obelisk. She should have recognized the other high-council member, but her memory of everything after leaving the North-west was missing.

My mind flashed to the flask Kale had been holding when we found her. Maybe she had been drugged. Maybe it had blocked that bit of time from her brain.

But it hadn't eliminated Padia from Kale's memory completely. Kale still remembered the council member, still knew she was behind all of this. Which meant Kale should still recognize Padia when she saw her.

I went to look for the other warrior.

I got as far as the backyard, where Jack seemed to be showing Bern how to juggle the knives, when a body burst through the trees.

It was Tess, her shirt sticking to her with sweat and her shorts stained with mud and grass. It looked as if she'd fought her way through the forest.

She came to a halt a few feet away, her body jerking as she searched for breath.

"Mels . . . they're planning an attack."

I didn't react to her statement, couldn't afford to. "Where's Cleo?" I asked, holding up my hand to keep the questions I could see burning in Jack's and Bern's eyes at bay.

Tess's eyes grew huge. "A new priestess arrived. She held some kind of ceremony, said there was a spy at camp. Then when she saw Cleo, she recognized her, knew she was related to Mel. They took her . . . Cleo, I mean . . . and dragged her off. I'm not sure where."

Padia. Mel was right. She was here. But it didn't sound like she had been here long. I'd been wondering if Thea might be Padia, but Tess's announcement laid that suspicion to rest, at least.

I glanced at the hearth-keeper. "Cleo's not at camp?"

Tess hesitated, then shook her head. "I don't think so. I'm not sure."

"Who? What has happened?" Mel appeared, her knees covered in dust and ash in her hair.

"They caught your mother. They know she's been spying on them."

"We have to get her," she replied, her voice matter-of-fact.

"There's more." I gestured to Tess.

The girl swallowed and repeated what she'd already said. "I think they may be taking Cleo with them, as some kind of trade or bait."

I frowned. "So you don't think she's at the camp?"

She shook her head, hard. "No, sorry . . . with the excitement . . . I'm getting confused."

I was too, but there wasn't time for that. Trying to keep my voice as neutral as possible so as not to rattle her more, I asked, "This new priestess . . . does she have a name?"

"Uh . . ." She looked around . . . looked afraid.

"Padia?" Kale asked. She'd come around the other corner of the house, having apparently been for a walk. I was glad to see it, glad she was recovering.

Lao appeared in the open doorway of the house.

"Yes, Padia. That's her name." Tess nodded and

glanced toward Lao. When the older hearth-keeper's gaze fell on her, she looked away.

Kale hopped from the porch onto the ground. "We need to stop her."

Her color was stronger and there was a glint in her eyes. She outranked me too, but I didn't let that factor into what I had to do.

I faced Kale. "We are going to Mel's."

"Are you sure we shouldn't go after Padia? If we get to her, we can undo everything she's done. I could go alone."

"No. There are some things that can't be undone." Death being the biggest one. If we went after Padia, and someone, anyone at Mel's paid the price . . . I bit down on my cheek. It wasn't an option. For once I was going to think about individuals before the tribe. "We need everyone."

Kale's jaw tightened. She glanced at Tess as if the hearth-keeper might offer something to strengthen her case, but Tess only stared back. Finally Kale nodded.

Glad I wasn't going to have to fight a battle here before going to fight whoever awaited us at Mel's, I started yelling orders. We had our weapons packed and were ready to go in ten minutes. We left the dogs behind with food and water. Everyone else piled into the truck. With Cleo missing, the car was missing. The truck was all we had, and we had no time to steal another vehicle. Kale, Lao, and Tess got the cab. Jack, Bern, Mel, and I lay flat in the bed. Only truckers and RVs would be able to see us there. We covered ourselves with an old tarp and hoped no one would notice us, or if they did, wouldn't bother to call in and report us.

The worry didn't keep me awake. I took advantage of the trip and the dark that had fallen to grab a couple hours of sleep. It would be early when we arrived at Mel's . . . barely dawn.

It seemed a good time for an attack.

I would be ready.

Chapter 21

I saw the birder as soon as we pulled into Mel's lot. Jack saw her too; I felt him stiffen beside me, but I beat him out of the truck. I threw myself over the side and was running toward the building where the older woman stood, a canvas bag over her arm, before Lao had even brought the truck to a stop. The woman saw me coming; her skin paled. I'd grabbed Bern's nunchakus as I'd leapt. They'd been loose on the floor and easy to reach.

I spun them over my head now but resisted the urge to yell. Just because I could only see the one birder didn't mean there weren't more. I expected there to be more, and I didn't want to alert them.

Kill this one, then move on to the next. That was my plan.

The nunchakus were spinning, the whirring noise they made reassuring and restful. Focused and ready, I prepared to strike.

Something hit me from the back, someone . . . big and strong, bigger and possibly stronger than me.

I tried to twist, to lash at my attacker with the weapon, but a second assailant joined the fight. A staff jabbed me in the trachea, cutting off my breath.

"Stand down! She's not a birder. Stand down!" Jack's voice, yelling in my ear. Adrenaline rushing through me, I gripped one end of the nunchaku in my closed fist and pummeled it into his skull.

Then suddenly a weight like a lead blanket dropped on top of me, on top of Jack too. He cursed softly. Only my face was free of the suffocating heaviness. I twisted my neck, searching for whoever had brought this new weapon into the mix.

Bubbe stood over me, her face upside-down in my view.

Her lips pursed, she made *tching* noise. "You kill my clients, it make it very hard for me to keep my business, *dorogaya.*

Client. Stand down. The words mixed in my head. Jack's attack and the staff jabbing against my throat. I closed my eyes and counted to ten. With my emotions under control, I opened them. "Let me up."

The weight disappeared and so did Jack.

I moved to my feet. The birder or, rather, the old woman who I had thought was a birder, stood hidden behind Bern, only the tip of her canvas bag and the corner of her purple shorts visible. Both were shaking.

With a sigh, Bubbe left me and went to comfort her customer. I made out a few murmured words, a spell, I guessed, and the woman seemed fine . . . or at least she didn't scream when Bern stepped away, leaving me a clear view of her.

She still looked like a birder to me. Her shorts came to her knees and she wore practical white-laced shoes. Her shirt was pink with a robin on the front, and her bag bulged with what could easily have been a stash of handguns or bombs.

I took a step, thinking to question her if no one else would. Mel dropped the staff in front of me, rapped me in the gut.

"I know her. Bubbe knows her. This entire neighborhood knows her. She was Harmony's principal for four years. She is not a birder—"

The woman reached into the bag.

My muscles coiled, ready.

She pulled out a pair of binoculars and slipped the cord attached to them around her neck.

Mel sighed. "Okay, She isn't one of *your* birders. She watches birds. The Arboretum is across the street. Lots of people watch birds there."

I kept vigilant, focused on the octogenarian. Older, perhaps, than some, but aside from that she looked exactly like the birders who had killed my mother.

Mel tapped me in the stomach again. "We're here because of Amazons, remember? Besides, you can't jump on every old lady with a pair of binoculars and leather walkers."

Amazons. Right, we were here because Tess had heard the Amazons were planning an attack on Mel's.

Still, I glanced again at the old woman in the robin shirt. "Check her bag," I ordered.

Mel rolled her eyes but marched off. After a few gentle words to the woman, she returned with her canvas bag. "Organic trail mix, an aluminum bottle of water, and a field guide. Satisfied?"

I wasn't. "Open the bottle." If I was going to do this right, I wasn't trusting anything.

Turning her back so the woman couldn't see what she was doing, Mel twisted the lid off the bottle and took a sniff. Her nose twitched.

I leaned forward, ready.

"You're right. It's not water. It's lemonade, with a kick . . . vodka, I'd guess." She screwed the lid back on and stared at me. "Okay?"

Still not completely satisfied, I waved her away.

In a few minutes the could-be birder was gone.

Leaving me to face an annoyed Bubbe and an amused Mel.

I passed both of them. At the corner of the building I took a right and kept walking. I walked the entire perimeter of the property before coming back to where the rest of them waited.

I gestured for Bern to join me and headed toward the gym/cafeteria. The building should be vacant; I wanted to make sure it was.

Mel and her grandmother stopped me. Standing shoulder to shoulder, the family resemblance was striking, or maybe it was just the grim set of their faces.

"You think perhaps we could discuss what is happening, what our plan is? And how we can accomplish it without assaulting any more customers?" Mel twisted the staff she still held in the dirt.

I stared her down. "Easy. Close down. Send everyone home."

With Bern right behind me, I continued on into the cafeteria.

We moved as quickly as we could through the building, hitting the main floor . . . cafeteria, kitchen, and gym first, then moving to the basement where the showers and a few offices were. The place was empty. It didn't appear anyone had been inside since my last visit.

Reassured, we exited out the front. Mel was waiting for me. "Let's get Bubbe to put some kind of ward on the doors and windows," I told her.

She twisted the staff parallel, then perpendicular to her body. "You think we hadn't done that before?"

"We got in," I reminded her.

"We know you, and for reasons I'm beginning to doubt, trust you." She stalked toward the main building.

I followed her into the basement where the rest of our group, along with Mateo, Dana, and both babies had gathered. Bern stayed outside and once I appeared, Lao joined her. They would watch for anything suspicious while the rest of us talked.

Tess started, repeating what she had told me about the safe camp's plans. When Padia's name came up, Kale jumped in to explain who she was.

As Tess got to the part of her story where she said Cleo had been captured, all eyes turned to Bubbe.

She held out her hands. "My daughter, she will prevail." And that was it. The old priestess seemed more worried with watching how Mateo held his son than with whether Cleo would survive being captured by the tribe.

I took this as a good sign.

"Zery wants us to close the shop—all of our businesses." Mel had stood against the wall most of the conversation, only now stepping closer. Dana, sitting cross-legged on the floor and holding Pisto, looked up, her interest clear.

"For how long? We have a class tomorrow." She glanced at Mel. "Mateo has been filling in for Cleo."

I stared at a dot on the wall for the count of three. Artemis forbid the mommy half of her "mommy and me" class missed a few situps.

"I think that is wise." Bubbe, agreeing with me again.

I looked at the old priestess, wondering why exactly she and Mel didn't get along better.

Dana started to object, but Bubbe stood her ground. "This is not human business, not what has happened here recently. We do not have the right to pull them into it, to risk they be hurt." She looked at me then, her gaze old, heavy, and judging.

I glanced at Mel. She raised an unsympathetic brow.

"What about the babies?" Tess, her voice meek, glanced around the group. "Shouldn't we get them somewhere else? Take them somewhere safe?"

It was a good point, one I hadn't thought of before. I looked at Mateo. "She's right. You and Dana need to leave with the babies while things are still calm."

"Except . . ." Tess held up her hand like she was in some human schoolroom.

I acknowledged her with a stare.

"Padia . . . she mentioned him . . ." Tess shifted her attention to Mateo, then back at me. ". . . had a description. The camp will be looking for him, know he has the baby."

Mateo stood. He looked strange, so tall and long limbed, holding a tiny infant pressed to his shoulder. "I am also the most qualified to protect my son."

"Avoiding the enemy is the best protection. Would you risk him being attacked because your pride said to stay with him?" If the tribe knew of Mateo and were looking for him, separating him and Andres made the most sense.

The bird son snapped his lips together. I could tell he didn't like my answer but also saw the wisdom in what I said.

"Who wouldn't they be looking for?" I asked, glancing around the room.

Tess raised her hand again. "Who would you least suspect?"

Hearth-keepers, the most likely of any of the talent groups to be entrusted with the care of a child, but the least likely to be given something others would kill for. And Andres wasn't a child to these Amazons, he was something to kill and kill for.

Thea would never expect me to send him with unaccompanied hearth-keepers. She wouldn't be watching for them; she'd be watching for me or Mateo.

Maybe not the perfect plan, but the best we had.

We sent Dana and Tess off in one of Mel's cars. No one at the safe camp, or Padia had seen the vehicle. Dana, like Mel, had a cell phone so we would be able to contact them when everything was over.

With them gone, the rest of us got ready for battle.

Mel closed her shop, telling her office manager a family emergency had come up and asking her to call the shop's clients to reschedule—from home.

With the shop empty and no fitness or fortune-telling customers on the property, we got to work.

Bubbe and Mel set wards. If anything bigger than a seagull entered Mel's property, they would know it. The person or animal wouldn't, however, know that we knew. Sitting in the middle of a city like Madison, we couldn't just zap trespassers. Which meant no deadly force—Mel insisted and I let her win.

I doubted she would have set the wards I wanted anyway, making my arguments rather pointless.

We set up watch and central command in the gym.

But knowing the basement or living quarters of the main shop was where they would expect to find the baby, Jack and I hid there. I took the basement, Cleo's workout room. Jack took the living quarters, Mel's bedroom.

Then we waited.

I have never been good at waiting. Playing sentry is an important part of warrior training but not one I'd excelled at . . . but, then, queens didn't have to be good at waiting and guarding; our role was usually more active. Pursue and defeat, that was my preference.

After three hours I was battling myself to keep from climbing the walls. I'd given up on just sitting, waiting, and listening, and allowed myself the luxury of lifting the occasional silent weight as I paced.

At four hours, I began to wonder if somehow I'd missed something, if there might be a battle raging or one already raged, that hidden in the basement, I'd somehow missed. Bubbe's and Mel's wards were supposed to notify me. I wasn't sure how that notification was to come, but I hadn't felt so much as a twinge or seen anything that could be taken as a message.

At five hours, I crept out of the room and up the stairs. First I checked the front doors. There was no sign of anyone, friend or foe, on the front lawn, which meant either my group was staying hidden as ordered or they'd all been killed and toted off while I paced alone in the basement.

I kept going, past the shop level to the upstairs where Mel lived and Jack was supposed to be waiting too.

I checked the kitchen and living room as I walked past . . . empty. I didn't open the rooms with doors, not until I came to Mel's.

The door wasn't latched; I pushed it open with my foot. The room was small and sparsely decorated—just a few childhood scribbles of Harmony's taped to the walls, a staff hanging over the bed, and a bag that I guessed contained either priestess or artisan tools hanging from a peg behind the door. The room had a second door too, one that led to the fire escape. It was open.

I cursed softly, sure now that I'd missed something.

I grabbed Mel's staff, hoping I'd find someone on my side who could still use it.

Then I stepped out into the noon sun and was blinded by the flash of steel.

My practice with Jack, fresh in my mind and my instincts, I ducked and kicked. My foot found its target; I was rewarded with a grunt. I grabbed blindly for the head I knew would be low now and pulled it toward my stomach. Then, falling backward, I used my leg to catapult my attacker up and over the low railing of the fire escape.

Back on my feet, I prepared to jump down on the body lying on the ground below . . . the male body . . . Jack.

Mateo stepped from behind a tree, looked down at the son I'd just thrown two stories, then up at me.

With a curse, I vaulted over the railing, landing on the ground beside them in a crouch.

"Now you see the benefits of wings over teeth." The bird son nudged Jack with his boot.

Jack rolled over, blood streamed from one nostril. He touched two fingers to his nose and groaned. "Again," he muttered.

I held my breath of relief, then covered my reaction by prodding him with the staff. "I didn't cheat this time."

He grunted.

Feeling generous, I looked away, leaving him to get back to a stand-alone, unobserved and with at least a pretense of dignity.

I addressed Mateo. "What have you seen?"

"*Nada*. Until Jack tried to fly without wings." He glanced over my shoulder, to where Jack was still struggling to stand. His expression was a mix of mocking amusement and disappointment.

"And the others?" I asked.

He glanced at me, his brown eyes annoyed. "I have seen no one, heard nothing."

Jack was standing now. He walked to the fire escape and scuttled up the stairs. In a few minutes he was back, four knives shoved into his belt and two in his hands. Blood was smeared across his face where he had wiped at it. His shoulders were squared and there was a determination in his stride.

"I haven't seen or heard a thing . . . except you," he said. His eyes held a challenge, a request for a rematch. Something I'd gladly give him when all this was over and settled.

We split up. Mateo took the west side of the property line; Jack and I headed east. At the walkway between the two buildings we split again, Jack going between the two, me past and around the far side of the gym.

I found Bern there, silent and still as a statue. She didn't look as if she'd moved an inch in hours, didn't move more than her eyes when I approached, but at my signal she fell into line beside me.

We walked the full eastern length, out to Monroe Street, then cut across the front yard and made our way back to the shop.

Mateo, Lao, Mel, Jack, Kale, and Bubbe were waiting on the shop's steps.

No one had heard or seen anything in the six hours that had passed.

"Do you think Tess heard wrong? Perhaps the attack wasn't planned for today," Mel offered, but I could see the unease in her eyes and I understood it. I'd ordered us to come here rather than storming the camp and taking Padia.

"Perhaps the plan is not real." Bubbe held a smooth stone in her hand; she rubbed it in a circular motion with her thumb as she spoke.

"When did the birders attack?" Jack reminded us. "When would you plan an attack?"

Night . . . the answer to both.

I sighed. Which meant we had to wait more.

Accepting this, we downgraded our status and left Jack and Bubbe outside this time to watch for signs of the tribe. Bubbe went to the front yard and proceeded to work through a variety of yoga poses . . . a strange sight given her age and choice of clothing—a bright red full-length dress with lots of embroidery. As she hiked the skirt to her knees to perform one pose, I turned and watched Jack climb the large oak that grew alongside the shop. Once in the branches, he was completely hidden, at least from my point of view.

With our lookouts positioned, the rest of us went inside, to the shop level. Mateo headed to the phone.

Placing my hand on top of the receiver, I stopped him. "What are you doing?"

"Calling to check on my son."

Realizing we did need to let Tess and Dana know what had happened or not happened here, I removed my hand.

Dana must have answered. He asked about Andres, then cursed in Spanish.

"How long?" His complexion darkened. "*Sí*, find them." He glared at me.

I jerked the phone from his hand.

Dana was on the other end blathering something about a diaper change and going to the bathroom now. Then she whispered, "They aren't here. I know this is where she said she was going, but they aren't here."

It took five minutes to figure out what had happened.

They'd left Mel's and driven to a truck stop between here and Illinois. They'd been there the entire time. At first they had stayed together, Dana following Tess when she took Andres for a diaper change or even once to buy a can of formula, but as the time went on and there was no sign anyone had followed them, they'd relaxed some too.

When Tess had said she was going to buy diapers and then change Andres, Dana, busy feeding her own son, had let her go alone.

That had been ten minutes earlier.

While we waited, Dana searched the truck stop and came up empty. Then she checked the lot and saw the car was gone too.

I slammed down the receiver.

Mateo was already moving; by the time I got into the front yard he'd already shifted and was flying toward the truck stop.

Yelling for Bern and Mel to follow me, I ran toward the truck.

Chapter 22

Mateo beat us to the truck stop; I could see him circling overhead. A few locals saw him too.

Binoculars and rifles with scopes were out and pointed at the sky. A fight almost broke out when someone, thinking he was an endangered species, threatened to call Wisconsin Department of Natural Resources.

I stood in the open, in clear view, hoping Mateo would see we had arrived and back off.

He did, but not before plummeting toward the building, shrieking as he fell. Ten feet from the ground he pulled back abruptly and soared back into the sky.

As I watched, he flew south. He'd be waiting for us, and he was pissed.

And I couldn't blame him.

I went looking for Dana.

She was sitting in a stained faded-blue booth with two baby carriers and one baby: Pisto. And she was crying. Not horrible gulping sobs, worse—steady slow drips.

And that was before she knew I was there. She was looking down, holding a pacifier to her son's mouth when I walked in. Her chin and the hand holding the pacifier were both shaking.

Mel stopped me from going further, cutting me off and approaching the distraught hearth-keeper herself. Dana fell against her.

"I know you told us to stay together, but it had been so long and we had all this stuff . . . and it's hard, but that's not an excuse—"

Mel shoved the girl's face against her chest, cutting off whatever other blubbering admittance she had to make.

I turned on my heel and left the building.

When I got outside, the rest of our group was waiting. They were in a four-door domestic that looked like it got about five miles to the gallon.

Mel stepped into the parking lot, loaded down with a baby bag and empty carrier. Dana trailed behind her, with the other carrier and her son.

"Makis's," Mel commented, looking at the car. "He doesn't drive it much. Left it with us to watch while he was gone. I didn't realize anyone knew where I kept the keys." She glared at Bubbe, who was barely visible behind the wheel.

She looked like every old lady you curse when trying

to make it across town in a hurry. Except as Mel marched forward, she gunned the engine in warning.

Mel rapped on the window.

While she and her grandmother argued, I addressed Dana. Her tears were gone, or at least they weren't flowing down her cheeks now. I took the baby carrier and led her to a park bench that sat in the grass a few feet from the parking lot.

"What happened?"

She told me pretty much what I'd heard on the phone. "Th-they must have followed us, b-been waiting for us to separate," she stuttered.

Jack walked up behind me. I glanced at him over my shoulder. His gaze flitted to mine and I saw my thoughts mirrored there. *Maybe, but why wait? It wasn't like a priestess of Padia's rank would fear taking on two run-of-the-mill hearth-keepers.*

We, I suspected, had been had. What I didn't know was by whom.

It was a long drive back to Illinois. Felt long anyway.

There had been some discussion of returning to Mel's, but none of us thought that attack was going to happen, not with Tess and Andres already missing.

No, the battle was in Illinois, probably had been all along.

It was time to return to my camp.

We left Dana and Pisto at Jack's neighbor's house.

The rest of us split into two groups.

Lao, Kale, and I would approach the camp directly,

walk in like we had every right to be there . . . which we did. We would try talking first, see if Kale's story convinced the Amazons that Padia had misled them, and that the high council they were following wasn't the high council at all but a rogue portion of it.

While we talked, the rest would come through the woods. They would search the outdoor areas, including the barn, for Cleo, Tess, and the baby. They would also be there to jump in if a battle broke out.

I couldn't imagine words would fix this, though, couldn't imagine a battle wouldn't break out.

I packed the truck and my body accordingly.

Lao drove. Kale and I rode in the back, ready to jump out and fight without doors slowing us down.

It was a silent trip down the bumpy drive, a drive I'd traveled too many times to count, but only one other time as an outsider.

An outsider among Amazons.

There was a time I'd have chosen death over that.

Things were quiet outside the safe house, but not normal, not completely.

The horses were in the paddock, looking as if they hadn't been ridden or groomed since we left. The gardens looked unkempt too. Nothing horribly noticeable, we hadn't been gone that long, just small things . . . a watering can left turned over on its side in the middle of a row of beans, mud caked in a few of the mares' tails, and no smells of cooking coming from the kitchens. It was after one on a Monday, bread baking day; the yard should have smelled of baking yeast and wheat.

As we climbed out of the truck, I glanced at Lao. She was frowning. She'd noticed too.

There were signs of life, however. Someone had set up a loom on the front porch, and there was a stack of spears fifty or so feet from the house plus a target hanging on a tree.

And then there were the two men in cable uniforms walking out the front door.

Thea was behind them. One man held a clipboard out for her signature. She signed it and watched them get into a white truck before turning to me.

"Zery, you came back."

She seemed unconcerned. She was studying Kale, who had walked a few feet away, and had her back to the priestess.

"Where is the tribe?" I asked.

Thea's eyes jumped, her focus shifting from Kale to me. "Inside. We've been doing some upgrades. There is a lot to learn." With a frown, she looked back at Kale.

I bristled at her disregard and the idea that she was bringing technology into my safe camp without my permission, but knew stating that now would get us nowhere.

Instead, I stepped forward. "You've met Kale." I stated it as fact. We'd found Kale at Artemis's obelisk.

Whether she remembered it or not, she had to have come from camp. I hoped her intense scrutiny of the place now meant the visit was coming back to her.

I glanced at the council member who was staring at the house.

"Kale . . ." Thea glanced around.

At her name, the warrior turned. As her eyes passed over Thea, her lips moved slightly. She spoke, but I couldn't make out her words.

Lines formed on Thea's forehead; she pressed fingers to them. "Why are you here, Zery? I don't know anyone named Kale."

After closing her eyes briefly, she took a breath and looked back at me. "Are you here to say you've decided to follow the high council's directive, to beg for a place back in the tribe?"

My hand lowered to my belt. I'd placed one of Jack's knives in a sheath there earlier. It was in clear view. I wasn't trying to hide that I was prepared to fight. "I wasn't aware I had left the tribe, only this house."

"Hmmm. Is that how you see it?" Thea shifted her eyes over the three of us and seemed to miss Kale's presence entirely. "How about you, Lao? You'd really choose one weak queen over the tribe you've helped to birth and raise?"

Tired of Thea's passive-aggressive insults, I touched the knife's handle. "Where are Tess and Andres?"

The priestess sighed. "Tess I know, but Andres?" Her voice was bored, almost condescending.

"The baby, the one you want to kill."

Her eyes flashed, but her body posture remained non-threatening. "You mean the one *the Amazons* want to kill, the one the high council *ordered* us to kill?"

"That would be the one. Have you seen him and Tess?"

"If I had, the job would have been done."

Kale stepped forward. "We know Padia's here."

Thea looked at her as if she'd forgotten the council member was standing next to me. "Padia here?" There was surprise in her voice.

Tense, I responded. "The visiting priestess. We know she was here. Does she have Tess and Andres?"

Thea growled. "I know who Padia is. She isn't here. You would know if she was. I would—"

I cut her off. "We have a new enemy, Thea, and it isn't the sons."

She laughed. "Not the sons? Don't tell me, you've been seduced like your friend? Have you been visiting her? Associating with sons?" Her voice rose, incredulous. "I knew you'd fallen, that you were too weak to carry out the council's orders, but I wouldn't have thought that of you."

I jerked Jack's knife from its sheath and held it under her chin. "We are here to get Tess, Andres, and Cleo. Turn them over."

Her eyes sparked. "I already told you Tess and the baby aren't here. Maybe she took the little mutant. Maybe she has the strength to do what you didn't."

This barb took, sank into my subconscious and ate away at it. Could Tess have taken Andres? Could she have been lying to us, deceiving us all along?

"And Cleo?"

"Cleo, the new warrior? Why would you want her?" Bored, polite, and well-mannered.

Her manner gnawed at me, worse than any direct insult.

The porch had filled with Amazons. I leaned closer to the priestess. Hissed in her ear, "Padia lied to you, Thea."

Louder, I repeated, "She's lied to all of you. Padia may be a member of the high council, but she isn't the only member. She's told you the high council is in agreement, but they aren't. I've brought a council member here, to tell you the other side." I nodded at Kale but kept my eyes focused on Thea.

I waited, expecting Kale to step forward and declare who she was, to force the deluded Amazons to listen, to out Padia and the Amazons who followed her for their worship of another goddess.

Thea's voice rose. "Why would you come here with such stories? Are you that desperate to regain the role you lost?"

The priestess was still talking. "I told you we would accept you back as a warrior, but that isn't good enough, is it? You failed as queen, failed the council, and thus failed the tribe. Time to face that, Zery. Time to face you will never regain the role again."

Her voice was strong, with a shade of sympathy, but

her eyes were cold, like the metal blade posed inches from her artery. *You've cracked, Zery. Cracked.*

The thought sprang from nowhere.

Startled, I glanced at Thea's eyes. They were steady and still cold. *Admit you aren't strong. Don't embarrass yourself and your tribe.*

My hand began to shake. A pain, concentrated and sharp, like a knitting needle being thrust through my brain, cut off my breath. Sweat broke out on my upper lip. I wanted to drop the knife, to cradle my head in my hands.

What was happening?

As the pain probed deeper, the priestess's eyes seemed to bore into me. Doubt sprang up from somewhere so deep inside me I hadn't known it existed.

The knife in my hand wavered, down . . . sideways. At first I thought it was nerves, my indecision showing. I tightened my muscles and ordered my body to obey my will. My bicep throbbed with a new pain, one I recognized from hard workouts and long battles, but I continued my struggle to stop the knife from its erratic jumping. I stared at it, unable to comprehend what was happening. The weapon was moving, but unguided by me, despite me.

Thea smiled, a calm, sweet smile, nothing menacing at all . . . I doubled my effort, the blade stilled for a second, then jerked again.

Thea's smile widened. Her eyes were laughing as she glanced down at the weapon. She found my predicament amusing, found me amusing. If the knife had been free, I would have pierced her through the heart without a flicker of hesitation.

There was a swirl of movement beside me. Caught up in what was happening, I'd forgotten I wasn't alone. So, it appeared, had Thea.

Lao, the hearth-keeper who before this adventure I'd thought of as someone to fold laundry, fix a broken washer, or order weeds to be pulled in the garden, curled her hand into a fist and slugged the high priestess with a short uppercut to the chin.

Thea's head shot up and her mouth dropped open. Her eyes wide and shocked, she fell back a step.

Feeling the release as clearly as if a rope had held me in place and been cut, I staggered.

Thea lowered her chin and opened her mouth to say . . . something. The words never came. The hearth-keeper balled up her fist and struck her again.

Blood leaked from the corner of Thea's mouth. The passive amusement disappeared. Her face drawn and angry, she circled her arm behind her head. The earth under my feet shifted. I knew immediately what was coming.

I shoved Lao back and covered her with my body. Rocks sprang from the ground. Thea moved again, this time making a throwing motion. Stones, sticks, and dirt pummeled into the truck behind us.

Another raise of her hand and the Amazons who had remained standing on the porch, watching, rushed forward. They dove at us, hearth-keepers, warriors, and artisans. The group seemed to have doubled since we had left.

I didn't know where they had come from or why, but it didn't matter. Innocent or fully knowledgeable of what was happening, they were all at this moment my enemy. And there were four of them for each of us.

Victory gleamed from Thea's eyes.

For all of five seconds.

Then arrows pierced the ground around us.

Thea whirled and cursed.

Bubbe stood in the front of the paddock, her red dress swirling and billowing. She dropped her bow and raised her arms, wind growing around her as she did.

Bern and Mel, astride horses, held bows too. Nocking new arrows, they kneed the animals forward into a gallop and leapt over the fence. They slid to the side, hung hidden behind their horse's necks, only the tops of their legs and the length of Mel's hair, dangling below, visible from this angle.

Jack and Mateo jumped from the roof to the ground on our side of the fence. Jack was the first to reach the Amazons, the first to strike. He jerked a knife from his belt and threw it as he ran.

A warrior, a female I didn't know but an Amazon all the same, crumpled, struck through the heart.

For an instant my world froze . . . instinct and logic warring inside me. One of my own had fallen, been killed by a son. A lifetime of loyalty said that was wrong. I stared at the knife in my hand, not sure what to do, who to attack.

Friend or foe? Who was who? When did it stop being simple?

Another warrior jerked the knife from her fallen companion's chest and pulled back her arm, ready to launch it back at the son. I didn't think; I didn't let myself.

I acted . . . my knife struck . . . two warriors down.

Thea spun and screamed, "Traitor! I thought it before, but here is the proof!" The stack of spears rose and turned . . . pointed toward us . . . me. There was death in her eyes . . . directed at me.

I ran away from Kale and Lao, praying I was right, praying the spears would follow.

They did. One by one they shot toward me like they were being flung by a catapult. I dove and leapt, not pausing from one movement to the next. I put what I'd learned with Jack into practice, let instinct guide each motion.

Beyond me, the two groups fought; knives flashed; staffs twirled. There were yells and screams. I couldn't tell from whom or why. My attention wavered. A spear grazed my neck, then shot through the length of my hair.

I cursed and rolled again, only to see another spear hurtling toward me. My breath was ragged.

I was losing a battle I hadn't even been allowed to fight. I cursed myself then, my own stupidity. I'd let the enemy define the conflict—a beginner's mistake, a mistake that could kill you. I flipped into a somersault but didn't come out, kept going toward the spears rather than away. Didn't stop until I was in the middle of the struggle and a sword was within my reach.

I grabbed it and spun; adrenaline pumped through me. Thea stalked toward me, her lips moving, but Areto cut her off, a sword in her hand.

I smiled at my old student and wondered if her time under Thea had served her well.

She jabbed. I parried. She jabbed again. Our swords met; metal slid over metal until the crossguards met. She stared into my eyes. "The barn. Look in the barn."

Then she stepped back, her eyes dead, her body poised to continue the fight.

The barn.

I spun and slapped her against the wrist with the flat of my blade. She dropped her sword and fell to the ground as if struck.

A horse flew toward me, with Bern on his back. I tossed her the sword. Still moving, she grabbed it midair. I ran and jumped, using both hands to propel myself into place behind her on the animal. "The barn," I yelled. "Cleo is in the barn."

Swinging the sword at Areto, who had recovered her own, Bern nodded, then reined the horse toward the barn and kneed him back into a gallop.

As we raced by Bubbe, I yelled, "Hold them off."

The sound of air whooshing and Amazons yelling told me the old priestess was hard at work.

The barn was dark and smelled of wet hay. There were bales piled up to the rafters.

As Bern slowed the horse to a walk, I glanced back over my shoulder. Bubbe had called up a wind and was spinning it into a shield, the Amazons on one side, my allies on the other. Mel had joined her, spinning a buckler of her own, smaller than her grandmother's but more agile. It darted around, following any Amazon who thought to work her way around Bubbe's magic.

The others watched, tense, ready if the priestess's magic faltered.

"We checked here. We didn't see anyone," Bern said, pointing with the sword.

"Areto said she was here."

Bern's nostrils flared. "Maybe she lied."

I could see Bern hadn't forgiven Areto for choosing Thea over me . . . over us, but there had been a light in Areto's eyes, an apology. I believed her.

I slid off the horse and approached the hay. "When we were little, we made fortresses out of the hay. Did you ever do that, Bern?" It was a rhetorical question. I really couldn't imagine Bern as anything except the warrior she was today.

I climbed onto the stack and grabbed the first bale by its twine wrapping.

I tossed it down. It landed next to the warrior. She pulled back on the reins, making the horse step back, and eyed the pile of bales.

I knew what she was thinking: that even an Amazon couldn't survive with a ton of hay stacked on top of her.

I tossed another bale onto the ground.

Kale appeared in the open doorway. "Padia has to be here somewhere. Maybe she's hiding inside the house, with Tess and the baby. We should search there."

Holding a bale, I grunted. The twine dug into my fingers. Normally you wore gloves for work like this.

"How are Mel and Bubbe doing?" I asked. I'd moved four bales now and saw no sign there was anything hidden in the pile except more hay, and maybe a snake or three.

Kale frowned. She took a step toward the house, but Mel and Bubbe were blocking her path. She cursed and looked back at me.

Bern, however, answered. "Holding," she said. "Should we attack?"

I shook my head. Two warriors had already died. Two warriors who had been misled into believing they were doing what was right, that they were saving the tribe . . . two warriors who could have been me. I wouldn't feel guilty for their deaths, they were necessary, but I wouldn't add to them if I could help it.

"Call everyone to the barn, everyone except Mel and Bubbe. Tess and Andres may not be here, but Cleo is."

Bern stared at me a second. Then without a word she sprinted to the others. Kale was in the barn too now; she had given up on getting past Mel and her grandmother. She stared up at me but said nothing.

When the others arrived, they climbed onto the pile with me and started tossing hay.

Kale stayed close to the door, glancing from us to the Amazons held at bay by Bubbe and Mel. Watching.

The barn was filled with broken bales before we found the hidey-hole. A piece of plywood had been dropped over the last layer, over a space about six feet long by eighteen inches by eighteen inches—casket size. A short casket for an Amazon.

With Bern's help, I pulled up the board. Cleo lay inside, pale and limp. I sat on the bale beside her and reached for her throat—to check for a pulse.

Above my head there was a scream.

An owl dove from the rafters and out the open barn door.

Mateo, who had been shifting bales behind us to keep them from tumbling down on top of us, froze, then ran after the bird.

There was another, louder shriek outside . . . one I recognized as the son in his bird form.

I glanced at Jack. He dropped the bale he'd been holding and ran after Mateo.

I didn't know what was happening, could see no danger in what had happened. Owls lived in barns; we'd startled one . . .

From outside Jack yelled and an engine roared to life.

A cloud of dirt descended on the barn . . . maybe the camp . . . I couldn't tell.

Mel's voice, yelling, telling me to hurry, urged me to action.

I grabbed the unconscious Cleo and tossed her over

my shoulder—the second warrior I'd carried this way in just a few days' time.

I hoped it was a trend that would go no further.

The truck we'd driven into the camp screeched sideways, sliding on gravel toward the barn.

Bubbe stood where we had left her, but her shield was smaller, almost half its original size. Mel screamed at her and threw up her arms. Dust billowed behind the old priestess, rolled down toward her, toward the Amazons still on the other side of her shield of whirling air.

"Get her!" Mel yelled at Jack, who was running toward them.

The son grabbed Bubbe around the waist. Lost in her spell, her body stiff, the priestess seemed oblivious; she kept chanting. He carried . . . dragged . . . her toward the truck.

Kale and I flipped Cleo over the side into the bed, and Bern raced toward the struggling son. She grabbed Bubbe by the ankles and the two of them jogged her to the truck.

Her lips slowed; her shield fell, and every Amazon who had been waiting behind it rushed toward us.

Chapter 23

Mel was the last of us still standing her ground. Her arms raised, her body shaking, she was holding back the wave of dust she had gathered.

"Drive toward her," I yelled at Lao, who was behind the wheel. The hearth-keeper gunned the engine.

I clung to the side of the truck, my body hanging out over the edge while I prayed we would reach my friend before she was hit by a knife or sword.

There was a war cry . . . a victory cry. Weapons smashed into the side of the truck. The Amazons thought they had us, thought they'd won. And if they got to us, managed to stop the truck—they would. We had no weapons now, and Bubbe, our strongest weapon, was in much the same state as her daughter, staring blindly and chanting.

But a new weapon had appeared—the Amazons' own confidence. They were focused on us, focused on what they saw as an easy win and completely unaware Mel was holding back a wave of dirt and debris that would ensure our escape.

At least I hoped it would.

Lao barreled the truck toward the rush of Amazons as if they weren't there . . . or as if she had zero qualms about mowing a line of them down. Which, after seeing her attack on Thea, I suspected was the more accurate scenario.

The Amazons were close, but we were closer. Six feet from my friend, I yelled at Bern to grab me and leaned out, far enough I would have fallen if the warrior hadn't taken hold of my legs. She stood between my knees, her fingers wrapped around my belt. My pelvis bounced against the top of the bed; I ignored the pain and focused on Mel.

We drove by barely slowing; I looped my arms around my friend's waist and jerked her off her feet.

Her arms fell and so did the wave. "Pull!" I screamed at Bern and in seconds the three of us—Mel, Bern and myself—tumbled into a pile on the hard truck bed.

A roar sounded behind us and we were pelted with tiny rocks, twigs, and dirt.

Coughing, I pulled myself up to peer over the side of the truck. I could see nothing but dirt, but I could hear the curses . . .

The truck roared up the drive blind, but unimpeded.

In minutes we were on the highway, headed back to Jack's neighbor's house.

We gathered behind the house. Cleo and Bubbe had both come out of their fog, but neither was back to normal. Mel watched them through half-closed eyes as she pretended to replace handles on knives Jack had retrieved from the ashes of his home. She hadn't said a word about Cleo's or Bubbe's condition, but I knew she was shaken.

I hadn't been close to my mother and losing her had blown my worldview to smithereens. Mel, despite her differences with her family, loved them. And they had always been strong . . . stronger than her, in her mind . . . although not in mine.

"What happened?" I asked, running a whetstone over one of the blades.

She shook her head. "I don't know. Things seemed to be going well. Bubbe was holding them off, seemed as strong as ever . . . then something happened. She didn't weaken. She went somewhere . . ."

"Here." Bubbe tapped herself on the forehead, then stood and crossed the yard between us. She wore the same red dress she had this morning, but it had lost its crispness and now hung limp and dirty from her shoulders. Her eyes, however, were sharp again as were her steps.

"I went inside myself." She pointed at her temple. "Went where others tried to go."

Mel glanced sideways at me. Both of us thinking the

same thing—she wasn't herself, whatever had happened back at the camp was still affecting her, might for a long time.

Bubbe sighed and grabbed the stone wolf that hung from her neck. Her eyes closed, and her lips moved.

Something shifted in the trees.

I glanced toward them, expecting Mateo, who hadn't reappeared since shooting out of the barn.

But instead I saw a wolf, gray and rangy. His nose lifted to sniff the air. I tensed. His eyes scanned over those of us gathered in the yard, coming to rest on the old priestess, her eyes still closed, her lips still moving. He padded forward until he stood next to her, then he lifted his nose and nuzzled her hand.

With a smile, she opened her eyes.

"See, the wolf, you think he comes to the crazy?"

The creature, Mel's family *telios,* turned eyes old and wise on me. I'd seen the priestess call him before but wasn't sure then or now if he was real or just mist gathered into his shape. His eyes were knowing. They held wisdom I knew I'd never gain, and I wished more than anything I could see through his eyes to know what he knew.

Bubbe laughed. "Not for you, queen. Your *telios* is like our goddess . . . jealous. Best you learn about him before you cheat with another."

She raised her hand and the wolf disappeared, answering whether the animal was real or magic. But she had made her point, whatever had happened to her back at the camp wasn't affecting her now.

She tapped her temple again. "Did you not feel it? The probing? Someone tried to get inside, but I hold that key close. There is too much hidden in here to let go easily." She laughed. I wanted to laugh with her, but I couldn't; what she had said was too chilling.

"You felt someone in your mind?" I asked.

She nodded. "Here"—she touched her temple—"but not here." She placed her fingers over her heart. "That was her mistake. The brain holds knowledge, but the heart . . . that is what makes an Amazon strong."

My mind whirled. The thoughts I'd had while staring down Thea . . . the doubts . . . they had come from nowhere.

"No priestess has such skill. We don't poke where we do not belong," Bubbe added.

Cleo had already shared her story, or what she remembered, with us. Like Kale, that was very little. But she repeated it now.

"I was in the barn. Thea and Areto walked in. They knew something, I could tell. I acted casual, positioning myself to fight, but then"—she frowned—"I didn't want to. I didn't want to do anything. I'd been feeling lethargic all day, since breakfast, but this was worse. It scared me; I forced myself to push through, but it was like swimming through oil. I bent for a broom, to use as a staff, but I was shaky, couldn't concentrate on more than staying upright. Then someone hit me from behind.

"Falling was almost a relief. Losing myself to the darkness was too." She looked down and shook her head.

"When I woke up, I was under the hay. I don't know if I could have escaped if I'd wanted to, but the fact was, I didn't want to. I was happy just to lie there staring at the darkness." She walked to the edge of the woods. Her back tense, she didn't move, just stared into the shadows of the forest.

I looked at Kale. "Did you see Padia there?"

She picked up one of the pieces of wood Mel was carving into knife handles. "I don't know." She dropped the wood and looked back at me. "I don't remember what she looks like. I've tried to remember, but whenever I try to recall her, I get a blank. I can't even tell you what her hair color is or how tall she is."

"How long were you on the council together? How many times did you meet? If you saw her, you'd know, right?"

She ran her hands down her shorts. She whispered, "Twenty years, hundreds of times. Would I remember her now? I don't know, but I don't think I would."

I licked my lips. She had to be wrong.

I looked at Bubbe. "Could Padia do that? Could she wipe Kale's memory?"

The old priestess pursed her lips. "No."

A bit of tension left my shoulders. Whatever had happened to the two warriors, to me . . . to Bubbe . . . it wasn't what we were thinking. There was some other explanation, some simple one that didn't involve someone probing around inside our heads.

"But then, she couldn't convince Kale to kill those

humans, make her forget what she'd done, make my daughter lose her will to fight or try to tip her toe into my head. She couldn't do any of those things. No one could, but someone did."

I'd been worried about recognizing the enemy; now I learned she might be inside me . . . or could get there.

Silence settled over us.

Mel broke it. "What about Tess? Was she at the camp and we missed her? We missed Mother."

I answered, "Thea claimed she hadn't seen Tess or the baby." Thea's other comments, her suggestion that perhaps Tess had taken on the job I'd refused, nagged at me.

"Thea lies." Lao stood on the porch holding a tray of sandwiches.

I acknowledged her comment with a nod. I didn't trust Thea either. I couldn't even be certain Tess wasn't hidden in the barn. Despite the mess we had made, there were still plenty of bales left stacked.

"She could have been in the house," Kale suggested.

"Or hidden somewhere else on the property," Mel added.

Both possibilities I'd already considered. I stared at the pile of knives Mel and I had repaired. I had two missions now: save Tess and Andres and stop Padia.

Unless what Thea suggested was true. Unless Tess was on the other side . . . unless she hadn't *been taken,* but had taken Andres all by herself.

An owl called from the distance. I searched the trees for him. Funny how I'd lived in these woods for over a decade and I'd never seen as many owls as I had in the last few weeks.

The thought pinged inside my brain like a metal ball in an old-fashioned pinball machine.

I looked at Jack. "Where's Mateo?"

"I haven't seen him since he flew out of the barn."

Literally. He'd seen the owl . . . shifted and taken off after the creature.

"Jack, do you speak wolverine?"

The group stared at me, their expression a tad too quiet, but the son answered. "If you mean do I understand what a wolverine wants when he makes a noise that sounds like a growl or a grunt, yes."

"And you can talk back?"

He tilted his head. "Communicate. Wolverines are not exactly the linguists of the animal kingdom."

"What about other animals? Do you understand them?"

"A few, if they are close to a wolverine . . . a badger, for example."

"So, Mateo, would he understand other birds? Say, an owl?"

Jack considered the question, then nodded. "Likely. Condors and owls are both raptors."

"So, when it looked like he was following the owl, he may have *really* been following it, may have understood something it said."

"Yes . . ." Dawning crossed through Jack's eyes. "Wait here." He crossed the six feet to the house in two steps.

Before anyone had a chance to question our exchange, he was back.

"Athena. The goddess they are worshipping is Athena."

I didn't know much about Athena, about any goddess except Artemis. Bubbe and Jack, however, knew a lot, as did Mel, and with the help of the Internet she was able to find out even more.

"You've never heard of her?" she asked. I could tell by her tone that she found my knowledge lacking.

"I worship Artemis," I replied, crossing my arms over my chest. Priestesses might spend time keeping tabs on the other goddesses; warriors had other things to worry about. Or used to. Now it appeared other goddesses, Athena at least, might be something we had to worry about too. Shamed by the realization, I dropped my arms.

"Here." Mel pointed at the computer. "She's the daughter of Zeus."

"Artemis's sister, then," I noted, happy to be able to at least show that much knowledge.

"Except Artemis had a mother, Leto. Athena didn't."

"She didn't have a mother?"

"Not one that gave birth to her. Zeus swallowed her mother, Metis, and later Athena came out of his forehead fully grown."

I frowned. Childbirth was very important to Artemis, and while not something I wanted for myself, it was a key part of what women were, what made us strong. To spring fully grown from a man's head . . . it stole that power from us. Who would worship a goddess like that? Why?

Disgusted and confused, I refocused on the most important question, at least as far as defeating Padia: "What powers does Athena have?"

Mel grimaced. "It doesn't work like that. We don't have Artemis's powers, our powers are just enhanced by hers."

"So what powers would Athena enhance?"

Mel pushed back her chair. "She's a warrior."

I frowned. "Like our warriors?"

"Yes and no. Artemis is a huntress."

Bubbe walked up and stared at the computer. With a *humph* she turned to me. "It is the heart against the head. Athena, she works with logic. She wins her battles with her head, thinking, plotting. Artemis uses her heart and instincts to bring down her prey."

I let that soak in but couldn't see how it would help me. "What else?"

"Athena loves invention."

"Invention? New things, like the Internet?"

With a glance at the computer and a sigh, Bubbe nodded. "My granddaughter has a bit too much Athena in her for my tasting."

Owls and the technology. We'd seen signs of both at the safe camp. And I associated both with the camp's new high priestess . . .

"What else?"

Mel read a list of things linked to Athena off the Web site. None of them stood out as something I'd noticed since Thea's arrival. "Is there a picture?" I asked. I don't know what I expected. I hadn't seen any goddess pictures or figures while at camp, but when Mel scrolled down and the image of the armored Athena appeared, I froze.

"What's that on her breastplate?"

"Medusa. Athena helped Perseus kill her."

My heart beat faster. "Can you get a close-up of her face?"

"Athena's?"

"No, Medusa's."

A few more clicks and a picture of the snake-haired gorgon filled the screen. Everything settled into place.

Kale was on watch. I sent Bern to get her.

When the warrior walked into the room, she froze, seemed mesmerized by the screen.

I waited, hoping my hunch would pay off.

Finally she looked at me. "How did you know?"

"What? How did I know what?" I didn't want to lead her.

She glimpsed from the screen to me and back. "I don't know . . . I think . . ." She shook her head.

Despite her confusion, I stayed focused. I hadn't ever liked Thea, certainly didn't after she declared herself queen, but that was a long shot from the suspicions that had been building inside me. But now I had hard evidence. All I needed was for Kale to confirm it. I whispered for Mel to change the screen, to go back to the owl we'd looked at before.

With both windows open, I looked at Kale again. "How about now?"

She stared at me. "Padia. Those are her tattoos. How did you know?"

As the question left her lips, my fingers loosened and my mind relaxed.

That happens when you know your enemy, when you can finally put a face on the person you intend to kill.

Once the block in Kale's brain was broken and we knew Padia and Thea were one and the same, it made our next move obvious. We had to capture the high priestess and force her to tell us where Tess and Andres were. And we had to do it fast before she carried out her mission to kill Andres.

"But what about what Tess said . . . that Padia had come to camp?" Mel asked.

I poked my tongue against the inside of my cheek. I'd been worrying over the question myself. It was one of the things that had made me doubt Thea's guilt before. "She didn't seem to be sure it was Padia, just another priestess. Maybe Padia has someone else working for her."

"Or maybe Tess lied." Mel's words landed hard, but I couldn't believe them, if for no other reason than Thea had said the same thing.

"Padia is powerful, always has been. Who knows what she is capable of now? She's obviously trying to shift suspicion on the hearth-keeper." Kale shook her head. "There's no telling what she did to confuse the girl."

"So, if Thea is Padia, why does she want Andres?" Mel asked.

"Because—" I cut off my own reply. I'd assumed Thea's reasons to kill my brother were to keep him from growing up to be a threat to the Amazons, but that was before I'd learned she worshipped Athena.

"Because she's afraid of the sons? What they will become?" I offered, but the reasoning didn't ring true, not with everything else. How could Thea/Padia's purpose be to preserve the Amazons, when by choosing Athena over Artemis she was breaking us in two?

"I don't think she cares about the Amazons," I added, still thinking.

"What does she care about?" Mel turned in her chair and looked at Kale.

The warrior's lips formed a thin line. "Herself. Power."

"She was already on the high council. What more power could she want?" I asked.

"Her own tribe?" Kale offered, her eyes flashing.

"She declared herself queen," I added. A safe camp wasn't a tribe, but it was a start. And now I realized I had no proof aside from Thea's word that my position had been taken from me. She had made the announcement after speaking to her "contact" alone. Which brought another question to mind. I had spoken to her contact. That contact had identified herself as Padia. If Thea was Padia, who had I talked with?

Still surfing the Internet, Mel lifted her fingers from the computer mouse. She spoke, interrupting my train of thought. "If she's a true follower of Athena, guided by logic, she has to have a plan. She had to realize she would be found out at some point. What then? Are the Amazons at the safe camp going to continue to call her queen?"

I gripped the back of her chair with one hand. "Maybe. We know she did something to Cleo, and Kale. She tried to do something to me and Bubbe. She has to be doing the same something to the Amazons at the camp."

"She didn't make any of you do anything you didn't believe in."

"I killed those humans." Kale shook her head. "With a gun. Even if the women attacked me first . . ." She frowned. "I wouldn't have done that. Padia is dangerous. She has to be destroyed."

"Maybe you killed them. Maybe Thea did and left you there to take the blame. Maybe they did kill each other. We don't know. When we found you, you were confused and, yes, I think you were acting under some influence Thea put over you, but it didn't last. It wore off." Mel stared at Bubbe, who had become uncharacteristically quiet. When her grandmother made no move to offer any additional comments, Mel sighed.

"The point is, if Thea is using some kind of mind control over the safe camp, we haven't seen any evidence that it will last. And I think if she could do it, she would have already. You wouldn't have been able to remember what you just have, and Mother wouldn't have been hidden inside a stack of hay bales. You are both warriors, valuable if Padia planned on taking on other Amazons. Why would she throw you away?"

Bubbe snorted. "Because the head does not control the heart."

"So, what does Padia want from killing Andres?" I asked.

"I'm not sure, but if Padia is getting her power from Athena and she really wanted to show her loyalty, there is something she might do." Mel twisted the computer's monitor so it faced us. A line drawing of an altar appeared, an animal of some sort lying across its top, its throat slit. "Sacrifice."

"And what better to give your goddess than the blood of your enemy mixed with the blood of those you desert for her?" Bubbe closed her eyes and began to murmur.

The image of the knife Thea had handled in the woods flashed through my mind. I described the object.

Kale tensed. Bubbe captured her wolf totem pendant between both palms. "That is not Amazon. The deaths of the sons were never for ceremony. Never to pay a price. Like our *telioses,* we killed to survive."

A chill tripped up my spine. The bowl of oil, the knife . . . "She had been setting up for the ceremony when I arrived."

"The knife will be with her, in the house," Kale murmured. "We need it too, to keep this from happening again."

I agreed. I couldn't wait to see Thea again, to call her Padia to her face and expose exactly who and what she was to the tribe.

I just prayed Mel was right and any power she had over the camp was fleeting. If so, all we had to do was separate her from them and everything would go back to normal.

Chapter 24

After much discussion with Mel and Jack, I accepted that we had to change our tactic if we wanted to stop Padia.

She didn't play by Amazon rules, but she knew them. Which meant she also knew what to expect from us.

The only way to defeat her was to do something she wouldn't have planned for, something completely out of character for Amazons.

Meaning we couldn't rush in, we couldn't depend on our hearts, we had to use our heads.

When I made the announcement, Bubbe muttered, but then she clasped her hands behind her back and didn't object further.

We had waited until full dark to gather in a crescent in view of the moon. Athena was a sun goddess, Artemis a moon goddess. From now on, if our battle went past this night, Mel insisted we plan our attacks for when the moon was in the sky, when Artemis was the strongest and Athena the weakest.

Kale had objected that it would be what Thea expected, but she was overruled. As Mel said, we had to assume the safe camp Amazons were under Padia's influence, at least for now. Which meant we were still outnumbered and in need of every advantage we could find.

So, change one: night was our friend.

Change two: we didn't attack head-on.

We were outnumbered. Approaching your enemy from the front might be honorable, but in these conditions it wasn't logical.

Tonight we would become spies. We would sneak into the safe camp and grab Padia without waking anyone else.

That, at least, was the plan.

Change three: we spent actual time discussing how best to unarm the priestess.

We had decided her powers were mental: putting thoughts into people's heads, blocking memories, and, I suggested, moving things.

"What kind of things?" Jack asked.

"Rocks, knife blades." I described the rocks exploding from the ground and the knife moving in my hand while I battled to hold it still.

No one spoke. We looked at Bubbe.

"It is possible," she replied, her face solemn.

"Anything else?" Mel asked.

I glanced at Mateo. He had returned an hour earlier. I hadn't had a chance to talk to him yet, but I suspected he had another of Padia's skills to tell us about.

"She has spies," he said, his accented baritone startling in the gloom. We hadn't lit a fire or torches. We weren't calling on the goddess and didn't want to risk a fire alerting anyone to our presence, something we hadn't worried about earlier . . . another change.

"What kind of spies?" Mel again.

"Owls."

Another wave of silence.

"When you found Cleo in the hay, an owl flew from the rafters."

"We startled him," Kale said.

Mateo moved, I sensed he was smiling although I couldn't see his expression in the dark. "Yes, but he didn't fly because he was afraid; he flew because it was his job. He was a lookout, there to let Padia know if Cleo escaped."

"Let her know . . ." Mel's skepticism was palatable.

"I followed the owl, kept him from returning to the camp, then snatched him from the sky. Owls here aren't used to having to fear other birds . . ." I sensed the smile again. "He screamed his warning, his message that the nest had been violated."

"The nest?"

"Cleo's storage place," Mateo explained. "He fought to

escape, but not for his life . . . to deliver his message. His message, the warning, consumed him. I held him as long as I could, to allow you all to escape, then I released him, followed him back to whoever had planted the mission in his brain."

"And?"

"The priestess, Thea. She was standing outside the barn with the warriors. He landed on her shoulder. . . ."

"He did?" Kale asked.

"He did," Mateo spat. "She broke him. His freedom is gone. His mind is gone. He sat on her shoulder for only a second, then flew off again. He seemed lost, searching for something he couldn't find. . . ."

"Perhaps he was looking for something else," I offered.

"No, Mateo is right. If she could do what she did to me and Cleo . . . imagine what she could do to a bird," Kale said, her voice soft but bitter. "She has to be destroyed. We shouldn't wait. We should find the blade and kill her tonight."

Kale's words had been harsh, and understandably so, but I couldn't give in to the temptation of acting on them. We needed Thea alive long enough to tell us where she had hidden Tess and Andres. I made sure everyone understood that before we set out to capture the priestess.

It was midnight. The moon was no longer full, but there was enough light that I could see the house clearly.

We had come through the woods. Our plan was to escape that way too, although escaping really wasn't part of my personal plan. Tonight I meant to take back my camp, or to lose the battle completely.

This time Jack would have to drag me out of the fight; I wouldn't let him reason me out of it again.

Bubbe had got us this far. She'd walked ahead of the group, checking for wards. She hadn't found any new ones, which meant either our visit wasn't expected or Padia was depending on her alternative alarm—the owls.

Mateo had taken care of them. Despite the foggy state he claimed they had been reduced to, the sight of the condor had roused three from their perches. He'd run them off, then circled the area. With the disappearance of the owls and the appearance of the giant condor, silence had settled over the woods.

Not even a tree frog or a cicada hazarded a sound.

Or maybe it was Jack keeping the forest quiet. He roamed the woods in his animal form, searching for any other sign things weren't normal in the trees.

The rest of the group had been assigned watch points too. Cleo and Kale took the barn where many of the warriors would be bedded down. Mel and Bern held positions at the front and back of the house. Lao had the driveway. And I had the house itself, the inside where Padia/Thea slept.

My fingers tingled as I strung the rope I meant to bind her with from my hand to the underside of my elbow and back up, forming an easy-to-manage loop. I was antsy, but controlled. I had to be . . . head, not heart tonight.

As I pulled the rope off my arm and hooked it to my belt, my hand brushed over my new art—not tattoos, no time for that—drawings compliments of Mel and a Sharpie marker: the praying mantis for patience and focus; the dog for his ability to read humans, to anticipate our next most likely move; the leopard for stealth; and the meerkat. I had to question Mel about that one.

"Snake charmers," she replied. "To help evade her efforts to charm you."

There were others after that, but I quit asking. I didn't need to know the reasons for the art, just trust that Mel's artisan skills would enhance my powers.

And I did trust her. Maybe that wasn't using my head, but I was an Amazon. I had to go with my heart some.

Once we were past the trees and the yard, Mel was in charge of checking the house for any last wards. I waited for her to make the circuit. After her nod, I approached the house.

I knew where I was headed. There was a window over the kitchen sink. It was small and higher off the ground than the other windows, but still within my reach if I jumped. It was also the opening farthest from any sleeping Amazons.

I jumped and grabbed the sill, then pulled myself up until my elbows balanced on the tiny ledge. Finally with one hand I shoved the window open. Another reason I picked this window; I knew it was never locked.

Amazons were lazy about locks anyway. Who needed them when you had wards? Wards were more dependable, at least at stopping humans. Obviously not at stopping a high priestess, but until now we hadn't realized one of our own could be a threat.

That was something Padia should have realized, but then, she'd had her owls to alert her as well. Too bad for her we'd had a way to combat that security measure as well.

Feeling satisfied that, so far, my invasion was going well, I belly crawled through the window.

The sink area was clean—Lao would be pleased. Using my arm strength to keep from falling, I slid over the sink. At the edge of the counter I paused, considering the best way out of the awkward position. Deciding there was no way except forward, I used the counter lip for leverage, pulled a bit more of my body into the room, then walked my hands down the lower cabinet until my palms hit the floor. From there it was one easy handstand and a flip up onto my feet.

My shoes landed harder than I had planned. I froze and waited to be surrounded.

But there was no response. No sound. No movement. Nothing.

The kitchen was dark. The house was dark. The farmhouse didn't even have most of the stray lights I'd seen at Mel's in the past . . . digital clocks and flashing answering machine lights. There were clocks on the oven and microwave, but the light on the stove had been broken when we got the thing and the microwave stayed unplugged more often than not to allow some other appliance a shot at the outlet.

Tonight must have been one of those nights because the only thing clearly visible in the room was the window I'd crept through and the moonlight beyond it.

I turned away from that small amount of light and let my eyes adjust to the dark. Then I headed to the high priestess's room. Outside the room I'd called my own for a decade, I paused. I'd planned on going up the stairs to the room I'd assigned Thea when she arrived at camp, but with my room empty, would she have moved in? The room was bigger and furnished better than any of the other bedrooms.

Of course she would have.

I reached for my belt, for another unAmazonlike tool that Jack had supplied—chloroform. We'd argued about it. I'd insisted I could subdue the priestess myself; I'd looked forward to that, knocking her out with a well-placed and planned blow to the temple. But the others had reminded me that I'd agreed to change things, to do the unexpected.

Chloroform would certainly be that.

So Jack had disappeared for an hour and come back with a bottle. I didn't know where he got it and I didn't care.

Lao had soaked the rag and placed it in a plastic Baggie. That felt strange too, standing there in the dark, reaching for a Baggie someone might use to store a peanut butter sandwich.

But I did it. This wasn't about me and my pride, this was about saving the tribe.

With the cloth in my hand, I turned the knob. The door swung open noiselessly.

I stepped inside.

The room was darker than even the hall had been. Someone had pulled the curtains, so no moonlight found its way inside. And, like the kitchen, there was no clock, nothing to provide even minimal light.

But I knew the room like my own heart.

I moved without pause to the bed and the head that rested on the pillow.

She didn't wake, not until I had the cloth pressed to her face.

She tried to get up, tried to lift her body to a sitting position, but I slipped my leg over her, straddling her and pinning her arms to her sides. She kicked out her leg and bucked her hips, trying to throw me off.

It was tempting to drop the plan then, to punch her instead, but remembering my commitment, I concentrated on holding her down and keeping the cloth over her nose and mouth, just as Jack had told me.

It worked. With only a few more bucks of her body, she fell still and her head slipped to the side.

It was horribly, disappointingly easy. I muttered the complaint under my breath, then heaved her body onto my shoulder and followed through with the rest of our plan. I opened the bedroom window and tossed her onto the dirt below.

She landed with a rewarding thump.

After closing the window behind me, I picked her back up and jogged to the woods.

We had Thea. Now to force her to talk.

Chapter 25

We trailed through the woods, moving as quickly as we could. Jack and Mateo stayed behind, watching, ready to warn us if the Amazons stirred.

In the woods I dropped the priestess back on the ground and unwound the rope I'd brought. I hadn't needed it at the camp, but I needed her tied up before she awoke.

We had her mind powers to deal with too, but I was trusting Bubbe and Mel to handle that.

As I bent to wrap the rope around Thea's hands, she didn't move. Her fingers were limp . . . and bare . . . no ring.

A moment of foreboding stopped me. I quickly wrapped the rope around her wrists, then grabbed her by her hands and jerked her body forward, into a sliver of moonlight that leaked through the trees.

I stared down into a face I knew well, a face I had for a while trusted . . . Areto.

With a curse, I took a step back toward the camp. Mel stepped out of the woods in front of me.

"It isn't Thea; it's Areto." I was too angry with myself to say more. I tried to shove past my friend.

She stopped me with her staff. "You can't go back. We took our shot and missed; there's no reloading this round. We will have to wait for another."

I kept walking. This time Jack stopped me. He was fully human and fully naked.

I growled and shoved against his chest. He wrapped his hands around my wrists.

"What are you doing?" he asked.

"Ending this." I twisted my wrists, pulled them free of his grasp.

He pivoted on one foot and grabbed me by the upper arm as I moved past him. "You're not thinking—"

I jerked my arm free and swung at the same time. "Thinking didn't work. Using my head instead of my heart didn't work. I got the wrong Amazon. I'm going back for the right one."

My fist missed him, but I accomplished my goal. He let go. I lengthened my stride, let my legs devour the ground beneath me.

Anger that I'd kept hidden even from myself was racing through me. I'd trusted in the others' plan and it had failed. Now I was going to do things my way, even if it meant breaking the house down board by board.

"She isn't there." Mel's voice carried. My anger carried me two more steps.

"She hasn't slept there since you left."

I stopped and forced a breath into my lungs, forced myself to calm enough to comprehend what she was saying.

"How do you know?"

"Areto. She's awake and she isn't fighting. I think she's happy we have her."

"She could be lying."

"Could be. Or could be she's realized she's been lied to by someone else."

I knew Areto. I had trusted Areto. Did I now?

I stared into the darkness, not sure what to do or who to believe.

"She said something else, something I think you are going to want to hear."

"What?" I called, but Mel, damn her, didn't answer. She had already walked away.

Annoyed that I'd lost the head of steam that had been propelling me back to the camp, I muttered a curse for my friend, then trudged back to where I had left Areto.

She was sitting up. Her hands were still bound and Bern stood beside, her a sword pointed at the other warrior's throat.

I nodded at Bern, letting her know I appreciated her vigilance.

"Where is Thea?" I asked Areto.

She didn't look at me, didn't look at any of us.

"Thea lied to us," Areto said. "I followed her because I believed her lies." She twisted her head then and looked me in the eyes. "I don't any longer."

I inclined my head, but only slightly. The warrior had told me that Cleo had been hidden in the barn. That bought her a small amount of respect, but not trust, not yet.

And respect didn't mean I wouldn't kill her.

But she knew that.

"Tell me," I said.

She didn't ask to be released, to have her bonds loosened, or even to have Bern lower her blade, she just talked. My respect grew a bit more.

"She worships in the day. Makes us worship then too . . . when warriors should be practicing, hearth-keepers working, and artisans creating. It isn't natural."

I didn't interrupt her or enlighten her as to why that was.

"She brings humans into the camp."

"The cable men," I replied, to encourage her.

"And the women."

I paused. "The birders," I murmured.

"The birders." She shifted her attention to Bern for a second. There was an apology in her eyes.

The dark-skinned warrior didn't acknowledge it, but I saw her blade waver.

Areto swallowed. She whispered the next words, so soft at first I thought I'd heard them wrong . . . believed I had to have heard them wrong. "They worship with us."

My shock must have shown.

She pulled her elbows in toward her body, as if she wanted to pull back inside herself, contract with . . . shame . . . or anger? I wasn't sure which. I knew I would have felt both. Shame that I'd let the priestess lead me so far away from my values, anger that she'd violated my trust.

"What about the three who were killed? Do you know about that?"

She shook her head, but she looked to the side, telling me she knew or suspected something, something she didn't want to say out loud. "The one . . . that was before any of this . . . while you . . ." She stopped. "The others, yes. A little . . ."

I didn't like her answer, didn't believe her. "What about Kale? Do you know what happened to her?"

She looked up, her face earnest. "I don't know the name."

"The dark-haired warrior who was with me at the camp."

She licked her lips. "I never saw her before then. There was another one, though."

"Another one?" I prepared for a shock; I could feel one coming.

"There was another Amazon. She was angry. Thea had already gone to the woods with the two women. Taken them to the obelisk."

Her eyes shone with outrage; I shared it, but I didn't acknowledge hers or mine, didn't give her an out to stop.

Her jaw tensed, and she continued, "This Amazon was looking for someone, a priestess, but not Thea."

"Padia," I offered, then to myself, "and she found her."

"I don't know, but she told me she was on the high council and ordered me to tell her where Padia was. I told her I'd never heard the name and she said, 'The priestess, tell me where the priestess is.' So I sent her into the woods."

Kale waited to see my reaction. I didn't give one. She had betrayed Thea to this mystery Amazon. Did I care? Not a whit.

"After maybe an hour, Thea came back. She had me go with her into the woods. She carried a body back with her."

A body, and not the birder's.

"It was the Amazon."

"Where is she?" I asked.

"The barn, under the hay. I think it's what made Thea think to put Cleo there."

I didn't know how to respond, didn't know what to think. There was a dead Amazon hidden in the barn. Who was she? Fariba or Valasca was my guess—one of the high-council members Kale had named who had supported Padia. They had probably found out she had deserted Artemis and were as outraged as I was.

I wanted to know who this dead Amazon might be, but I wasn't done with my questions either.

"What about the sheriff. Who called them?" I asked, putting the body to the side for now.

Her chin rose. "I did. Thea thought I was arranging the hay bales, but I went into the woods and saw them. I knew Thea had killed them and the council member too."

"But you didn't see Kale?" I asked.

She shook her head. "No, but I didn't stay long. I knew I had to get back to the barn before Thea discovered I was missing. I returned to the house and called, told the police we had trespassers."

"You didn't mention Thea."

Another shake, this one slow, ashamed. "I couldn't."

A chance at shedding her sheep's wool and Areto had balked. Of course, only a sheep would call humans to do what an Amazon should take care of herself.

"And when they arrived, Thea talked to them," I prompted.

"She did. I think she was worried they'd go in the barn. Hay was still everywhere. She directed them to the obelisk, but I could tell she was angry."

"Did she suspect you?"

"She trusted me enough to get my help in hiding the Amazon. It would never have occurred to her I'd call about two dead humans. She also didn't know I'd seen them."

The muscles in Areto's neck were tense and her eyes were hard, but the emotion wasn't directed at me, it was turned inward.

I gave her a moment, realizing I'd misjudged Thea in at least one respect. She hadn't brought the human authorities to our property. Of course, that was a small issue compared to everything else she had done . . . or was trying to do.

"So where is Thea?" I was still curious about the Amazon in the barn, but Thea was my focus right now. I had to find her.

"I don't know. She has hardly slept at the safe camp since you left. She told me to take your room."

"She said you could have my room?"

"No, she *told* me to take it, and she had another warrior sleep in hers."

So even when she did stay at the camp, it wasn't in either of the rooms I might have guessed.

Mel was right; Thea was a follower of Athena, a plotter. But if she wasn't sleeping at the camp, where was she sleeping?

I looked at Mel. "I think we need to find out who these birders are. Find them, and we will probably find Thea."

I gestured for Bern to pull Areto to her feet. I wasn't sure what to do with her. A lot depended on what happened next, if I discovered what she had told me so far was true or not.

I glanced at her. "Do you see Thea come and go? Does she drive herself, or do birders come with her?"

"She leaves at dusk on foot and comes back at dawn."

So wherever she was staying was close. But our woods covered fifty acres, and a number of houses were within jogging distance, cross-country. She could be in any of them, or she could be staying in a tent pitched on our property or an adjoining property . . . there was no way to know.

"There's more."

Bern held Areto by the arm. The captured warrior didn't struggle. She lifted her face and met my gaze.

"There's something planned in two days. I don't know what, but we were told to stay at the camp, that we would all be expected to participate."

"Night or day?"

"Day, little before noon."

I nodded, then moved to walk past them.

"Zery?" Areto pulled in a breath. Her chest expanded. "I accept my fate, whatever you decide, but I want you to know . . . Bern too . . . I'm sorry."

I walked past her then. She was sorry; I was sorry. But regret wasn't going to get us out of whatever Thea had planned . . . action was.

While Mel revisited the computer, looking for anything that might tie the date Areto had mentioned to Athena and give us some clue as to what Thea had planned, I sought out Jack and Mateo.

In a strangely normal tableau, they were sitting in the kitchen, drinking beers and eating peanuts. There were two empties in front of each of them and the floor was littered with peanut debris. As I entered, Mateo crushed a shell under the heel of his boot, then shifted his foot to smash another.

I filled them in on what Areto had said.

The bird son didn't look up until I'd finished.

Like me, they were more interested in where Thea might be now than in who might be lying dead in the Amazon's barn.

"I didn't see any sign of a tent," he replied. His face was drawn and his eyes tired. I didn't think it was the beer causing either. It was easy to forget he was Andres's father. That he had as big, in some ways bigger, stake in what happened than I did.

"But you weren't looking for one either," I said. I kept my tone pure business. There was no room for pity, and certainly no time. "And if there is one, I don't think it would be obvious."

Looking at Jack, I asked, "How are wolverines at tracking?"

He scissored his fingers around the beer bottle's neck, then swung it back and forth. "Better than humans."

"Better than Amazons?"

He looked up. His eyes were filled with challenge.

"See if you can pick up her scent," I replied. Then, at Mateo, "And see if you can find a tent, or anything else that she could be staying in overnight."

He brushed a pile of peanut shells onto the floor and started to rise.

I paused, for some reason feeling propelled to say more. "He's alive, Mateo, at least for now. I don't know what she has planned, but I'm sure whatever it is, it involves Andres . . . which means we have until . . ."

I hesitated, calculating. Areto had said two days, but it was morning now—had she meant from yesterday? Realizing she probably had, I finished, "Wednesday, noon. We have until then."

Then I left. A day and a half. That was it. It wasn't much; I prayed it was enough.

By five I was still wide awake, as was Mel.

She was at the computer, a cup of coffee at her elbow. The beer sounded better to me, and since neither would have much effect on my Amazon metabolism, I walked back to the kitchen to get one. Mateo and Jack had left. Kale was missing too. She seemed to like to be alone; considering what she'd been through, I could understand that.

Crunching peanut shells under my shoes, I returned to the office with a longneck.

As I twisted off the lid, Mel leaned back in her chair and watched me.

"So, there's another Amazon involved."

I lifted my head in the affirmative. "From the high council."

She slid her fingers through the coffee cup's handle and tapped them against the ceramic. "Any idea who she is or why she came here?"

I lowered the bottle I'd just pressed to my lips. "Kale mentioned two other council members who were on Padia's side. I figure one of them found out about her worshipping Athena and weren't happy with being duped."

Mel seemed to accept my explanation. "Makes sense. Too bad she didn't find us instead. It would have simplified things a lot."

"Or Kale. Thea . . ." I was having a hard time deciding what to call the priestess, Padia or Thea. For now I had settled on Thea. I'd thought of her that way for too long. "Thea must have already done whatever she did to her before the council member Areto saw showed up, otherwise the pair of them might have been able to stop her."

"But she only killed the second arrival. I wonder why?"

I shook my bottle, checking how much I had drunk. "She needed a patsy? She'd already killed the birders too and wanted someone to take the blame?" Maybe if Areto hadn't called the sheriff's office, Thea would have.

"Maybe." Mel didn't seem to buy it. "And you said Thea didn't seem to know Kale."

"She was obviously acting." I shrugged; I was past understanding why Thea did anything. To be honest, I didn't want to understand her; I just wanted to stop her.

Mel picked up her cup and took a sip. "Do you think Andres's still alive?

"According to Areto, there's a big event coming up. So, yeah, I think he is."

Mel pulled her fingers free from the cup. "Well, that's what confuses me. This event . . . it's huge." She tilted her head toward the computer monitor. "Panathenaea. Athena's birthday."

On the screen was an image of Athens, people thronging the streets. They were gathered around a statue I now recognized as Athena. "What are they doing?" I asked.

"Giving gifts." Mel's face was grim.

"What kind of gifts?" I asked, but I already knew.

"Sacrifices. During Panathenaea, they made sacrifices."

"And what better sacrifice than the blood of your enemy mixed with the blood of those you betray," I murmured, repeating Bubbe's words.

Mel nodded. "None, but the thing is, Panathenaea didn't just pop up. If Padia wanted to kill Andres for Panathenaea, and it makes sense she would—any sacrifice made then is going to have one hundred times the power of one made any other day—why would she have tried to kill him earlier? That doesn't make sense."

"Maybe she hadn't thought about Panathenaea being so close, but by the time she stole Andres back, she realized she was missing an opportunity."

"An Athena worshipper forget her birthday?" Mel scoffed. "Athena's about planning, remember? What kind of plan is that?"

She was right. Like many things about Thea, it didn't make sense. Panathenaea had only been a week away when we stole Andres. What was a week? Nothing. Not if it meant increasing your power by one hundredfold.

The beer seemed to be giving me a headache, or maybe it was trying to figure out the indecipherable priestess.

I set the bottle down. "I don't know. I just know we have to stop her."

Chapter 26

I shook off the questions my conversation with Mel had uncovered. I didn't need more questions. I knew what needed to be done; the details of Thea's madness could be sorted out later.

Hoping some caffeine would stop the headache that was ticking to life inside my skull, I'd followed Mel's lead and gotten a cup of coffee from the machine in the kitchen and carried it to the back deck.

Bern and Cleo were asleep. I'd ordered them to bed as soon as we'd gotten Areto squared away in a windowless room in the basement. Kale was watching her, or at least I assumed she was; I hadn't actually checked in on them for hours.

Bubbe was off doing whatever Bubbe did in the early bits of day, and Lao was in the kitchen cooking breakfast.

Actually, she was fussing over a mess Kale had made while helping her. I was impressed a warrior would even try to help in the kitchen, but apparently Lao had thrown out more than one of Kale's efforts since the warrior's arrival and was nothing but annoyed to have to do it again.

Sipping my coffee, I wandered toward the woods. The mother dog followed me. Somewhere not far away an owl hooted. I tensed and considered searching for the creature, but the thought was fleeting. I couldn't fly. I could maybe find the animal and shoot it down, but it would be no use to us dead.

I had to trust in Mateo, trust he had heard the owl too, and would do what I couldn't.

I turned back toward the house.

Something rustled in the trees behind me. The mother dog stiffened. She positioned herself in front of me and raised her lip in warning.

Taking a cue from her actions, I reached for the nunchakus I'd tucked into the top of my pants.

Tess burst out of the woods.

Dressed in the same clothes she had worn when she had left Mel's with Dana and Andres, she glanced around the clearing. Leaves and twigs were caught in her long hair. Her eyes were wide and wild, and her breasts moved up and down as she fought for breaths.

"They have Andres. They're going to kill him. You have to come with me." She grabbed me by the hand and tugged me toward the woods.

Remembering the questions I'd had about her, I held firm. "Calm down. Tell me where he is, who has him."

"Thea. She's going to kill him. You have to come with me now."

Behind her the owl called again.

She jumped. "Now! You have to come now." Then she turned and raced into the forest.

I hesitated, but only for a second. Tess was already out of sight, the sounds of her frantic running already growing distant.

With a curse, I jogged after her, sure I could catch her and hopefully calm her before she alerted Thea that she had escaped. Or, if she was responsible for any of this herself, just catch her.

The girl was faster than I had imagined. Trusting my instincts, I jogged the direction I sensed she had gone. I was at least one hundred yards away from the house when I caught sight of her again.

She was standing by a tree; she seemed to have come to her senses and was waiting for me.

I held up one hand. "Don't run. We need to talk. We need to plan—racing in will just get Andres killed."

"Oh, I wouldn't waste energy worrying about Andres right now." Thea stepped out from behind the tree. She held a box, similar to what the birder had used to ignite the explosion at Mel's.

I lunged forward, but the action was futile. She pressed the button.

As my foot hit the ground, it shifted beneath me. Machinery ground above my head. I fell backward, realized I'd been caught in some kind of a net. It closed around me; I grabbed the rope it was made of and tried to tear my way out.

Thea laughed. "I'm sure that with the use of the blade you disguise as a belt buckle you could free yourself, but not in the time I'll give you." She raised her hand.

Tess stepped forward and pressed a tube to her lips. I stared at the hearth-keeper, my brain not cooperating, not comprehending what was happening.

She blew through the tube.

Something small flew out of its tip and zipped toward me. I hurtled my body to the side in an attempt to dodge the tiny missile.

Metal bit into my side. I pinched the dart between finger and thumb and jerked it from my flesh. My mind flashed back to the darts Thea had used on Mateo when I'd thought we were on the same side. Darts I'd never questioned her about.

Another projectile hit, then another. There was no stopping them, no avoiding them and, as each dart hit, I moved slower, until I wasn't moving at all.

Thea, her face pressed close, laced her fingers through the net's weave and pulled me toward her. She whispered, "Sleep well, queen. You have a big day ahead of you."

I clenched my fingers, trying to form a fist, and then nothing . . .

*   *   *

When I awoke, I was no longer in the net. I was lying on my back on a bed. My feet were bare and tied. My hands were bound too, palm to palm. My belt with its hidden blade was gone, and I could tell by the lack of pressure to the small of my back that the nunchakus had been taken from me as well.

The room had a cheap disposable look, and it was small, barely larger than the queen-size bed. I could tell I was in an RV and that it was daylight outside, but I had no idea how much time had passed. It could have been minutes, hours, or days. Days was doubtful, though. That would have taken us past Panathenaea, and I suspected my capture had something to do with Athena's birthday.

There was a door straight ahead and two windows, one on each side of the bed and both out of reach in my current situation, but if I could stand, that would change. I wiggled my way to a sit, until I was propped against a wall.

I glanced around again, looking for something to smash through the glass.

That's when I saw the owl perched on the top of the closet door. Its eyes were round and expressionless; its gaze locked on me like I was a fat mouse it planned to have for dinner. I twisted my body, intending to place my feet on the floor.

The owl fluttered his wings and shrieked. The sound was otherworldly. Despite knowing it came from the animal, a shiver shot up my spine.

The bird settled back down, tucking his wings back against his body, and resumed his disturbing observation. I shook off the moment of unrest and lifted my feet again.

The door I'd noticed earlier opened and Thea walked in.

The bone spear-shaped knife she'd given me the night of our first meeting was in her hand.

She motioned for me to put my feet back on the bed.

I stayed where I was.

"Tess, bring the darts," she called.

The hearth-keeper appeared behind her.

I jumped to my feet and lunged forward, intent on head-butting the pair out of my way. The owl shrieked again . . . right before a dart hit me in the shoulder.

Then the net was back, dropped from the ceiling. I stumbled and fell and was hit with three more darts. My head began to swim.

"Enough. I need her awake this time."

There was silence, then the sound of footsteps and the door closing behind someone.

When I opened my eyes, Thea was staring into them. Her eyes were gray; I'd noticed that before, but now I could see the color was deceptive. They weren't a solid gray, a shade somewhere between black and white. Instead they were like prisms, many colors, all the colors I had ever seen before broken into such tiny bits that from a distance they appeared gray.

They were mesmerizing . . . my head began to sway, my body too.

"There you go. You see it, don't you? Now you need to listen, listen carefully. I'm going to tell you secrets, secrets you need to know, secrets that will make everything all right."

I felt my head nod. Secrets. I wanted to hear Thea's secrets.

I held very still and let her whisper in my ear.

Her words flowed over me like water, warm and reassuring. She knew what I wanted, what I needed . . . I just needed to listen.

"Are you with me, Zery? Do you hear me? Raise your hands and let me know that you do."

I raised my hands, or tried to; something was holding them down, keeping me from complying. I jerked with all my strength and they flew up.

Thea laughed. "Good, good. I think we can get rid of this now."

A weight lifted off my body, the net pulling free.

I was sitting on my butt, my legs bent at the knees in front of me. She knelt beside me. The knife was in her hands, but it didn't bother me. I trusted her, wanted to hear her secrets.

"You know Padia's plan, don't you?" she asked.

I nodded. I did.

"And you don't want her to succeed, do you? Would you do anything? Sacrifice anything to stop her?"

I nodded again. She smiled and patted my hand, like a toddler who'd drunk all of her milk. She leaned close and whispered, "That's my secret. I want to stop her too."

Some part of my brain scoffed. I didn't believe her; I knew who she was.

Thea . . . Padia . . . brushed her thumb over my arm. "What's this?" Her thumb stood out against my skin and the black ink underneath.

"Your artisan friend playing? Thinking she can outdo me with markers?" There was disbelief and disgust in her voice, but my attention was mainly focused on the art she had ridiculed—the praying mantis . . . the leopard . . . the meerkat. What had Mel said when she'd drawn the meerkat? What was his gift?

The tiny animal's eyes glistened; it swayed, like I had swayed. It barked, yelled at me, in Mel's voice. "Think, Zery. Remember. Be strong."

I blinked and looked at Thea. She wasn't watching me. She was still staring at the art my friend, my best friend, the one person I had always been able to trust, had drawn on me . . . to save me.

And suddenly the fog thinned. Thinned but still there, like looking at the world through sheer fabric. The floor was hard beneath my buttocks. The air in the place was stale and smelled of old food, sweat, and septic, but all of it was dulled somehow, ever so slightly surreal.

But Thea, my enemy, I knew was within my reach. That I knew with a certainty. The thought swirled through my mind. She was close. I could loop my arms around her neck and snap it through. Or I could have, should have been able to, but my arms and legs were leaden. Without the priestess's instructions, I seemed unable to do more than breathe and swallow. And even if I could have moved, even if I could have killed her as I so longed to do, I wouldn't have Andres, didn't know who the birders were, where they were. Didn't know anything.

Mel and Jack had told me to think, to plan, to quit just reacting. This was my chance.

"I'll tell you another secret," she murmured. I gritted my teeth to keep myself from replying.

She ran the edge of the stone knife down my throat. "Padia isn't as strong as she thinks she is. Isn't as smart as she thinks she is. I know how she got on the council; it wasn't because she was the best. Not by a long shot." The blade paused, poised over my artery. "She's bossy too. I hate bossy. Do you hate bossy? Wait, you are bossy, aren't you?"

I didn't reply. None seemed required.

"But bossy won't work for her this time. Do you want to know why?"

I did.

"Because I have the knife." She held it up; twisted it so light seemed to pulse off of it. "She may have the child." Thea's hand stilled. "But I have the knife she wants and needs for the ceremony and now I have you . . . a queen! That's as good as a baby, don't you think? If you were a goddess, which would you rather have? A baby who has barely lived a life, or a queen with almost one hundred years behind her?"

Her brow furrowed. She pressed the knife against my arm. "Answer me, which?"

"A queen," I croaked.

She smiled and leaned in again. "You want to hear another secret?"

This time I didn't think I did, but I nodded anyway.

"Tess suggested you. It was sweet of her, wasn't it? Thinking of you. You should thank her, you really should."

I intended to, I really did.

"It's perfect, actually. You are the person who stopped me from ending this a week ago. Because of you, I lost the child. It's only fair you take his place . . . for now."

I realized then what she meant to do . . . to sacrifice me and then, later, Andres.

I curled my fingers into my palms, fought to keep from reacting.

She brushed her spider ring against my arm. I could feel the tiny hairs on the spider's legs as if he were real, could feel him crawling off of her ring and onto my arm.

I shivered.

She smiled and lowered her blade.

The spider climbed higher, until he was covering my heart.

"He's poisonous. One bite and you won't be able to move, you'll fall paralyzed to the ground. Your breathing will stop too, but that will take a while . . ." Her voice changed to a hiss. "That would ruin my plan a second time."

"What plan?" I asked, hoping my words wouldn't make her question if I was under her spell.

"My plans to be queen, of course. Not"—she stroked my arm—"a small-time queen like you . . . Padia thought she could buy me off with that." She blew air out her nose in disgust. "I want what Padia wants, to rule a tribe, my tribe, a tribe I created, who follows me and only me. A tribe of logical females, who appreciate the value of keeping up, not hiding their heads in the millennia-old sand."

Padia. She kept saying the name as if she and Thea weren't one and the same.

The spider shuffled to the left; I could feel its eyes on me. I lowered my gaze, stared down at the monster. It was bigger now, huge. It covered my entire chest. Its fangs hung down, brushed my shirt. I couldn't take my focus off of it, was afraid if I did, the fangs would puncture not only my skin but my chest, sink into the cavity and pierce my heart and lungs.

"You see him, don't you? He's beautiful, isn't he? I could have called something else, but for you . . . this seemed perfect." She leaned close and whispered, "One of my secrets. Padia can't do this, not like I can. The goddess hasn't blessed her like she has me. I am stronger. I deserve to rule."

She sighed and patted my arm. "Enough talking. I can see you're ready now. You weren't before." The spider's eyes, eight of them . . . I counted . . . winked at me, or seemed to. It had no eyelids . . . my mind grappled with that, blinking with no eyelids. It was impossible, as was the gigantic arachnid on my chest. But the creature was there; I could see him and feel him.

Panic shot through me. I wanted to pull away, but I couldn't . . . knew if I did, I'd feel those fangs, hear them as they popped through my chest, then sank in toward my heart and lungs.

Somewhere Thea was still talking. I could barely hear her now; the spider was my entire focus, keeping it calm and happy my only concern.

"Later, we will go to the obelisk. My tribe is gathering now. Padia will be there too, with the baby. I haven't met her yet in person. Tess heard her plans before she escaped. I should thank you for that I suppose, eh? See, until you came to camp and told me Tess and the baby were missing, I didn't know. Didn't know Padia had already arrived here either. It's what put me on alert, stopped your feeble effort to kidnap me." She laughed. "So Padia will be at the obelisk with the baby, but we will get there first. You, unfortunately, won't be able to greet her when she does arrive . . . won't technically be there then."

She tapped the blade against my cheek. "Smile. It's a happy day. We both get what we want. You save the child from Padia and I become queen."

Chapter 27

They walked me through the woods, Thea telling me
when to move my feet. Like a puppet or a zombie, I complied. My cooperation wasn't an act. My legs moved
whether my head wanted them to or not.

The sun was high and hot, even through the trees. Sweat
beaded in my bra, like it had that day so long ago when I'd
gone into the woods and found Andres there with Thea.

Tess was with us, but there had been no sign of Andres
yet, or the birders.

The hearth-keeper had shot me twice more while I had
lain on the bed. The darts had left marks and still stung,
but I didn't rub at them or flinch when she lifted the pipe
yet again. Thea told me it would help, make everything
easier, and I believed her . . . or thought I did . . . but somewhere deep inside I felt a scream building.

I nurtured that scream, concentrated on it while my feet followed the high priestess's directions.

Our pace was slow and the RV they'd had hidden beneath a pile of brush was far away from Artemis's clearing, barely on Amazon property.

After what felt like hours of drudgery, we arrived.

The obelisk stood tall, proud and regal as always. The sun shone off its glossy sides. I wanted to press my face to it, soak in that heat, use it to feed my secret scream.

But Thea told me to stop while I was still fifteen feet away, still standing in the trees and, damn my obedient feet, they complied.

She held up the knife. "Give me your hands."

My arms rose, steady and sure, as if pulled by a string. She slipped the blade beneath my bonds. The bone was cool and smooth against my skin. There was a slight tug and the rope fell to the ground.

I waited, the scream wasn't ready yet, wasn't strong yet. It flitted away, then came back, unsteady, untrustworthy.

Thea murmured something. My head nodded. She smiled and motioned for Tess to follow her.

From where I was standing I could see the entire clearing, the obelisk, the packed dirt beneath it, and the birders who slowly filed into the space. They wore their usual uniforms of Bermuda shorts and pastel tees. They looked like every grandmother you see at the mall.

Thea held up the knife for them to see. "Today all promises become real."

The brush to my left rippled. I shifted my eyes, the

only part of my body I seemed to have control over, to the side. Jack in his wolverine form poked his head out of the underbrush. He sniffed, then watched me standing there doing nothing. He lifted his lip in a silent snarl. I thought for a second he was going to attack me or rush the circle, I wasn't sure which.

How I was standing . . . cooperating . . . He knew I had failed, or worse, thought I had been turned.

I stared at him, trying to put words into my eyes, to tell him I wasn't there willingly, but he only pulled his head back and disappeared.

"Zery?" Thea called from the circle.

My legs pulled my feet through the bed of dead leaves and weeds that covered the ground. The tip of my shoe caught on a root. My leg jerked, pulling it free. I staggered forward and into the clearing.

Thea held up her hands. "Our gift! Who could ask for more?"

Gray, grandmotherly heads nodded. They slipped their hands into each other's until they formed a tight circle around us.

Tess stood behind them. She glanced over her shoulder and licked her lips.

Thea gestured and Tess hurried forward, a bowl of oil in her hands. The priestess dipped her fingers into the liquid and drew an arrow . . . a spear . . . on my forehead. Then she began to chant.

Her head bowed, she murmured over the blade, speaking words of wisdom and sacrifice, knowledge and power. She asked for things I didn't think possible, channeling my power, the power of my ancestors into the women gathered around us.

Then she raised the blade.

"This gift I give in the name of the greatest of goddesses, in the name of Athena."

I tried to fight then, tried to remember what Mel had told me, how the art on my arms combined with my own will would protect me. But as I stared down at her work, all I saw were marker lines . . . no magic, no faith . . . failure.

I stiffened, ready to feel the blade ram through my chest, ready to lose my life, only praying that somehow doing so would save Andres's.

"A gift? For Athena? I don't think so." Kale stepped into the clearing. In her hand was a sword, and behind her was an army of Amazons—or what appeared to be an army in my defeated state—all the Amazons from the safe camp, the ones I knew and the ones who had arrived since my exile.

I closed my eyes and prayed my thanks. Artemis hadn't deserted me. She hadn't released the power of Mel's magic because I didn't need it. I had my tribe.

One of the birders reached for her pocket. Kale raised her hand, and a knife, previously tucked into another Amazon's belt, flew at the woman's throat. A millimeter from piercing it, the blade froze and quivered, hung in midair.

"Unless you are willing to give your life for her, I wouldn't move."

The birder didn't and I didn't either, and not only because of Thea's power over me.

Kale was a priestess, and her magic was just like Thea's. The realization stunned me.

She smiled. "Good job, Zery. You figured me out." Then she swung the sword overhead. It tumbled end over end, heading toward me.

The birders gasped and ran. The bone knife grasped tight in her hand and her eyes wild, Thea spun.

I gritted my teeth, willed my feet to move, but I was still frozen, trapped under Thea's web.

Her eyes glittering, Thea stepped in front of me. She raised her arm. Words ordering the sword to fall flew from her mouth, but the sword kept coming. She yelled again.

The while her lips were still open, her body arched and a grunt replaced her commands. Skewered by the sword, she stumbled to the side.

Released from whatever spell she'd put on me, I grabbed the weapon and jerked it from her corpse.

I was armed, but so were the Amazons surrounding me. Knives, swords, staffs, nunchakus . . . an arsenal of weaponry . . . all directed at me.

Kale sighed and strolled forward. At Thea's body, she stopped. "She really was a pain in the ass. I don't know how you put up with her as long as you did. Of course, your mother might have said the same thing about me."

"Who are you?" I asked. Inside I knew, but with everything that had happened, with my mind still fuzzy from Thea's control, I needed to hear the words.

"She tried to steal my sacrifice, offer it as her own—before Panathenaea. What a waste that would have been! I was already on my way here when I talked to the two of you on the phone. I could tell she was lying to me, thought she could outsmart me.

"I sneaked into camp to watch her. Saw her kill Kale and two of them." She nodded toward the birders. "Then you came along. At first I thought to just kill you too, but then I realized it was a chance for me to learn more, to get the baby and the knife." She glanced at Thea. "She had found it, through her network. I should have taken it from her as soon as I knew she had it, but she'd seemed trustworthy, seemed to understand who was in charge. I never dreamed she would try to keep the knife from me or be stupid enough to think sacrificing the baby early would help her overpower me."

The baby. Andres. I still didn't know where he was, how he was. I held up the sword. "Where is he?"

She squinted her eyes and glanced up at the sun. "He'll be here soon."

I wanted to shove the bloody tip of that sword through her heart more than I had ever wanted anything, but twenty armed Amazons surrounded me. I might succeed in killing Kale . . . Padia . . . but then what? The others would kill me and Andres would arrive with no one here to protect him.

She tilted her head and studied me. "That sword must be getting heavy . . ."

And suddenly it was; suddenly it weighed more than fifty swords. My bicep burned; I gritted my teeth.

"So, all of you are part of this—you, Thea, Tess?" I spit out the question, hoping she couldn't keep up a conversation and toy with my mind at the same time.

"Don't forget Areto. You didn't really think she was on your side, did you?"

My arm quivered. Areto . . . I'd trusted her and she'd betrayed me, again.

"Thea, Tess, Areto . . ." Padia shook her head. "Who can you trust?"

The weight of the sword increased again. It felt as if an army was hanging from my bicep. A groan escaped my gritted teeth.

She laughed and waved her empty hand in the air. "Enough. I'm tired of this. Kill—" She bit off her own words and stared at me again. The blade moved back to her chin, tapped once, twice, a third time. "Tess gave Thea the idea to sacrifice you, did you know that?"

I did. Thea had already enlightened me.

"I can see you did . . . But did you know where Tess got the idea?"

At my lack of response, she tilted her head. "From me. I needed to get Thea here unaware and with the knife. She thought Tess was on her side and had set up a trap to delay me, that by the time I arrived you would be dead and Athena would have already gifted her and her birders with the goddess's powers. She was wrong, obviously. But the idea . . . it isn't a bad one. What goddess wouldn't want a queen as a gift?"

"Padia?" Tess's voice, calling from the woods.

Padia smiled. "Bring him in."

Tess moved into view, the blanket-wrapped baby held against her chest.

The priestess glanced at me. "Baby's first. You understand. He's the main course; you're just the candles on the birthday cake."

Tess slipped the infant into Kale's arms.

"Don't kill her. Hold her," Kale yelled over her shoulder at the Amazons. Four sets of hands grabbed my arms. My mind free of Padia's hold, I jerked my body, strained to escape. Still locked in my grip, the sword swayed erratically. It sliced into the cheek of the closest warrior. She didn't let go.

A dead voice, one of the Amazon's, muttered in my ear. "It's only a son. His death will increase our power."

"I don't steal my power from others, I make my own." I jerked again, and this time I broke free.

The scream I'd held inside, while Thea tormented me, while Padia boasted, exploded from my lungs. I spun, slicing through the bellies of four Amazons as I did. They stumbled back, their hands pressed against their bleeding guts.

I screamed again and jumped toward Padia. She had Andres and the knife; I had nothing to lose.

But another warrior cut me off, and this one had a

sword of her own. I parried and lunged, thrust and dodged. Pulled every trick I could think of to get past the Amazon, but she was well trained and met me blow for blow.

I could beat her, eventually, but there was another Amazon to take her place, and another . . . then another . . . and Padia had the knife . . . and Andres.

The warrior took advantage of my wandering mind, lunged and sliced my side. With a curse I jumped back.

I didn't have enough time *or blood* to defeat them all.

Where the hell was Jack? Even if he'd believed I'd switched sides, he wouldn't have left Andres like this.

That thought kept me strong, gave me the resolve to swing my blade again and again.

Over my current adversary's shoulder, I saw Padia repeating what Thea had done to me, drawing an arrow on Andres's forehead. The baby, quiet seconds earlier, opened his mouth and screamed.

I spun and slashed, willing the Amazon who stood between us to fall. My blade caught her on the neck; her eyes turned glassy and her arms lowered slowly as if released click by click—like an automaton rather than a feeling, thinking being.

I got it then. They were automatons. They were under Padia's power, probably had been for days.

Tess might be too.

Thea had used darts on me, to weaken me so she could control me more easily. Who knew what Thea and Padia had done to the others? How long either had been working on them? Perhaps since I had left, perhaps some of them . . . the newcomers . . . longer.

I was lucky Thea hadn't done the same to me, but I realized *Padia had tried*. There was the food Lao had fussed over and thrown out. Padia had probably been poisoning us, thought she was weakening us, but thanks to a hearth-keeper her efforts had been scotched.

I smiled. If Lao could do that, why couldn't I take on an army?

I raised my sword, ready to battle, ready to save Andres and myself.

Something glimmered in the woods. Without shifting my gaze, I willed my brain to see what it was: Mel with a bow and arrow, the Amazons' most traditional weapon, Artemis's most treasured tool, was perched in a tree.

Mel was here. She pulled back the string.

A thought . . . a plan coming to me, I shook my head.

Padia expected me to fight and she had the band of Amazons programmed to hold me back. I was making the mistake I'd made before, letting my enemy dictate the rules.

I didn't want to fight these warriors, didn't want to see them dead. I only had one enemy here, one heart calling out to be pierced.

I dropped my sword.

A warrior hurtling toward me faltered, tripped, and fell. She'd been told not to kill me. I'd heard Padia myself. I didn't have to fight these Amazons . . .

Sensing something had changed, Padia turned and stared at me. "Zery?"

I stepped to the side, forcing her to move too if she wanted to see me past the waiting warriors. She did, giving Mel one clean, clear shot.

With a ping, the arrow left the bow.

Padia raised her hand. The arrow shot off course as if swatted away. She smiled. "Don't think I've forgotten your merry band of misfits. I thought I had them all accounted for . . . I didn't realize one had slipped my trap."

Another arrow and another flew toward us.

Padia swatted each to the side. "Get her," she yelled at two of the stupored Amazons.

They left their positions and jogged into the woods.

"Now, back to what I was doing." She closed her eyes and raised her arm.

I moved to attack her, but something grabbed hold of my feet. They wouldn't move. I stared up at the tree where my friend had been. She was gone.

Then a few feet away there was a glint, another arrow, this one pointed at me.

My best friend was about to shoot me.

And then she did.

Pain sliced into me. My knees buckled; unsure and confused I stared down at the metal shaft that protruded from my shoulder—an arrow, Artemis's arrow.

Suddenly, understanding my friend's plan, I jerked it out of my flesh, turned, and stared at my target . . . at the priestess who was trying to tear my tribe apart. Then I threw it with all the frustration, anger, and faith I could summon from my soul.

The anger alone would have done the job.

The arrow hit, slammed in and through Padia's throat. Still holding Andres, she turned. Her mouth opened and closed, but no sound came. The bloody arrow, protruding from her throat, shone in the sun.

She stared down at the child, then up at the knife she held overhead.

My feet free, I lunged to the side, grabbed the sword I had dropped and, swinging it overhead, raced forward.

The blade easily accomplished what the arrow had started.

Blood sprayed, blood beyond anything I had seen before. It seemed to coat Padia before her head had even separated from her body, well before it clunked onto the ground.

A growling snarl sounded from the woods. Jack in his wolverine form shot forward. The air waved and the animal was gone. Jack, the man, naked and covered in Padia's blood too, grabbed a screaming Andres before the baby's body could collide with the packed earth.

Somehow Padia still stood; her headless body tottered backward into the obelisk . . . slid down its side and collapsed onto the dirt.

Still holding the sword, I followed my brother's example, I let go of a scream. This one in victory.

With Padia dead, I turned to face her followers.

The Amazons lowered their swords, dropped their

knives, and stared at each other. Then they turned to face the birders who were still lined up and waiting to receive their powers. The T-shirt-wearing women, unaware what had happened, their view blocked by the massive Amazons, moved closer . . . until they saw Padia.

A shudder went through them, like a football-stadium wave. Moving as one unit, they lifted their gazes again . . . to me, blood-coated me.

I picked up the sword from where it had fallen after slicing through the priestess's neck and held it overhead. "So, you want to become Amazons?"

They ran.

And this time I didn't think they would be coming back.

Mel walked out of the woods, the bow over her shoulder. She nocked an arrow and let it fly. It hit a tree only feet from the slowest birder. The old woman doubled her stride.

Our attention on the birders, we didn't notice Tess break into a run. Mel lifted her bow again, but I placed a hand on her arm.

Jogging through the trees toward us were Bern and the others. Seeing the fleeing hearth-keeper, my new lieutenant changed direction. She caught up to Tess in two strides, and with one strike of her nunchakus, she took the hearth-keeper out.

With Tess crumpled on the ground, Bern stood over her. "She betrayed you," she said.

I nodded and turned away. I didn't look back to see if

the warrior took my nod as permission to kill the girl or left her lying there unconscious, but alive.

Tess might have been under Thea and Padia's spell, but her betrayal had been more complete than the others and longer lasting. I couldn't believe they had turned her that completely, not without some desire of her own.

The other Amazons stood quiet, waiting. I was within my rights to take their lives too. And they all knew it.

I didn't, though. They had dropped their weapons once Padia fell, and unlike Tess they hadn't run in guilt.

I'd take their names, keep track of them somehow, but I wouldn't order them killed, not today.

Jack, human and naked, walked up with a shirt in his hand. He pressed it to my shoulder. "Sorry we were late. I hate to miss a good party."

I grunted. "You could have stayed the first time."

"And taken all this glory away from you?" He shook his head. "Besides, I thought you'd want to share the fun with friends." His tone turning serious, he added, "They were drugged. I don't know how. Its effect on me was different, it froze me in my animal form, but the others were unconscious. Mel came out of it first, her body anyway, her priestess skills . . ." He shook his head. "She insisted on coming ahead anyway, though."

Hearing her name, Mel approached. She held two arrows in her hand.

"You shot me," I said.

She smiled. "I've wanted to do it many times. Be glad I waited this long."

"And that your aim is good," I replied.

"Is it?" she asked.

I ignored the jibe. I knew if she had wanted me dead, I would be.

"It was smart," I said. "Shooting me."

She took Jack's place, lifted the cloth, and studied my wound. "Padia was focused on stopping me from shooting her, but it never occurred to her I'd shoot you."

"She didn't know you."

She pressed the cloth back down, a little harder than necessary, but I ignored the flash of pain. "No, she didn't know either of us, didn't know how strong an Amazon you are."

I grunted. I hardly planned on bragging about the events of the past few days.

She grabbed my arm. "You killed her. You stopped her from whatever the hell she was trying to do."

Not knowing how to reply, I changed the subject. "Something needs to be done with Athena's blade." I nodded to where the stone blade lay, white and sinister, in the grass.

She twisted the cloth around my shoulder and tied it in the back. "That's a job for the high council."

"If there is a high council."

She sighed. "With Padia's influence gone there should be, but they definitely have a few openings. Seems like the perfect time to get things going."

"And . . . in what direction?" I asked.

Her face solemn, she met my stare. "Don't play that with me. We both know this has changed you. You see what has to be done. If you won't leave the damn tribe, you might as well step up and lead them in the right direction."

Lead them in the right direction. My friend who hated the Amazons, but hated the high council more, had just suggested I join them.

Denial formed in my brain. I wasn't ready; I had almost failed here. The council wouldn't respect me or listen to me.

It would be a wasted effort to even try.

But Mel pressed a finger to my lips and said, "Shut up and just do it."

And for once I decided to take her advice without arguing.

My decision made, a cloud lifted off of me.

Yes, I had screwed things up here, but I had made them right, and by joining the council I could stop things from getting screwed yet again.

Areto walked up, Bern beside her.

Since the smaller warrior was still breathing, I assumed Bern didn't think she had betrayed us again. Actually, I knew she hadn't. Jack had told me she had been unconscious too. Padia had lied about that, to shake me, I guessed.

"They are going to need a new queen," I said.

"You aren't coming back?" Areto asked.

Bern stared off to the side.

"I'm going to the Northwest, to find the council." I

didn't know where they met, but I would place a call. Someone would answer and someone would find me and let me know if they would hear my claim for a position.

They had three vacancies . . . one my mother's. I'd been queen for sixty years and served well.

I had also just uncovered their biggest failure. If word of the Athena cult growing under their noses got out . . . there would be more than three positions to fill.

"Oh," Areto studied her hands.

"I was thinking someone familiar with the camp should fill the role, at least until the council is back together and someone can be officially appointed."

Bern nodded. "Areto will serve well."

I nodded. "I'm sure she would, but I think there's someone else who would do better." I glanced at Areto.

She closed her eyes, agreeing, then walked away.

I stepped into Bern's space, stared into her eyes. "Anyone ever call you a sheep, Bern?"

Confusion rippled her forehead. "No."

I smiled. "I didn't think so."

A few hours later I'd told a silent Bern I was leaving her in charge of the safe camp, and I'd said my good-byes.

With my staff and a few other belongings stashed into a duffel, I set off through the woods back to Jack's neighbor's house. Mel, Cleo, and Bubbe were still there with Lao, cleaning up.

By the time I got there everything was set to rights. Lao swore the place looked better than when we had arrived.

"These people will be leaving all the time, hoping the brownies will come back and fix the place up again," she declared before taking off through the woods back to camp.

I hadn't thanked her for anything. She didn't coldcock Thea or throw out Padia's tainted food as a favor to me, she'd done it because it was who she was, what she did. To thank her would have cheapened that.

She didn't thank me either, just shoved a couple paper-wrapped sandwiches into my hands and told me not to bleed to death too soon.

With that heartwarming thought, she was gone.

Mel stood beside me on the porch, watching her disappear.

"There may be more, you know," she stated.

"Hearth-keepers?" I asked, although I knew that wasn't what she was talking about.

"Deserters, Amazons trying other goddesses, or at least fighting for the tribe to return to the old ways."

I nodded. "Discovering the sons shook things up. They are afraid."

"But you aren't." She stated it as fact, but she was wrong. I was afraid, afraid that no matter what I did or what I became, it wouldn't be enough . . . that I wouldn't be able to save the tribe I loved.

I didn't say it to her, though. She'd told me only minutes earlier that she was resuming the search for her son. He was the son of a son. A perfect sacrifice when Panathenaea came around again . . . or whatever other ceremony was important to any other goddess who might think to challenge Artemis's hold on the Amazons.

Mel didn't need to know my fear. She needed to believe in my strength.

And, honestly, that's what I needed to do too.

"I'll take care of your mother, get her body returned to the tribe," she said, perhaps realizing I needed to change the topic. "Bubbe will do the rites, if you want."

I nodded. She knew I did. I wouldn't trust it to anyone else.

We stood there another five minutes saying nothing, but finally I couldn't put off my future any longer. I said one last good-bye, picked up my bag, and headed to the highway. Trucks ran down this road at all hours.

I just needed one.

It was getting dark. I walked along the shoulder, lost in my thoughts.

I'd left the tribe and I'd come back. I'd lost my mother and found a brother. The position of queen had been taken from me, and now I was going to force my way onto the high council.

Not one damn thing was like it had been just two weeks earlier.

Behind me a horn sounded, a car . . . a beater covered in dents and rust pulled to the side.

I sighed. Not the best candidate for getting to the West Coast. Still, he could surely at least get me to town.

Before I could lean down to check out the driver, the passenger door flew open.

Cautious, I stared inside.

Jack stared back at me.

"Heard a queen needed a ride."

"Nope. Wrong Amazon. No queens here." I placed my hand on the door, ready to slam it shut.

He called out, "Sheep?"

My fingers stilled. "Definitely no sheep."

"That's good; wet wool smells."

I looked up and realized it was raining. Big giant plops of water landed on the hood.

His foot pressed the door open further. "How about a fairy godfather? Could you use one of those?"

Thunder boomed in the distance. Lightning zig-zagged across the sky. I adjusted my bag on my shoulder. Staring at the horizon, I said, "You know, I never thought I did, but lately . . . I've learned I've been wrong . . . a lot."

I got in the car.